Anita Hendy's

The Furlong Spirit

Anita Hendy ©

Published by
Anita Hendy
Prefix 0-9549641
Ballyteague Sth,
Kilmeague,
Naas,
Co. Kildare,
Ireland.

December 2006
1st Edition.

ISBN 0-9549641-4-4

Check out Anita's Web Site www.anitahendy.com

This book is the second part in a Trilogy
by Anita Hendy
The other two books are called
'A Girl Called Molly'
'Father William'

*'This 'Trilogy' is dedicated to
any reader whose lovely character
may have been hurt, & to whom Christian comfort
is weakened by the destructive influence of evil.
This 'Trilogy' was written so
that the grace of holiness may become a visible light
in all our eyes, giving love, forgiveness and peace
to the gentle hearts of all peoples in this beautiful world.'*

Anita Hendy 2006

CHAPTER 1.

The sun rose over the city of Dublin. Fingers of light crept silently into the dark crevices chasing the shadows away. Birds stretched their tiny necks towards Heaven, as they sang their sweet songs of joy. Cats having returned from night adventures, lay contentedly in the warmth of the rising sun.

However, the peace of the morning was broken when a large removal truck drove past a row of Georgian houses and stopped as it reached no. 28. Inside the house, Hattie Thornton, a widow in her mid fifties, and her housekeeper Julie Clancy were rushing anxiously about. They were trying to decide what to leave and what to take with them to Wexford. On hearing the bell ring Julie dropped a heavy box and hurried to open the door. Outside on the step two big strong workmen removed their caps and having introduced themselves, quickly stepped aside and they entered the hall. A third, smaller and rather thin man remained outside in the street. Having opened the large heavy doors of the truck, he proceeded to light an Afton cigarette, leaned against the railings and with shifty eyes kept a careful watch.

Inside the hall Hattie gave her usual strict instructions. A smart formidable middle-aged lady, she stood in the middle of the beautiful wide staircase pointing at the wooden tea chests in the large hallway.

'Be careful with those my man, all my good glasses and china are in there,' she said sternly.

From the top of the stairs a little girl of eight sat watching. Aunt Hattie had told her to keep out of the way in case she got hurt. Her little cheeks were squashed as she pushed her small face through the narrow banisters. Big blue eyes danced with excitement as she watched the commotion below.

An hour later with the removal in full swing, nobody noticed a lonely sad figure walk silently into the hallway.

Since the tragic death of her husband J.J. some years ago now, Jessie McDermott's health had slowly declined. Her once plump contented face had grown taut and drawn. Instead of hurrying about in her usual busy way, she now moved slowly from place to place. She did not fill her clothes like she used to, and the fabric hung limp and from her shoulders.

'I suppose I'll never get to see the child now?' she said, looking down at the floor sadly.

On hearing her voice, the two other women looked at each other and stopped in their tracks. Walking quickly down the stairs towards her, Hattie, really concerned, reached out and gently took her frail hand. Steering her gently out of the workmen's way and towards the kitchen she said kindly;

'Come now Jessie, We didn't see you there. Let's go into the kitchen and have a cup of tea shall we?' Then raising her voice she called back over her shoulder,

'I think the men know what I expect of them by now. Hopefully I can leave them to it.'

Guiding Jessie into the kitchen she nodded tactfully at Julie to give her a few moments alone. Then pulling out a chair at the table she said,

'Sit down there dear and I'll put the kettle on.'

'I suppose I'll never get to see the child now,' repeated Jessie in a voice that had lost all hope.

'Come come now,' said Hattie drawing up a chair beside her.

'We are only moving to Wexford. Then I'll be back to visit Seamus and Eithne when they move in here. Their little twins are adorable but quite a handful you know I only hope they don't wreck this old house.' Then leaning over to Jessie she whispered secretively,

'I believe there's another one on the way.'

Jessie looked thoughtfully out the window,

'It was J.J. ya know, he had the mumps ya see when he was young. I always wanted children of me own. I loved Molly but it wasn't the same.'

'I'm afraid life will never be the same again Jessie.' said Hattie, 'But you know, we've both been so lucky to have had the chance to rear such special children. Molly's mother touched our lives in a way that nobody else could. I miss her too.'

Then patting Jessie's hand affectionately she sighed deeply as she bravely said, 'We must carry on.'

In a dark world of her own, Jessie's attention was drawn to the kitchen window. The little girl had left the staircase and was now running around out in the back garden.

'If only her mother could see her now,' she said sadly and started to cry.

' Oh but Jessie we both know that she is always with her in spirit. Now listen, you come to Wexford and stay with us as often as you like. There's the kettle now let's have that tea?'

Hattie chatted on gaily, but no matter what she said it did not seem to cheer Jessie up. The sadness just would not leave her tired weary eyes.

Suddenly the little girl ran from the garden into the kitchen. Holding her hand out she also seemed to have a worried look on her young face.

'Auntie, Auntie,' she said anxiously, ' I've got a sore thorn in my finger?'

'Let me see,' said Jessie as she pulled her small hand towards her.

'No,' said Molly pulling it back quickly, 'I want Auntie Hattie to fix it'.

Hattie felt embarrassed for Jessie and tried to distract from the awkwardness of the moment.

'Now dear we will both fix it and then it will be twice better,' said Hattie comfortingly.

Then she carefully removed the thorn with her long pointed nails.

Standing up slowly, Jessie said quietly;

'It's alright Hattie, the child needs you to make it better and that's how it should be. I'll be on me way.'

'But what about the tea?' asked Hattie, disappointedly.

'I won't bother you with it thanks. I can see yer busy.'

Seeing that Jessie was in a severe depressed state, Hattie told Molly to go over and give her a kiss goodbye.

The little girl ran over with open arms and Jessie hugged her tightly as if she could not bear to let her go. Then, releasing her quickly she turned for the door. Hattie hurried to catch up with her. Then pulling her back gently by her arm she said thoughtfully;

'Jessie we've shared too much in the past to let distance separate us now, we must keep in touch.'

'Yeah,' replied Jessie sadly, 'we'll keep in touch.'

The two women embraced and Jessie walked out the door and down the steps. Nobody heard her say, with a voice that had lost all hope;

'No, it'll never be the same again.'

By early afternoon the removal truck was packed and ready for Wexford. Seamus Thornton arrived in his vauxhall car to collect his mother, Julie, and little Molly.

3

'Uncle Seamus,' shouted Molly excitedly, as she ran down the steps and jumped up into his strong arms. Carrying her towards the car, he put her down gently when they reached it.

'My but you're heavy girl, what's my mother feeding you at all?' he joked.

Ignoring his comment Molly looked earnestly into the car. She was disappointed to see that the baby twins were not there.

Back in the house Hattie and Julie stood alone in the hallway. They listened to an unfamiliar silence. Then they looked around at the emptiness. It was as if they seemed to hear all the voices that had passed through the lovely, welcoming old house in the last thirty years. Words were not needed. It was all said with the deep thoughtful expression in their eyes.

Then as Julie pulled the heavy grey door behind them, she felt a little anxious about leaving Dublin for a whole new life in the country. As for Hattie Thornton, Hattie was going home.

CHAPTER 2.

Doireann Furlong woke to the sound of the phone ringing in the hall. Fumbling for the light switch she brushed her thick brown hair back with her hand and strained her sleepy eyes at the clock on her bedside locker. It said two a.m. Pulling on her old dressing gown she hurried down the stairs. Lifting the receiver, she was glad to hear Lady Gowne on the other end of the line. Racing back upstairs to her bedroom, she dressed quickly, grabbed the keys of the car, and hurried out into the cold night air.

Driving up the road, her thoughts went back over the last few months. Now at last the waiting was over and hopefully it would all have been worthwhile.

The front yard at 'Mount Benedict' was deserted as she drove in. Parking her car, she got out and walked quickly towards the stables. It was a cool spring morning. Peering over a half door, she saw Lady Gowne dressed in a warm sweater, trousers and rubber boots. She was sitting on her hunkers watching a mare.

'Has she started yet?' Doireann asked in a low voice.

'It could be any minute now,' came a whispered reply.

Looking at the mare Doireann noticed the sweat on the side of her neck.

'I'm exhausted,' said Lady Gowne as she ran her fingers wearily through her blonde grey hair. 'I've been up all night. This is the third mare to foal.'

'Thanks for ringin' me,' replied Doireann 'I really wanted to be here.'

'Well I'm glad you came, I'm a bit nervous as neither of the other mares held.'

The two women were watching closely when suddenly two hoofed feet appeared at the rear of the mare.

'Oh look! she has started,' said Lady Gowne excitedly.

Doireann remained outside the door. She did not want to frighten the horse. Reaching over, Lady Gowne removed the sticky mucous from the foal's nose. Then the mare's muscles contracted, and the long head followed the feet.

'Look Doireann it has Cuitoeig's white star,' she whispered excitedly.

'Oh good,' whispered Doireann as she strained her eyes to see. With two feet still inside the mare the women remained quite still. They waited while the foal's lifeblood pulsated into its body through the umbilical cord. In a few moments the birth was over and the foal slid down onto the fresh golden straw. The tired mare stood up clumsily and this rough effort broke the cord. Lady Gowne bent over the foal with gauze soaked in iodine. Applying sufficient pressure she managed to stop the bleeding.

Remaining outside, Doireann watched the mare. She noticed her ears go back and her eyelids open wide.

'Oh my God,' she thought anxiously, 'something is wrong.'

'Out quick,' she shouted as she ran into the stable

Lady Gowne turned immediately almost stumbling over the straw, and ran out the door.

She had only seen this once before.

The mare's eyes bulged in their sockets and she took on the face of a demon. Tossing her black head back she shook it wildly. Her breath blew hard through her open nostrils and her lips drew back to reveal her large teeth.

Suddenly she turned and charged the foal. Her hooves kicked out viciously trying to squash it against the wall.

Doireann dashed between the helpless foal and its violent mother. Catching the foal's forelegs she dragged him out of the stable and Lady Gowne slammed the door behind them

'God that was close.' she said panting in a shocked voice 'what on earth got into Firefly? She could have killed us.'

'Its not over yet,' said Doireann heaving and struggling to drag the foal into the next stable.

'We've got to get milk for it within the hour.'

'Right Doireann, leave him and come with me.'

The two women ran quickly across the yard towards the house. On entering the back kitchen, Lady Gowne reached up, took a bottle with a large teat and a saucepan down from the shelf and handed them to Doireann.

'Go back out to Charlie,' she said urgently 'he's in no.3 stable and ask him to milk the mare. She has beastings, and when he's finished tell him to look in on Firefly. She might have calmed down by now. I'll ring the vet and start looking for a foster mother.'

The early morning air blew cold on Doireann's face as she hurried across the yard. An unfamiliar feeling of importance came over her. She was glad her experience with horses was now useful.

It took almost ten minutes for Charlie to get the milk from the mare, and then she left him to deal with Firefly.

When Doireann returned to the stable and the little foal, she found him stretched out resting on the fresh straw. Kneeling down she pulled his head gently onto her knees, and coaxed the teat into his mouth. In a few moments she felt him suckling. Then she heard the gurgling sound as he swallowed his first milk. She smiled and breathed a great sigh of relief. Only now, did she realize that she had just saved the foal's life. Warm feelings of affection came over her towards him.

With long firm strokes she began rubbing his black wet fur. Looking down at his feet she noticed he had one white sock on his hind leg. She pointed this out to Lady Gowne when she returned to the stable.

'Look,' she said in amazement he's the image of Cuiteog.'

'Oh so he is, so he is, thank God.'

'I'll stay with him till morning.' offered Doireann, 'He will need feeding every hour, why don't you try and get some rest?'

'Well, I might nap in the chair in the kitchen. I'm waiting for calls about the foster mother, but I'll be near if you need me.'

Shutting the stable door she stopped for a moment to watch Doireann nursing the newborn foal. She looked affectionately at her. Realizing the enormous help she had been she earnestly thanked her again.

When the dawn broke and the sun rose over 'Mount Benedict', Doireann was still tending to the foal. He drank thirstily from the bottle and lay down beside her to sleep. By now, he was well able to stand on his own, and Doireann could see just how beautiful he was.

Three hours later, after some well earned breakfast, the two women returned to the stable and stood together admiring the foal.

'I'll never forget what you did last night,' said Lady Gowne gratefully.

'We were lucky,' said Doireann bashfully, 'We were very lucky.'

'You know,' said Lady Gowne thoughtfully 'He has the great bone of his sire and with the wild spirit of Firefly he should be a real champion.'

Doireann watched him. He twitched his short tail, turned his little head and for a moment it almost seemed as if he winked at her.

CHAPTER 3.

Walter Furlong's rubber boots squelched in the muck as he shut the big iron gate behind his herd of cattle.

Leaning his arms on the top bar he rested his chin on his hands and with his thin white hair blew gently in the breeze, looked out thoughtfully across his fields he wondered had she arrived yet.

When his sister Hattie told him she was buying the old rectory, he had mixed feelings about it. On one hand, he was glad she was moving back home. However on the other, he wondered if she could ever settle in the country again, with her rich lifestyle and high felutin' ways. Forty years ago he had not given much thought to her leaving, he had just met his Doris then.

Turning around slowly he leaned his back on the gate, and rested his left foot on the lower bar. He began remembering that meeting as if it were yesterday. Doris's father was a rate collector, and that particular day he had sent her to collect the money owed to him by his tenants.

Walter had been sitting on a bridge watching the fish swim beneath, when suddenly he heard a girl cry out. Jumping down quickly off the wall, he saw Doris a little way off struggling with her bike. Her hair shone like gold as it caught the summer sun. Walking towards her, he smiled when he saw anger on such a pretty face.

'Howya,' he said cheerfully, 'have ya a bit of bother with the bike?'

'Hello,' she said shyly, 'The chain keeps coming off and I'm covered in oil.'

Walter looked down at her delicate white hands. Even the black oil could not spoil their beauty. He was a good foot taller than she and was nervous in case he might knock her delicate frame over. Kneeling on his hunkers to take a closer look at the chain, he kept stealing glances at her. He liked what he saw. The blue of her summer dress matched the grey blue of her eyes.

'Can you fix it?' she asked hopefully

'I think I can if we walk it as far as my house.'

'How far is that?' she asked curiously.

'Just down the road, do ya know 'Riversdale House?'

'Well I've passed it a few times but I don't know anyone there.'

'Well now ya know me, I'm Walter Furlong,' he said smiling.

'I'm Doris Kenny,' she replied and extended her hand.

They laughed when they looked down at their blackened hands.

He walked her all of a mile back to his house, and it was the quickest mile he had ever walked with anyone. His mother made some tea, and Walter purposely delayed fixing the bike to keep Doris with them a little longer.

Time went quickly after that first meeting, and soon it was as if everyone in Wexford was talking about their little romance.

'Get down Shep,' said Walter sternly, as his sheep dog jumped up on his trousers, interrupting his precious thoughts.

The dog obeyed, gave two more jumps in the muck and lay down on the grassy verge. Walter was soon lost in thought again.

He remembered that dreadful day Dr. Purcell told them that Doris had tuberculosis. He remembered the shock he felt, and how it was she who took his hand and told him not to worry. A few months later she was dead.

Coming back to the house after the funeral, he found the loneliness closing in on him. How he wanted to run from that house, run, run, and keep running. The memories of Doris were in every room. Someone handed him a glass of whisky and he swallowed it without tasting. The pain in his heart was unbearable.

Turning back, he leaned his arms on the gate once more and looked far out across the fields. He wiped a tear from his eye.

'I wonder has she arrived yet?' he thought.

Then he began thinking about the day Hattie walked with him from Doris's grave back to the house.

Linking his arm she had suggested bringing Doireann, his daughter, who was only two at the time, to live with her and James in Dublin. He knew she meant well for now he had to face rearing three children all on his own. It was hard on her being childless, but he knew she had asked him at a weak moment.

In his confusion, he was almost going to let her take the child, but for Aggie Cullen. His housekeeper was a wise woman. It was she who opened his heart to what he had in his children. She had brought him back from a state of limbo, to the reality of a second in time.

That Sunday, when James and Hattie were ready to return to Dublin, Walter called them into the kitchen.

'Well Walter,' Hattie said hopefully, ' have you thought anymore of what I said?'

He looked down at his daughter playing happily on the floor. Hattie held her breath. He reached down slowly and picked Doireann up in his arms. Looking up with tears in his eyes he said in his own quiet way,

'Ah sur how could I let her go. No, I think I must keep my children together.'

He saw the disappointed look on her face. He knew he had hurt her but he never meant to. From then on a coolness came between them, and they never seemed to recapture the closeness of their childhood.

Suddenly his thoughts were interrupted again by the noise of a tractor. Turning around, he saw his eldest son David driving towards him across the field.

Yes, David would know exactly how Walter felt. He had Doris for fourteen years, but poor David had his wife for just one.

Strange how he never wanted to talk about her! Walter knew by the empty sadness in his eyes that he missed her terribly. Since her death, David was spending a lot more time on the farm.

It pleased him when his two sons worked well together. Mind you, sometimes it was as if they were ganging up on their father with their big talk of modernisation, specialisation, and intensive cereal growing. It was so different to the way he had been brought up to farm. Yet, deep down he knew all these changes were necessary for growth and development. The cost of new machinery worried him, but he got strength and courage by Frank and David's common purpose and determination. It had united the three men in a way he had not seen since Doris died.

David spent a lot of time riding his wonderful black stallion Cuiteog. Galloping across the fields at dawn, he had become a familiar sight. Faster and faster he galloped, his body only a means to carry his spirit. Friends and neighbours would mention that he was seen quite often in the local wood. Lord how Walter's heart ached at the thoughts of what his eldest son was going through. He wanted to go to him and put his arms around him, but he just could not. Men did not do that sort of thing.

Switching off the tractor, David opened the door and leaned out.

'I've just finished rollin' the fields for silage Boss,' he said in a loud voice.

'That's great,' replied Walter as he walked over to him.

'I'm going away for the weekend but I'll be back on Sunday, Do you want a lift to the house?'

'No son, you go on, it's a fine evenin' I'll walk back.'

David restarted the engine of the tractor

'I'll see ya then,' he shouted over the noise. Raising his stick Walter shouted back,

'God bless ya son.'

He wondered where David went at the weekends but he could never ask. Buttoning up his jacket he turned and whistled for his dog.

'Come on Shep,' he said quietl, 'It's time for the supper.'

The sheep dog rose quickly and ran to his master. Bending down, Walter patted the dog affectionately and once again thought;

'I wonder has she arrived yet?'

CHAPTER 4.

Father William Thornton raised his right hand. Making the sign of the Cross, he blessed the small congregation that had gathered for morning Mass in the neglected church in County Laois.

Returning to the sacristy his thoughts went back over the previous eight years. From the day he arrived here to his first parish it had been like a honeymoon. He was young and full of enthusiasm and joy. He was willing to commit himself totally to the people. He cared so much about everyone and tried to be all things to his people. He was a parent to the parents, a child to the children, and even a judge in the confessional.

'Will I take your vestments now Father?' asked Mrs. Stapelton as she broke into his thoughts.

' Oh yes, sorry to have kept you,' he replied as he began disrobing. Kissing the sacred stole, he placed it in the drawer and wandered over to the window. He smiled to himself when he remembered those last eight years.

How the young girls in the parish would giggle as he walked by. Some even believed they were in love with him.

'I'll be away inside now Father,' said Mrs Stapelton as she picked up her straw bag and opened the church door. She was a small plump woman with bright eyes and a questioning mind.

'Right thank you.' he replied 'I'll be in for breakfast in a few minutes.'

'Right Father God willin' she said wearily, as she struggled impatiently with the heavy church door.

Smiling at her usual remark William took his coat from the hook, draped it over his arm and left the sacristy. Walking back into the main body of the church, he began comparing it to the splendour of the chapel in Maynooth. This was a very plain building indeed. The smoke from the extinguished candles, and the aroma of fresh flowers mingled with the familiar smell of the church. He sat down in the front row of seats and looked up at the window behind the altar.

'Yes,' he thought, 'the last years were good ones'.

He had been the centre of attention and was wanted by everyone. Young couples came to be married by him. A new church was needed, but Fr. Breen the parish priest wanted things left as they were. Fr.William tried to tell him that now, in 1968 Ireland was in a time of change, that they must look forward and not back, but to no avail.

Eventually Fr. William found, that to get anything done, he would have to go through organizations such as 'The Gaelic Athletic and Pioneer Associations'.

Suddenly, a little butterfly distracted his thoughts. It flew quickly from flower to flower. The little creature brought a delicate hint of life to the cold marble of the altar. He rose from his seat and crept up very quietly behind it. With outstretched arms he tried to catch it, but the butterfly only flew higher and landed on one of the stain-glass windows above. Smiling at his defeat, he walked back to his seat and was lost in his thoughts again.

Only for the men of Laois he would have given up doing things long ago. He knew he could depend on them. They were sound. Whether physical or fundraising, they were always glad to be in on his projects. Work was scarce and seasonal, but the men had a great generosity about them. The building of the new church had forged a great bond between them. They liked the way Fr. William would sometimes slip off his jacket and get stuck in with a shovel. They supplied the physical work, and he the drive to get things done.

Take the old handball alley. It had lain in decline for years, but now it echoed to the sound of young men's cheers as they took turns to crack the ball off the resounding walls.

Rising from his seat, Fr. William walked down the aisle of the church. He was indeed a striking figure. His hair was a little grey at the temples, but despite that, he still had a youthfulness about him. His face was pleasant, not handsome. When he spoke, his words were penetrating and strong. Like his mother Hattie, his manners were impeccable, and he was easy to approach. But it was his eyes that captivated everyone's attention. They had never lost the innocent depth of spiritual expression they had as a young boy.

Walking out into the sunshine he passed by the men working on the new church. Five years ago the fundraising had begun in earnest and now the church was almost completed.

'Have ya come to mix the cement Father?' they called to him as he walked among them.

'Not today lads,' he replied cheerfully, 'I'll leave that to the experts.' Today he was going to visit his mother. He was glad she had moved to the country but a little relieved that she was in another parish.

CHAPTER 5.

Hattie Thornton had arrived indeed. She had taken up residence in 'The Rectory'. This beautiful old eighteenth-century house stood at the end of a long avenue. Tall beech trees lined the driveway on both sides. Overhead large thick branches and green leaves gave welcome shade from the hot summer sun.

Entering the house the breakfast room was on the right hand side of a spacious hall, facing east. The morning sun streamed through a large bay window across the dining -table in the centre.

The drawing- room on the opposite side of the hall was large and spacious. A new flower-patterned couch with two matching armchairs gave a feeling of comfort, while an old rosewood piano stood invitingly in the corner. Like Hattie's previous home in Dublin, the ceilings were high with wonderful plaster mouldings. At the end of the hall, three steps led to the large homely kitchen, and on the opposite side was the pantry and stairs to the cellar.

The main staircase, on the left-hand side of the hall led up to the second floor. A large lobby window gave light to the landing, and the doors of four bedrooms and a bathroom led from it.

After the first week of moving and cleaning, the two women found the second one more relaxed. The house responded well to the care and attention to detail that Hattie lavished on it. She took a particular interest in the bedroom her son, William, would sleep when he would come to visit.

Having considered all four, she chose the one at the back of the house. In this room, the view across the countryside was breathtaking.

'Yes,' she thought 'My son can have some peace in here.'

When the room was ready Hattie shut the door, locked it, and slipped the key into her pocket. Her grand niece Molly was delighted with her new bedroom and kept bouncing on the bed. It was at the front of the house and just across the landing from Aunt Hattie's as he wanted to keep an ear for the child during the night. The little girl would slide happily down the banisters of the wide staircase, and run her hand slowly over the colours of the old tiles on the hall floor. Pretty soon, it seemed as if she had lived in the house all her life.

Like any other eight year old Molly found the countryside an adventure. She seemed to have no fear and would explore a little more everyday. The walks and the fields seemed endless.

Because she was little, her eyes were always on the little things. Nooks and crannies carved out by time in the barks of trees, and flowers and weeds growing side by side in the long grass. Pebbles and stones with all the little creatures climbing over and around them. She would gleefully run up and down grassy banks and climb on the fences and gates. Being very aware of her surroundings, she loved the freedom of it all.

Unlike her late mother who had a delicate femininity about her, Molly was a strong sturdy child. She was more like her father David. She thought nothing of scraping her knees and tearing her clothes. On one occasion Hattie told her to go and clean her legs not realising that they were covered in bruises.

Molly liked her long black hair to hang freely and hated when Hattie tied it up in large satin ribbons.

Walter Furlong was past being surprised when he saw his granddaughter coming across his fields towards 'Riversdale House', although he worried about her safety with the animals and machinery. At such times, Doireann would remind him that she did more or less the same thing at that age.

'Hello Grandad, ' Molly would say running breathlessly towards him and hugging his leg. His trousers smelled of machinery, but that was Grandad's smell and Molly loved him.

'Who have we here?' he would say looking down at her.

'It's me, Molly.'

'You can't be Molly,' he would reply jokingly 'you're too big.' She would then burst out giggling and run away.

Walter loved teasing her, for she brought new life back to the old place. He would watch her as she tried to catch the pigeons. They cood round the courtyard then flew high up onto the roof of the barn.

There was always so much to see on the farm. Molly would climb on the iron of the stable door to look in at the horses. Boley the carthorse would oblige by putting his long chin over the half door. Then, baring his big lips, he would smile at her with large brown teeth. Bending down she would pick up the loose hay lying on the ground, and struggle to climb back up on the door with it. She was happy when she heard Boley munching it from side to side in his large mouth.

She never knew quite what to make of the pigs however. They were so fat and lazy. She did not like the feel of their bristly hair and it always seemed to be covered in muck. She noticed that each animal had a different smell, some stronger than others. Strange though, she was not upset by these smells, she guessed they were part of the animals.

Following Biddy, the dairymaid around, Molly never tired of asking questions.

'I remember your mother, God rest her,' Biddy would say. Then again whenever Molly was naughty she would scold her saying;

'Your mother would never have done that.'

Sitting in the cowhouse watching her milk the cows, she would listen intently as Biddy remembered the week Molly's mother came to Wexford. She loved to hear how much in love her parents had been. While Biddy reminisced, her mother came alive in Molly's imagination.

One hot lazy summer's day Molly was running around the farmyard playing with Shep. She had been teasing him with some twine. Having pulled it roughly from his mouth, he ran after her. Molly screamed and ran like the wind. Glancing back from time to time, she failed to see Biddy come out of the cowhouse with two fresh buckets of milk.

Biddy cried out 'watch it miss.' but it was too late.

Molly bumped straight into her and knocked her down. The milk spilled over her apron and flowed out across the yard. Shep began licking it up thirstily.

'Now look what you've done. A whole mornin's milkin' wasted. Wait 'til the Boss sees this,' she said angrily, struggling to get up. Molly bent down to pick up the buckets but they were empty.

'I'm sorry I didn't see you,' she said sincerely.

'Ya won't be allowed in the yard after this young Miss,' said Biddy crossly taking off her wet apron. Molly became frightened.

What would she do now? She would have to hide. Maybe if she stayed out of the way Grandad and Biddy might forget about it.

As she turned and ran towards the gate, she ignored Biddy calling her back.

Molly ran and ran across the fields. The sun was hot and there was no wind to cool her face. Eventually she spotted some large trees. Running over to them she sat down under their shady branches. She felt lost and lonely. She could see the farm in the distance, but everything was spoiled now. She could not go back there. She hugged her knees tightly and rested her nose on them. Her skin had a comforting earthy smell. The large roots of the trees were hard to sit on so she kept changing her position. Eventually, she grew tired and thirsty.

Then in the opposite direction to the farmyard, she saw smoke rising from a chimney. Whoever lived in that house might give her a drink of water. She would not tell them about Biddy and the milk.

Molly ran quickly across the fields towards it. On reaching the house she found it surrounded by a thick high hedge

Finding a small opening she climbed through.

'Oh' she thought excitedly 'This is a funny looking house.'

The roof was thatched with golden straw and the white walls were small and bumpy. Standing, tiptoes she looked in through a small window. There was no one inside. Realizing that she was at the back of the house she walked slowly around to the front. Suddenly she spotted what she thought was a witch's broom leaning against a wooden bench. She grew frightened. But then she saw the cats.

'They don't look like witch's cats.' she thought to herself and walked over to them.

One big fat one got up, and Molly's eyes widened when she saw four little kittens following. Oblivious to anything else she knelt down and began stroking them. They in turn, clawed playfully with the belt of her dress that had come undone. She laughed and giggled, forgetting all about Biddy, the milk, and the witch.

Inside the cottage Aggie Cullen wiped her brow with her floured hand. The old woman strained her ears to listen. Looking left and right through the window she could not see anything, yet the chuckling continued. Wiping her hand in her long apron, she walked slowly to the door and looked out.

She was pleasantly surprised to see a pretty little girl playing with her kittens. Molly turned to grab one of them, looked up suddenly and saw Aggie.

The wrinkled skin on Aggie's face tightened. She drew a quick gasp of breath as she looked down into those familiar blue eyes.

She did not have to be told who's child she was, for in her heart she knew.

Oh she yearned to reach out and cuddle her, but she did not want to frighten her. So instead, she decided to sit down on the bench outside the door and watch her closely.

'Are you a real witch?' asked Molly curiously.

'Oh bless your heart child,' she said with a broad smile 'Indeed I'm not I'm Aggie Cullen.'

'Oh I heard Daddy talking about you. You looked after him when he was a little boy?'

'Aye I did and I knew your Mammy too.'

'Did she ever come here?'

'Aye, but only once.'

'Was it to play with the cats? '

'I can't remember.' chuckled Aggie.

'Mammy's in heaven with the angels.'

'Yeah, I know,' said Aggie quietly.

Then to cheer the little girl up she suggested,

'Would you like a glass of milk and some of me griddle cakes?'

'What's a griddle cake?' asked Molly as she stood up and ran over to the old woman. Trustingly she reached out, took Aggie's old hand and looked up innocently at her.

Aggie looked down at her little hand. Her long fingers closed slowly on it. She was not just holding a hand, she was holding a life. A link back to the past, to David and Molly's love, a love that she had been privileged to witness.

Oh! How good that little warm hand felt in hers. Her eyes filled up as she squeezed it tenderly. Then she rose from her seat. Still holding Molly's hand tightly she turned and together they walked into the cottage.

The kitchen was dark with a funny smokey smell. Over a large open fire hung the picture of the sacred heart. All around chipped mugs and pots held wild flowers. There was a funny looking bed in the corner, and Molly gasped excitedly when she saw even more cats on it. There were some old coats hanging beside the chimney-breast.

Aggie wiped a stool for Molly to sit down on. The cottage was so different from the Rectory, and Aggie did not make a fuss when the cats wandered in and out. Auntie Hattie would go mad.

Gulping down delicious griddle cake Molly tried to tell Aggie all about Biddy and the milk. The child became worried and anxious.

'Hush there now and don't be frettin'. Everythin' will be alright. Ya won't be the first child to spill milk and ya won't be the last. Tomorrow ya must go to the Boss and tell him yer sorry. It'll all be forgiven and forgotten.'

'Oh really, do you think so said Molly hopefully.

'I know so,' replied Aggie happily.

A big broad smile spread across the child's face and she sat back and relaxed. Aggie leaned forward and reached over to her. With the corner of her apron she wiped the jam from her little chin.

In that moment a bond was formed between them that was to last the rest of Aggie Cullens life.

CHAPTER 6.

Molly loved Sundays. There was something special about a Sunday. She woke to the sound of the church bell ringing in the village. Everyone dressed differently on a Sunday as if they were going to a very important place. Having run wild all week in the freedom of her old clothes, she did not mind being a little lady on a Sunday.

Returning after Mass to 'The Rectory' she went running down the avenue. Today Uncle William was coming to visit, and she wanted to wait for him at the gate. She liked having a priest for an uncle and yet she did not know why. She felt he was different. Maybe it was his strange clothes, or the way she felt goodness coming into the house when he came to visit. Whatever it was she was always pleased to see him.

Fr.William was by this time just a mile away from 'The Rectory'. He bumped along the winding roads in his old Wolseley car and carefully negotiated the potholes. His thoughts were about the day ahead and how Molly would be there to greet him. However pangs of loneliness still haunted him when he thought about her mother. Could it really be eight years since she died?

Suddenly he turned the corner and there as usual was Molly waving at him as if he could not see.

Stopping the car beside her she sat, legs dangling, on the old wall. 'Hello Father,' she said excitedly.

'Well hello Molly,' he said smiling 'If mother sees you up on that wall, in your good Sunday frock, she won't be too pleased.'

Doing a quick jump down Molly ran over to the car.

Fr. William leaned over, opened the door for her and she climbed in. Sitting quite happily beside him, she fingered the red leather of the seats as he drove slowly up the avenue. He wanted to hear all about her little discoveries since the last time he visited. Parking the car at the front door, they got out and walked into the house. Hattie met them in the hallway.

'Hello son,' she said kissing his cheek.

'Molly where have you been? Look at the state of your dress. Didn't I tell you to be careful and we going up to your Grandad's for dinner.'

Then aloud she said crossly, 'Where's Julie?'

Hattie bent down and was brushing the green moss stains from Molly's dress with her hand when Julie came rushing up from the kitchen. Hattie instructed her to take Molly upstairs and help change her dress. Linking William in the direction of the sitting room she suggested a small sherry while they waited.

Upstairs in the bedroom while undressing, Molly hopefully asked Julie:

'Will Daddy be in Grandad's Julie?'

'No, you know your Daddy goes away most weekends.'

'Where does he go?'

'God only knows child,' replied Julie as she quickly pulled a fresh dress down over the child's head. Molly felt that if Julie did not know where her Daddy went then nobody did.

Downstairs Hattie stood waiting impatiently. When everyone was ready to leave she suggested they take William's car.

Over in 'Riversdale House' Biddy was rushing about the large kitchen. This time she had excelled herself with the cooking. Vegetable soup was followed by delicious leg of lamb, mushy peas, and crunchy roast potatoes. For once, the fresh mint sauce had turned out perfect. She smiled as she placed it proudly on the table in front of Hattie.

Molly loved trifle for dessert. Her spoon scraped off the sides of her glass dessert bowl as she tried to get every last bit. She knew it was special for Fr. William and she wished he could come to dinner everyday. After the meal, there were compliments all round for Biddy, who looked bashful as she poured out the tea.

As the conversation took on a more adult tone Molly became restless and fidgety. Noticing this, Walter excused her from the table. She left the room and went to play in the yard.

'Has anyone heard from Jessie lately?' enquired Walter as he sugared his tea.

'I called to see her when I was in Dublin last week,' replied Fr. William. 'God love her, but her mind comes and goes you know. Mostly she lives in the past. Her brother Mick is a great help now that he's moved in, and of course Seamus checks on her regularly. You know, she thought I had come to take Molly's Mother out to a dance'

'How long is J.J. dead now?' asked Julie helping herself to a biscuit.

'Two years almost,' replied Hattie blessing herself quickly ' it's hard to believe a man, so careful about his driving could come to such a tragic end. I believe the other car was speeding.'

'Lord have mercy on him,' said Julie 'but wasn't it great he didn't suffer. A death like that is easy on the victim but so hard on the loved ones left behind.'

Not particularly liking the turn of the conversation, Doireann tried to change the subject.

'Have you been up to Lady Gowne's yet Aunt Hattie?' she enquired.

'No, not yet. Of course I have been invited to 'Mount Benedict.''

'I hear her indoor stables are finished now,' said Doireann excitedly.

'Maybe its indoor stables she wants,' said Frank begrudgingly as he poured some tea from his saucer back into his cup

Just then Molly ran into the dining room.

'Daddy's here, Daddy's here,' she shouted and just as excitedly ran out again.

Everyone looked surprised when David walked into the room. Dressed in a new brown suit, his tall broad shouldered figure looked very handsome indeed. His attractive brown eyes had an added twinkle to them and Walter knew that look on his face. It was the same one he had as a child, when he did something mischievous.

'Glad to see you here Father,' said David winking over at him, 'Em I've something to tell you all.'

'Now I know this will be a bit of a shock to you,' he continued as behind him, holding Molly's hand, a very attractive young woman walked into the room.

'I've just got married and I would like you all to meet my wife, Alishe McManus Furlong.'

If the roof of Riversdale House had crashed in on top of them it could not have caused a more dreadful sensation than this announcement. Everyone was startled for a moment. Then a long blank pause followed in which everyone began to show their feelings in their features. Walter's happy smile spread quickly across his face, while Doireann looked on in amazement. Frank looked at David with a half-idiotic grin of delight, while Father William remained calm. But Hattie's look was worth them all.

Sitting pale and motionless in her chair she reached for her packet of cigarettes. William immediately reached over and extended his hand reassuringly towards her.

Alishe was tall and slim with short brown hair cut in the pageboy style. The brown makeup on her young face enhanced the bright green eyeshadow on her eyelids. Black false eyelashes blinked quickly as her sharp eyes took in everyone in the room. She held her chin up in a proud way. On the fourth finger of her left hand were two beautiful shiny new rings. She wore a brightly coloured summer dress and white high- heeled sandals on her feet. Molly noticed that all her toes were painted red. Everyone rose from the table to congratulate them. Walter slipped out into the hall. He asked Biddy who was listening at the door to rustle up two more dinners.

'And don't forget to put Aggie's to one side. You can drop it into her on yer way home.' He walked back into the dining room to hear David say, 'I hope you can all be happy for us.'

Coming up behind them Walter put his arms on their shoulders and replied, 'We surely can son, we surely can.'

Then he shook hands with his new daughter-in-law and kissed her awkwardly on the cheek. Everyone moved around the table to make room for the happy couple. Doireann was busy setting two extra places. Walter watched David and Alishe closely and began to feel a little envious. He thought back to the loneliness he had endured for so many years.

How he would have loved to have found someone to love and to share good times as well as bad. He loved his children, and he had his farm, but it wasn't enough. As he sat thinking, he wondered if now, even in his sixtieth year it was not too late. He smiled at the thoughts of David finding love. He watched Alishe's eyes twinkle when she looked at him.

Then Biddy arrived in with two piping hot dinners, and Molly ran over and sat up on Hattie's knee. From the security of her lap, she watched Alishe eating her dinner.

'Is she going to be my new mammy,' she whispered into her ear.

Noticing a sudden paleness coming over his mother, William asked her if she was okay.

'No son, I don't believe I am. It's one of my headaches. Would you take me home please? Molly, you can stay and maybe William, you might come back and pick her up later?'

'Of course I will,' replied William.

Having said her quick goodbye's Hattie hurried out to the car.

Once in the refuge of her home she calmed down a bit and suggested a walk down the avenue. Under the beech trees the crows could be heard squawking from the tops of the high branches.

With her brow drawn in and tears in her eyes she said fretfully

'Oh William, what will I do if they take the child from me? Molly is like one of my own'.

'Now calm down, we don't know what will happen yet.'

'But that woman we know nothing about her.'

'You're wrong there,' replied quietly, 'I have met her several times, and she is a lovely professional lady.'

Hattie stopped suddenly and folded her arms. Standing in front of William she said angrily,

'You met them? You knew about this and you never told me?'

'I cannot break a confidence not even to you, Mother.' he said sincerely.

Thinking for a moment an idea came into her head.

'Well perhaps for me, you might go to them and find out what the situation is about Molly,' she pleaded.

'Look,' he replied, gently taking her by the shoulders, 'Please don't ask me to do this. I can't interfere unless I'm asked to do so. But I can tell you this, David would only want what's best for his child. You've got to trust him.'

Hattie did not reply but began to think deeply. Suddenly a real fear gripped her heart. She knew from the past what it was like to lose a loved one, and because of that she felt she could trust no one.

CHAPTER 7.

'Doireann have you ever thought about riding to hounds?' asked Lady Gowne as the two women watched Cuiteoig's foal, Propeller, run wildly around the field.

'I've often thought about it, but I never got the opportunity. Anyway, I don't have the proper clothes.'

'Well that's easily solved,' she said, smiling. 'Come with me.' Taking Doireann's arm, she led her across the yard towards the house. Removing their boots, they went upstairs in their stocking feet to the bedroom. Opening the door of a large mahogany wardrobe, Lady Gowne proceeded to take out an assortment of riding clothes and lay them on a big four-poster bed. Then she encouraged Doireann to try them on. Both women were almost the same size having kept their figures in trim by years of horse riding. But for Lady Gowne, being twenty years older, they could have passed for sisters.

A few minutes later Doireann stood amazed at her reflection in the long mirror. Her thick brown hair was neatly tied up in a black hair net. A white riding shirt was set off by a hunting stock complete with gold pin. A black fitted jacket complemented the cream riding breeches, and as Lady Gowne placed a black bowler hat on her head, they both agreed that she really did look the part.

'But will I be allowed to go on the hunt?' asked Doireann anxiously.

'Of course you will, I'm an official and I can have you whipped in with a phone call. Now, there's a meet next Wednesday on 'Hawthorn Estate', and we are invited guests of Major Tim Fennel. It should be a great turnout.'

Sitting down to rest on the side of the bed, she suddenly had another thought.

'Listen, I don't think your horse, Pacha, would be up to it,' she began 'I have a five-year-old gelding out there and I'd love to start him off with a bit of light hunting. You'd be doing me a favour if you rode him instead.'

For the next few days Doireann could think of nothing but the hunt. Feeling's of anxiety and anticipation kept welling up inside her. By Tuesday night these feelings had peaked and she hardly slept at all.

Wednesday morning at eight o' clock she arrived at 'Mount Benedict'. Lily, the maid, showed her into the large dining room. Seated at the head of a rather long table, Lady Gowne was eating a hearty breakfast.

'Gosh you're up early,' she said, rather surprised when her friend entered the room. 'Have you had your breakfast? Tell me are you looking forward to the day?'

'Yes I've had my breakfast thank you,' replied Doireann smiling, 'and yes I can't believe I'm actually going on a hunt.'

Trying to restrain her excitement, she wandered over to the large window and looked out across the lawn. Reaching for another cup, Lady Gowne smiled to herself and poured out some tea.

An hour later, the two women walked confidently under the arch into the courtyard. Doireann carrying an ordinary riding whip, while Lady Gowne had a most expensive looking riding crop. Charlie, the senior stud groom, had the two horses saddled and loaded in the horse box, which was hitched up to a big rover car.

'Everything is ready, my Lady,' he said happily as they approached.

'Good man,' she replied getting in behind the wheel. Doireann sat up in front beside her, while Charlie slipped his thin small body into the back.

Approaching the estate an hour later, a young man quickly opened the gates, tipped his cap and respectfully stood back. A lull came in the conversation as they drove up the avenue. They were lost in their own thoughts of the day ahead.

Looking out the window, Doireann admired the beauty of the enormous old trees as if they were painted on the landscape. Draped in cloaks of reddy gold, their giant branches spread far out across the autumn sky as if claiming their territory. Doireann's excitement was now taken over by a strange sense of nervousness as she lightly fingered her hairnet.

When the car pulled up alongside the other horse- boxes she got out quickly to help unload the horses. After greeting and introducing Doireann to other members, Lady Gowne motioned to Charlie to give them a leg up.

Then the horses walked out with hooves of steel clattering on the hard cobblestones, and echoing off the walls of the old courtyards.

Lady Gowne proudly led the way. Riding directly behind her, Doireann could not help but admire the perfection of her seat on the horse. As she approached the front of the house she presented herself to be greeted by Major Fennel, rather heavy red-faced man with a distinctive grey moustache. His bulging dark eyes danced with excitement as he looked around at the assembled crowd.

The morning sun lit up the cold autumn sky, giving the scene an elegance and sociability known only at that particular time of year.

On the front lawn Doireann noticed a table covered by a white linen cloth. In the centre was a large solid silver stirrup cup.

Taking a silver ladle, Major Fennel's butler took a measure of hot mulled wine and poured it into smaller cups. Then his staff walked around with these on silver trays offering them up to the riders seated on their horses. Lady Gowne raised her cup, smiled reassuringly at Doireann and wished her luck. As Doireann sipped the warm beverage she began to feel more relaxed. One maid provided lemonade for the children mounted on ponies and still on leading rein.

Two whips, seated on their horses beside the gates of a field, kept the mixed pack of hounds in total silence and control.

Then with the empty cups handed back, the tall beefy huntsman mounted his horse. Dressed in his bright red jacket he took his place at the head of the hounds. Raising the hunting horn to his lips, he gave two sharp blasts to signify the field moving out. Leading the way towards the woods, he was followed by his two gaffers, the pack and two whips. In a slow trot the forty riders, made up of people from the business and farming communities, were strung out behind.

Trekking across the field they headed for the first fox covert. The huntsman blew once on his horn to command the hounds to enter the covert. The hounds hunted on beautifully as they concentrated drawing the covert. The two gaffers took up point duty, while the huntsman rode with his hounds encouraging them through the thick undergrowth. Doireann nudged her horse up slowly beside Lady Gowne and they exchanged excited glances.

The minute the hounds picked up the scent of the fox they gave a wonderful tongue. This eerie curling sound caused Doireann's blood to rise, and the hair to stand up on the back of her neck. Suddenly the man at port duty saw the fox, but counted to twenty before he called out. The huntsman galloped out of the covert to see where the fox was hollered away. Recognizing his throaty call, the hounds also rushed out and the exciting sound of full tongue brought the countryside to life. Then the hounds raced on and hit the line.

Keeping up with them, the huntsman blew long and hard on his horn. From the other side of the covert, the field master stood up on his stirrups, and signalled to the field to follow.

'We're off,' shouted Lady Gowne excitedly, as she spurred her horse into a full gallop leaving Doireann slightly behind.

Now it was everyman for himself.

Urging her horse on, a strange physical arousement welled up inside Doireann and she lifted her rear off the saddle.

Following the sounds of the hunt, the riders galloped across the front of the fox covert, and cleared the first ditch. With horses and riders rising up in the air, she felt exhilarated.

Onwards the raced under the beech hedge, hooves thundering on the exposed roots of the large trees. Wild ducks fluttered noisily from the lake, at the frightening sound of the hunt in full flight. Reaching a small gap in a large double ditch, the horses jumped and clawed their way up the steep clay bank.

Once on top the riders could see right across the glen. Although briars prevented them from getting a good view of the hounds, flashes of the huntsman's red jacket could be seen clearly in the sunlight.

'Come on,' cried Lady Gowne encouragingly as she left Doireann behind once again.

A flurry of excitement ripped through the riders as they galloped furiously down the open glen, only to be stopped in their tracks by the fieldmaster.

'Hold,' he shouted angrily, 'The little bugger has doubled back.'

Doireann found it hard to hold her horse. It snorted heavily and strained on the reins. They riders watched anxiously as the hounds and huntsman raced furiously past them. The full tongue of the hounds encouraged the riders and horses to face the hard steep climb back out of the glen.

Once on the headland, the field was strung out in single file, and in full gallop made towards an open gate. Observing the hunt from a distance, members of a local gun club held their dogs. With shouts and gestures they encouraged the riders on.

Once again in the short grass, they could see the fox scurrying for the swamplands on the other side of the field. The hounds howled desperately as they chased after him. The pace was speeded up and the riders galloped swiftly across the big field.

As the hounds disappeared into the wetlands the huntsman galloped on muck and clods flying. The fieldmaster held the riders on the hard top land. Through odd breaks in the hedges, the riders caught glimpses of huntsman and hounds.

Suddenly, the fox was spotted heading towards the carriage road. Jumping the low ditch at an angle, the horse's hooves clattered loudly on the stoney surface. Racing on, Doireann noticed the hedges on either side getting higher, and was relieved when two large stone peers appeared at the end of the lane.

Onwards they galloped, past the ruins of an old house. Then rising once more up into the air, the horses jumped over a crumbling stone wall. Then to their surprise, the people found themselves back in the field where they first started. With the fox gone to ground, the huntsman called the pack to heel.

Then the riders, horses and hounds, panted perfusiously as the chase wound down slowly to a reluctant stop.

With a big red face, Major Fennel turned to Lady Gowne and said in a very serious tone,

'Damn good chase Maureen? Certainly gets the passion rising in one, what?'

CHAPTER 8.

On the first Friday of every month Fr. William could be found attending the sick of his parish. His last call was to a lovely old couple, Jack and Annie Bermingham.

They lived in a wild isolated part of his parish at the end of a long twisting laneway. Their little stone cottage had only three rooms in it and Fr. William often wondered where they had put the ten children they had reared. The roof was made of old galvanized sheeting and the chimney puffed out smoke from the turf fire burning continuously in the big open hearth.

Jack, now in his eighties, had been a good husband and provider down through the years. They had been tough ones. But for his little plot of land where he grew potatoes and vegetables, his family would have been hungry. He had laboured for farmers all his life, and many an evening, due to their kindness, he had brought home fresh eggs and milk.

His face was heavily lined, and gave evidence of a life outdoors. He was a thin man, with a funny round face, and he always had a kind smile and a welcome for everyone.

His wife, Annie, was seventy-six years old. A tall woman, with yellow white hair tied neatly in a bun. Having given birth to all her children at home, she had, over the years neglected her own health. Now her old hands were twisted with arthritis, and her legs discoloured with varicose veins. Now and again, the bulging purple veins would break out in painful ulcers, and she would be confined to bed.

Having improvised themselves rearing such a large family, they now found themselves alone. Thanks to the curse of emigration, their children were scattered all over the world. Their acceptance of old age and serious illness impressed Fr William, but it angered him too. He didn't like the way the Irish state took advantage of their religious beliefs. Nobody seemed to be doing anything to help.

Inside the house, the Berminghams sat quietly listening for the familiar sound of the priest's car. Annie kept getting up from her chair and wandering over to the little table in the corner. Checking that everything was in place, she would smooth the white cloth out with little strokes of her wrinkled hand.

On turning into their yard, Fr. William found their front door already opened for him. Returning their reverend greeting of;

'Good mornin' Father.' the young priest would enter the house carrying the sacred host in a small silver box.

Annie would take his coat and hang it on the back of the door. Jack would strike a match and light two candles on the table. Then blessing themselves, they knelt down in front of a small crucifix.

Fr. William would pray with the old couple and he found that their blind faith and humility served to strengthen his own. When the time came to receive the communion he too could feel their expectation of the Heavenly Visitor.

Afterwards, over a cup of tea and sandwiches, he would delay his journey home and chat with them awhile.

'Isn't it terrible Father that they done away with the Latin Mass?' Tom remarked sadly.

'Would you think so Jack? 'replied Fr.William.

'Yes Father, sure it's not the same at all"

'But surely the message of God's love is getting across to people more clearly?'

'Ah no Father' he replied pulling on his crooked pipe's shank, 'Sur its what we were used to.'

Fr. William smiled at the thought of them mourning, the loss of something they could not understand. He knew they had a deep loyalty to the mysterious but he wanted them to understand in their language the real meaning of Christianity.'

'Will ya have more tea Father? asked Annie rising slowly from her chair.

Taking up a tea towel, she protected her hand as she carefully lifted the handle of the black kettle and added some hot water to the pot.

'Yes, thank you I will,' he replied as he reached for a biscuit.

Reclining back in the armchair he felt so relaxed. In this little cottage it was as if the outside world did not exist. Looking into the open fire, he began to wonder about the old people. They seemed to be guided by their emotions more than their thoughts. Then he thought of the enormous task that the Church was facing.

'We both managed to get a lift to the last night of the mission.' Interrupted Jack, 'it was packed out mind you father,' he said, leaning forward and reaching for the matches 'that missionary is the man to put the fear of God into people.'

Fr. William's eyes darkened.

'God is love Jack,' he said firmly 'not fear.'

How many times must he explain this to them? Priests who preached sermons like that only served to distance the congregation from God.

'Aye,' replied Jack, lighting his pipe and sucking on it,

'But that priest had a power about him.'

'Yes it probably seemed that way,' said William seriously. 'But you know something Jack, all the power of the catholic priesthood, all its honour and influence, purity and holiness, strength and invincibility has its source only in the Eucharist.'

'Well I never knew that Father,' he replied puffing thoughtfully on his pipe. Stroking their little terrier dog that had just strolled in, Annie said seriously: 'We know God is love but he must be obeyed as well.'

Obedience and authority, words that haunted William since his ordination. How could he explain to them that they should obey out of love and respect, not fear.

However, before he could gather his thoughts together Jack rose slowly from his chair and leaned over to a large black wicker basket in the corner. Picking up three sods of turf he threw them carefully into the fire.

'Is it true the Bishop's being transferred Father?' he said, changing the subject.

'He is indeed. Bishop Lennon has been transferred to Cork, and we don't know yet who the new man will be. However there are lots of rumours.' replied William with a thoughtful look.

'Will we have more changes then?' asked Annie worriedly.

Fr. William smiled at their innocence. Replacing his cup in the saucer, he thanked them for their hospitality and stood up to leave.

'Sur there will always be changes Annie,' he said as she walked towards him with his coat.

'Yes Father,' she replied crossly, 'but there's none of them for the better.'

CHAPTER 9.

Hattie Thornton woke from a restless sleep. She had too much on her mind to relax. David and Alishe were returning from their honeymoon today and they had arranged to meet her for lunch at the Presbytery in Laois. She arrived down to breakfast dressed smartly in a tailored brown suit.

'I'm not really hungry Julie,' she said worriedly, 'I'll just have some toast.'

Julie's heart went out to her, but she knew from past experiences that it was best to say nothing.

'You take your time now Hattie, and don't worry about the child. I'll look after her,' she said reassuringly.

After breakfast Hattie set off in her car and Julie and Molly waved until she was out of sight.

'Well Molly, what are you going to do with yourself today?' asked Julie as she turned to go back indoors.

'Can I go over to Aggie's please?' asked Molly earnestly running in after her.

'Poor thing,' thought Julie, 'She hasn't been to many places in the last two weeks with Hattie been a little overprotective.

'Well I don't see why not, but you mustn't tire her out, you hear? And I want you home by two.'

A little while later Molly set off happily across the fields. Carrying a pot of Julie's homemade raspberry jam, she hummed to herself as she walked along. The warm summer breeze blew gently and the wild daises made a muffled sound against her sandals as he walked. Because she had discovered Aggie's cottage all by herself, it held a magic and freedom all of its own. Sitting at the open fire in the kitchen with Molly perched on the stool, Aggie told stories of long ago.

Her hoarse sandy voice spun tales with such sincerity that wide eyed, the little girl would conjure up vivid pictures in her mind.

After awhile Aggie would root in her apron pocket. Taking out a small white clay pipe she would wink at Molly. Holding the pipe up between her index finger and thumb she whispered mischievously,

'Sur ya won't tell anyone child? This'ill be our little secret.'

Catching it carefully between her stained teeth she would encircle the shank with her lips. Then picking up a small slip of newspaper from the hob, she lit it in the fire. Placing the flame over the bowl of the pipe, Molly watched in amazement as she sucked vigorously on it. Her thin jaws going in and out like a bellows. Eventually white puffs of smoke began to appear. Throwing the bit of newspaper into the fire, she leaned back contentedly in her chair to enjoy her smoke. Molly could not help giggling at the thoughts of what Auntie Hattie might make of this. Yet she was glad that the pipe gave Aggie such obvious satisfaction.

Later when the pipe was extinguished and replaced in her pocket, Aggie's eyelids started to close. Molly tried to sit very still so as not to wake her. Resting her chin on her hands she listened to Aggie's slow heavy breathing. Below her Adams apple, she noticed a little hollow. In amazement, she watched it as it went in and out with every breath. Then her eyes wandered down to her hands resting on her lap. They were long and slim, with large blue veins running crisscross under her thin brown skin.

Her clothes were darker than Aunt Hattie's and always covered by a long apron. The laced up boots on her feet shuffled as she moved, and she always moved slowly.

While Aggie slept, Molly got down off the stool carefully and wandered around the kitchen. In the quiet of the cottage, only the ticking of the clock could be heard.

The ornaments and crockery seemed to have been there for a very long time. Everything had a brown yellow colour to it. Over on a little table in the corner, she saw a handsome solider smiling behind the brown glass.

With Aggie asleep, Molly could now take a closer look at him. She liked his smile and his eyes looked happy. Suddenly Aggie moved in the chair, and Molly jumped. Turning back to look at her she saw her change her position slightly, but she continued sleeping.

Turning again to the little table, Molly noticed a gold locket intertwined with a wedding ring lying beneath the picture. She fingered it carefully and thought it was really beautiful. Then she began to yawn tiredly as the stillness caressed her into sleep.

To escape from it, she tiptoed slowly to the door. Raising the latch carefully she stepped into the yard.

Then she closed the door gently behind her. What could she do while Aggie slept? Noticing the broom leaning against the wall, she began to sweep the step.

The cats crept silently up behind her and rubbed their furry coats against her legs. Molly giggled but she had to be careful that they did not trip her up.

Like all children it was not long until Molly needed to go the toilet.

She knew Aggie did not have a bathroom in the cottage, because on her first day there she had shown her the outhouse. Now she really needed to go.

The outhouse stood at the end of the small garden. There was a narrow path down to it through the long grass. Its walls were made of mud, and someone must have painted it white a long time ago. The wooden door creaked as she opened it, and even though she was feeling a bit frightened she stepped inside. When the door closed behind her, she found she was in darkness, so she ran out into the garden again.

Maybe she should wait until Aggie woke up, but she knew she could not, she had to go now!

Cautiously she opened the door again, slowly this time and stepped in. Holding the door ajar with her foot she stared at a delph bowl set in the centre of a long wooden seat. There was a square box of shiny toilet paper on one side, and a big white enamel jug full of water on the other. Looking nervously into the bowl, she smelt the familiar smell of disinfectant. Sitting down carefully on it her feet dangled off the floor.

Alone in the outhouse, she kept looking up at the beam of sunlight coming through the top of the door. She could hear the wind blowing eerily, and it sent shivers down her spine. It was a strange toilet all right, but somehow Molly liked it. In the semi –darkness, she stayed a little longer watching the little spiders and ants crawling busily on the cracked cement floor.

A little while later inside in the cottage Aggie began to wake slowly from her nap. Not remembering having dozed off, she strained her sleepy eyes and looked over at the clock. The moving hands confirmed the passing of the hour. She rubbed her cheeks with her hands and rose slowly from her chair. Taking up the long tongs she stooped and poked the fire. The flame had died down so she threw some sticks into the hearth to rekindle it. The kettle would boil soon and then she could have some tea.

Looking around the kitchen worriedly she scratched her head as she suddenly remembered Molly and noticed she was gone. Walking to the door she called out in a loud voice

'Molly are ya there child? '

Hearing her call, Molly, carrying a small bunch of white daises, came running quickly through the long grass. Holding them out to Aggie she said affectionately,

'These are for you.'

The old woman was very moved by her gesture. Bending down, she took the flowers graciously from the child and patted her head lovingly. Then turning back they went indoors, and together they picked out the best jam jar to put them in.

CHAPTER 10.

Stopping her car outside 'The Presbytery' Hattie Thornton took one last look in the mirror. Her makeup disguised the worried tiredness in her eyes. All her emotions were tense inside her. Twice before she had been disappointed when she missed her chance to rear a little girl. At that time she had youth on her side but now, with the passing of years she could feel a frailty creeping in.

Adjusting her brown hat in the mirror she began to take a closer look at her face. The sunlight shining through the car windscreen revealingly showed up every crease and line. She ran her fingers slowly over her skin. From years of smoking she looked older than her years. The eyes looking back at her seemed not to be her eyes. Little bags under them did not help either. Tilting her hat until the small feather sat at the right angle, she turned the lying mirror away from her and instead began to think about how much she loved Molly. A special closeness had developed between them over the years.

Her mind went back to the time she first held her in her arms with her mother lying dead in the bed upstairs. How precious and delicate that new life was. She remembered how David, in his grief, came down the stairs and asked her to take care of his little baby. Jessie McDermott was too upset. She remembered the excitement that she felt at getting the chance to rear such a beautiful and special child.

Then these thoughts had been taken over by dreadful feelings of guilt. Guilt that she herself was alive, while Molly's mother lay cold in the bed upstairs. Looking in the mirror now she could see tears threatening and she blinked quickly.

All the nights she had lain awake listening for a cry, a movement. The nights she took the sobbing child into her own bed to comfort her. She remembered changing nappies and making bottles. She could have easily asked Julie to do all that, but Hattie needed to mother this special child herself.

Once again, her eyes filled with tears and she fought them back. This was no time to show any kind of weakness. Like a solider going into battle, she took a deep breath and arched her back. There was so much at stake here. But through all her fears she was very aware that David was, after all, Molly's father.

Just as she was getting out of the car, the happy couple pulled up alongside her. David, looking fit and tanned, as was his new wife sitting beside him. Smiling, they greeted one another with kisses, and together they walked towards Fr. William who was standing at the front door.

Over small glasses of sweet sherry, they told Hattie and her son all about their wonderful honeymoon in Rome. The tours of 'The Vatican 'and 'The Sistine Chapel', the moonlight walks by the fountains and the fabulous statues that were everywhere.

'Wait a second,' David said, jumping up from his chair, 'I have presents in the car. I'll just nip out and get them.'

He returned a few moments later carrying three gift- wrapped boxes, one particularly large one. For Fr. William, there was a replica of Michelangelo's sculpture 'The Pieta' and for Hattie, two expensive bottles of Italian red wine. Pointing to the large box on the floor David said, smiling: 'There's a porcelain doll in there for Molly. Alishe picked it out. It's really beautiful. How is my darling?'

Hattie looked at the box and thought to herself 'Little does Ailshe know that Molly doesn't play with dolls,' Then aloud she said smiling:

'Molly's fine and looking forward to your return of course.'

Then Mrs. Stapleton, the housekeeper, knocked on the sitting-room door and announced lunch was ready in the dining room.

Walking behind Alishe and David, Fr. William put his arm reassuringly around his mother's shoulder.

Over delicious wild salmon salad and homemade brown bread, Hattie listened to and watched Alishe closely. She could not but help but admire her confident way of speaking brought about by her training as a solicitor. Her short hair and classic cut suit gave her a definite air of sophistication.

'I could have had a career like that,' thought Hattie 'If I hadn't given it all up for James.'

Then she found herself comparing Alishe to Molly's late mother. They were two completely different women and yet they had only one thing in common. David's devoted love.

Because of the occasion, Fr. William opened a bottle of dry white wine and filled their glasses. Raising his own, he invited his mother to toast the happy couple in their new life together. Then the conversation turned towards horses.

'I was speaking to Doireann on the phone,' David said excitedly, 'and I believe the foal is the image of Cuiteog. I can't wait to see it.'

Hattie put her knife and fork down on the plate. How could they talk about horses at a time when Molly's future guardian was in doubt.

'Would you like more salad Mother?' inquired Fr. William passing her the salad bowl.

'No thanks, I'm really not hungry.'

As the meal continued, the young couple seemed to dominate the conversation as Hattie sat in silence. Only William guessed what could be troubling her. But he knew she could not bring herself to ask them the question, and by the way David and Alishe were engrossed in each other it could be some time before they would think of bringing up the subject.

So not being able to stick it any longer he picked up his serviette and decided it was up to him. Patting his lips, he cleared his throat and turned to his guests.

'I presume David, that you will be bringing Molly to live with you in Dublin?'

'Well,' replied Alishe, 'we did discuss this while we were away and…'

'Sorry darling,' interrupted David then taking her hand he said quietly, 'let me explain.'

Leaning over towards his aunt a sudden seriousness came into his voice:

'There is something I have to ask you?'

Hattie's face drained of all colour and she felt a funny tingling in her legs. Swallowing hard she replied,

'Yes David go on.'

'Well Alishe and I were wondering if you would mind keeping Molly with you in 'The Rectory'. What with Alishe trying to build up her practice and me to'in and fro'in, we feel it would only unsettle the child. Of course we will visit as often as possible, and I'll continue to take care of everything.'

Fr. William smiled broadly. Putting his two hands behind his head, he leaned back in his chair. Then looking over at his mother's surprised and relieved face, he said cheerfully:

'Mother would you like a drop of brandy?'

CHAPTER 11.

By the time autumn had made its blustering presence felt across the Irish countryside, Molly's life had settled into a routine. Driving to her new school with Hattie each day, she could only stare in wonder at the glorious colours of the trees around her.

The sun streamed shafts of light through the thick wood and the morning mist rose up to meet it. The dying leaves clung in vain to their bare branches as they danced their last dance with life and glided effortlessly through the air, gracefully landing on the cold damp ground. Mother nature was busy gathering her summer children under her dark cloak. Then she wisely coaxed them into a winter slumber.

The winds came rushing in to help her spread havoc across the Wexford countryside. Wildly they blew, pruning the dead foliage from the hedgerows, trees and gardens. Birds followed the farmer's plow waiting hopefully for the brown earth to yield up its food. Others gathered with military precision on the telephone lines for the inaudible order to fly south towards the sun.

Looking out the large window of the classroom, Molly noticed the angry clouds gathering in the sky. She wondered what winter was going to be like in the country. Then she began wondering what Aggie might be doing. With the days getting shorter, she missed her daily visits to the cottage. Saturday was the only day she could go there now.

Rapping the ruler noisily on the desk, her teacher, Miss Short, interrupted her thoughts.

'Miss Furlong, when you're quite ready maybe you might like to join us. Take out your English book please and read aloud from page 10.'

Molly jumped, startled back to reality.

'Sorry Miss,' she said apologetically.

The other children stayed very quiet and put their heads down in their books.

Miss Short came from a small village in County Kerry. A matronly figure, she wore silver- pointed framed glasses and flowery dresses. But it was her blue permed hair that held Molly's attention. Such a

41

peculiar colour, and yet she admired her for wearing it. Aunt Hattie never would. She also noticed the way she pulled her cardigan over her ample bosom time and time again, as she folded her arms.

Wandering over to the window during reading lessons and gazing up at the sky, Molly often wondered what she could be thinking about. Whatever it was she would move her lips and begin talking to herself. Noticing this, the other children would giggle among themselves. On hearing their giggles, Miss Short would turn back and in an instant there would be silence.

Although she was kind and the children liked her, she could give a fair whack with the ruler. Molly discovered this when she was caught talking during class. Oh the embarrassment in front of her friends, that hurt more than the painful tingling in the palms of her hands.

Molly had settled in well at her new school. She really liked the Wexford children. But she found them a little quieter than the Dublin ones. They in turn found her ways exciting. She would teach them new games and they would follow her lead. Running around the large playground their screams and cheers could be heard in the distance. They were all so wild and free. At the end of break they were always reluctant to return to the classroom.

Sometimes during play, Molly would leave her companions and steal away to the parish church next door. There was something mysterious about being there on her own. In a strange way she felt she had God's full attention. Looking up at the ceiling, she would feel very small indeed. The strange quietness of the building only heightened her sense of discovery.

On reaching the altar, she would stare nervously at the golden doors of the tabernacle. The thought of Jesus being in there filled her mind with wonder and she always felt she was in a special place. At this time Molly's faith was unquestioning. Walking back down the aisle she would gaze sadly at the pictures of Christ's suffering on the wall. In her childish innocence she would think: 'I'm glad Jesus is safe behind those golden doors, nobody can hurt him again.'

While she lingered in the church she was quite unaware that He was forming a one to one relationship with her.

Then the school bell could be heard in the distance and she would leave quickly and run across the yard. She would resume her seat in the classroom just as the teacher finished writing on the blackboard.

One day, Miss Short asked a girl called Francine to go to the shop and buy some Jacob's Mikado biscuits. The child returned with the biscuits and some change.

The children watched closely in amazement as their teacher scraped all the gooey fondue off the biscuits and rolled it into a ball. Then, holding it up, she asked the children to pick a number between one and ten. A poor girl said four, and smiled broadly when she was presented with her present. While Miss Short dipped, what was now a plain biscuit, into her tea, all the children gathered excitedly around the child.

While Molly dipped her finger into the gooey fondue with the others, she could not help wondering why the teacher did not buy plain biscuits in the first place. But then, as she swallowed the sugary treat, she was so glad that she didn't.

CHAPTER 12.

It had been a fortnight since Eithne and Seamus Thornton's third child was born. Hattie, Julie, and Molly were in a happy mood as they travelled the road to Dublin. As well as the excitement of seeing the new baby, Hattie and Julie were very curious as to what changes the young couple might have made to their previous home at no. 28.

When Seamus opened the door Molly's eyes almost popped out of her head. Clutching shyly on each side of his long legs were the twins. In the ten months since she had left Dublin they seemed to have grown so much. The little boy and girl were now running around, or rather waddling around in their bulky nappies. Their small mouths sucked on bottles half filled with milk and their soothers were pinned safely to their jumpers. Molly could not help laughing at their antics and she kept trying to pick them up in her arms.

'Be careful now, Molly they're are not toys you know,' said Hattie as she reached up and kissed Seamus on the cheek.

'Don't worry mother,' he replied 'they're Thorntons, made of strong stuff isn't that right Julie?'

'Indeed it is.'

Then putting his arm fondly around his old housekeeper and friend he said wearily:

'We could do with someone wonderful like you around here just now.'

Julie looked on a little bashful.

Then bending down, he scooped a twin effortlessly up in each arm and carried them in the direction of the kitchen. The women followed behind. In the hall Hattie noticed to her distaste, vibrant bright colours painted on the old walls.

'Now mother,' said Seamus sensing her disapproval, 'It's our choice and we happen to like it.'

In the kitchen, Eithne sat beside the Aga cooker nursing the sleeping baby in her arms. She looked well but tired. Hattie went over and kissed her warmly. Then when she saw her latest grandchild she sighed lovingly and threw her arms up in the air. Molly was hoping she would get to hold it, but Eithne offered it to Auntie Hattie's outstretched arms instead.

As Hattie sat down to nurse the baby Molly slipped her finger into its tiny hand. She was so amazed at the size of it and fingered it gently. The baby's eyes were shut tightly and every now and again she would give a little jerk, just to remind them that she was alive. She had a lot of black hair, and everyone agreed that she was very beautiful. But it was the twins James and Josephine that drew Molly's attention. They kept running around, playing with their toys and trying to climb on the furniture.

Seamus suggested that Eithne and his mother might have more peace if they moved to the sitting room.

'Yes, good idea,' said Julie 'and I'll make the tea. Tell me Eithne how do you find cooking in the Aga? Are you used to it yet?'

'Well I haven't had much time with it as you can see. I have my hands full. But the young girl who comes in three times a week to help finds it great.'

Taking no objections from anyone, Julie rolled up her sleeves and put the kettle on what had been her cooker for years.

Seamus stayed playing with Molly and the twins for a bit, but then he had to go on his rounds at the hospital.

The warm glow from the coal fire was very welcoming when the two ladies entered the sitting room. Hattie was relieved to see that the dreadful loud colours and modern furniture had not been imposed on this room. It was left it as it was. After all she had paid quite a bit for the hand painted silk wallpaper and she was glad they appreciated it.

Hattie cherished this time with her daughter-in-law.

Seamus had met Eithne when she was nursing at the same hospital. She was a nice country girl with a pleasant appearance. Short thick blonde hair framed the high cheekbones of her tiny face, and two little dimples only enhanced her lovely smile.

She was a real homemaker and Hattie had been very pleased when they announced their engagement. She always feared Seamus might marry one of those other silly girls he dated.

Just then he popped his head round the door.

'I'm off now, and I'll see you at dinner. I should be back around six.'

'Okay darling.'

'Bye son,' said Hattie.

Then turning to Eithne Hattie informed her that she was going to visit Jessie McDermott in the afternoon.

'Now I know her brother Mick is taking care of her since J.J. died, but heaven knows what that's like. I mean he wasn't able to take care of himself all those years he was away. I think I'll bring Molly with me, Jessie likes to see her.'

'Well,' replied Eithne earnestly, 'Seamus calls to them as much as he can. He says she's well looked after. But it's very difficult to take care of somebody who's mind is wandering.'

'That may be so but I want to go see for myself, anyway I owe it to Molly's mother.'

That afternoon Hattie helped Molly into her warm winter coat. The cold November wind blew sharply round the corners of the streets as they walked over to McDermott's. People hurried by with their heads bent against the stiff breeze. In the months she had been away in the country Hattie had forgotten just how crowded the city streets could be. Reluctant to go, Molly kept lagging behind. She would have preferred to stay in the warmth indoors and play with the twins.

On reaching McDermotts, Hattie knocked twice on the door. When it opened suddenly she was amazed to see Mick Mcoy dressed in flared grey slacks and a bright coloured jumper. Two large shirt lapels over lapped each other at the base of his thin long neck. She was pleased that his appearance was at least neat and tidy. A cigarette dangled from the edge of his dry lips as he squinted his eyes to see through the smoke. Then his dark wrinkled face suddenly broke out into a smile when he recognized his visitors.

'Ah is it you Molly come to see yer ould grandad?' he said, ignoring Hattie and bending down to shake hands with the child. His voice was hoarse from cigarettes, and his hand felt cold to the touch. Molly giggled nervously.

Breezing past him into the hall, Hattie enquired about Jessie. Throwing the butt out on the street, Mick looked left and right then closed the door behind them. Winking at Molly he replied:

'Jess is havin' a little lie down. But come on up to the room and see her, Sure we're all family.'

Unable to reply to his absurd remark, Hattie followed him, one pace back, and up the narrow stairs.

With the curtains drawn the bedroom was in semi-darkness. A heavy haunting smell lingered in the air. Hattie lifted her arms to open the window but Jesse's voice spoke crossly from the bed:

'No, leave it. There'll be a draft.'

Hattie stopped and straightened her fur jacket. Then she went over, took Jessie's hand gently in hers and sat on the edge of the bed.

'Well, Jessie, I said we'd keep in touch, and here we are. So tell me, how have you been?'

Jessie did not reply. She withdrew her hand from Hattie's grasp and returned to folding and scrunching her white cotton handkerchief. Her empty sad eyes stared blankly at the opposite wall.

Mick McCoy reached for a large glass. Hungry looking false teeth lay in water at the bottom.

Then helping to steady Jessie's hand, he watched carefully as she put them clumsily into her mouth. Hattie too watched closely. She noticed Jessie had put on a little weight. Her black permed hair was now straight and grey. But apart from that, Hattie thought she looked quite well.

Although Molly was used to Aggie's ways she found Jessie a bit frightening. So she decided it would be safer to stay back beside the bedroom door. Noticing her there Hattie beckoned to her to come stand beside her chair. Mick McCoy went over, took the young girl by the hand and led her to the bed. Although she had known Jessie since she was born, Molly now found her a little strange.

'Hello Aunt Jessie,' she said politely.

Ignoring the child, Jessie pulled anxiously at Mick's sleeve,

'Have I had me medicine today?' she asked crossly.

Feeling a little awkward Molly stepped back. Hattie put her arm around her reassuringly.

'I must say Mr. McCoy,' whispered Hattie 'you've been doing a great job under very difficult circumstances.'

'Is J.J. home yet?' interrupted Jessie.

Winking and nodding at Hattie, Mick released his sleeve from her grip and gentle tucked her hand under the bedclothes.

'Don't ya worry now Jess, he'll be in soon, any minute now.'

A worried frown spread over Jessie's forehead.

'He'll be wanting his tea, she said 'and I'll have ta lock up the shop.'

Struggling with the bedclothes, the confused woman made to get up.

Mick reassured her that J.J.'s tea was ready and that the shop was safely locked up.

'What do you think of our little Molly Jess?' he said trying to change the subject, 'she's got very big hasn't she?'

'Course she's big,' she replied crossly 'Isn't she married now?'

Suddenly, with all modesty gone, Jessie threw back the bedclothes and tried to get up. Hattie grabbed the sheet in an effort to cover her. Steering Molly out the door, Mick suggested lemonade and biscuits. Molly was glad to leave the room. She felt uncomfortable and kept looking back to see if aunt Hattie was coming too.

On the way downstairs, Mick reassured her that her aunt would be down shortly.

In the sitting-room, Molly ran over to look at the large wedding photo of her parents hanging just above the sideboard.

Upstairs Hattie sat down at the side of the bed again. Gently she took Jessie's cold hand in hers. Unable to find the right words, she felt very sad. Jessie's condition had deteriorated quite a lot in the last six months.

'It's strange,' she thought 'but for Molly's mother, I would never have had a close relationship with her.'

She remembered how independent and strong Jessie had been all down through the years. It seemed as if nothing could shake her. But then, nobody counted on the shock coming from the inside. Molly's death had shattered her heart, but J.J.'s had broken it in two.

Tears welled up in Hattie's eyes and she reached over and stroked Jessie's hair gently. Childlike, Jessie smiled back at her. Hattie felt so helpless. She wanted to make everything better, but it was impossible. Jessie had become a prisoner in the intricacy of her own mind.

A little while later Hattie walked slowly down the stairs. Molly was sitting at the warm fire engrossed in tales of Mick's seafaring adventures. He stood up quickly as she entered the room. Hattie refused his kind offer of tea, using dinner at Seamus's as the excuse.

'Finish up your lemonade now Molly, we have to get back, its getting dark,' she said, pulling on her warm suede gloves.

Molly gulped the fizzy red drink so fast it came back up her nose and made her cough.

Hattie asked Mick if he had ever thought about moving Jessie to a home.

'Ah, no mam, sure it gives me a chance to make up for all the years I've missed. Anyway, there's property here to mind with the fish shop closed up, and that little flat up over. Now your Seamus, God bless 'im, he's been a great help to us.'

Thanking him for his hospitality, Hattie ushered Molly outside and offered Mick the limp paw.

He bent down and, while planting a kiss on Molly's forehead his brown fingers slipped a 2 shilling piece into her hand.

'Won't ya come again soon to see your ould grandad?' he called after her as they hurried away. Molly turned and waved until they were out of sight.

When they arrived back at no. 28, she was happy to return to her games with the twins. Eithne was feeding the baby and Julie had a lovely dinner prepared.

'Well, Mother,' said Seamus, dropping his bag on entering the kitchen, 'Have you had a good day?'

'I'm feeling a bit perplexed actually,' she protested while drawing on her cigarette.

'Now what's the matter?' asked Seamus as he walked over to greet Ethel and admire his beautiful daughter.

'I shall ignore that remark,' said Hattie crossly. Then pacing up and down the kitchen floor she continued,

'Well first of all I go over to McDermott's this afternoon and I find Mick McCoy dressed in clothes suitable for a man half his age. Then he proceeds to inform me that we are related. Can you believe the nerve of that man? As for poor Jessie, one can hardly make sense of her at all. She's up in that bed, God love her, and she's not fully dressed."

'Yes mother, that is one of the difficulties in nursing patients suffering from Alzheimer's'

'But you don't understand Seamus,' she continued, lowering her voice 'She went to get out of bed with no panties on, and…. him in the room.'

Smiling over at Julie, Seamus tried hard to stifle a laugh. With great difficulty he replied seriously,

'Well then, wasn't it a good job you were there mother?'

CHAPTER 13.

Having thoroughly enjoyed the success of her day at the hunt, Doireann was delighted when Lady Gowne invited her to 'The Eadestown Meet'.

'This hunt is a more vigorous one,' she said in a serious tone, 'so I suggest you take out Firefly. I noticed you were a little underhorsed the last day, and Firefly could do with the exercise. I have decided not to breed with her, I'm going to develop her as a hunter instead. Then later on, perhaps, I'll sell her.'

Doireann was delighted to accept and was pleased that Lady Gowne thought she was capable enough to handle Firefly.

Meeting outside 'The Royal Oak' that Friday, Doireann noticed that the hunt lacked the elegance of the previous one at 'Hawthorne Estate'. It seemed to her there were twice as many riders there, and from all walks of life. Some of them looked a little inexperienced, sitting on their Irish draught horses. This was a more rugged and serious hunt altogether.

After the customary drink of hot mulled wine, riders and horses walked down the road for a mile to get to the field. Others riders were waiting at the gate to join them. The now familiar huntsman blew his horn for the field to move out. The sound of the hooves echoed over the River Slaney. Once in the field the large crowd of riders behaved perfectly.

Riding behind the Fieldmaster, a small man with a high pitched-voice chatted with the riders, but Lady Gowne and Doireann kept to themselves.

Onwards they went towards the hills, crossing at their brow. Stag deer could be heard bellowing up on higher ground. Reaching a small wood, the huntsman blew his horn, and the hounds, having been kept under strict control, now charged in.

Once again that familiar sound of tongue echoed back from the hills above them. A gaffer stood back while the others encircled the rath. Suddenly a large black- tailed fox darted out. Seeing the riders, he weaved to his left and headed across the open countryside. The huntsman called his hounds and the field-master held the riders. This gave the fox a more generous head -start.

The fields were endless, as the hounds in trained pursuit, and full tongue hit the line. Then on a signal, the riders surged forward with great enthusiasm.

Doireann, riding Firefly, was this time more than a match for Lady Gowne on Rioja. The two women galloped across the field. Suddenly a young rider came up alongside Doireann, causing Firefly to take on a faster pace. Racing on, the man drew up level with the field-master. Noticing this, the latter got annoyed and shouted angrily at him.

'What the hell do you think you're doing?'

'Tally ho.' shouted the young man merrily as he whipped his horse onwards.

'Get back, get back,' the Fieldmaster shouted anxiously.

But still the young rider pressed forward.

Then lashing out with his whip, the Fieldmaster shouted again: ' I'll give you tally ho, get back ya Bastard.'

The young man immediately drew back and veered to his left. Relieved, the Fieldmaster turned back to continue the chase.

Then looking causally to his right he stared in disbelief when he saw Doireann on Firefly galloping past him.

'Now where the hell do you think you're goin?" he shouted angrily.

Whipping his horse on, he tried to catch up with her, but the more he tried the more spirited Firefly became.

Galloping on, Doireann tried desperately to gain control of the horse. Catching up on the huntsman, she passed him out too, then, to her horror, she ended up scattering the hounds. In their confusion they ran quickly on towards a large ditch.

Doireann suddenly became terrified. Pulling even harder on the reins, she realized to her dismay that the horse had a bad mouth. As the hounds went down into the ditch, Firefly stopped came to an abrupt stop right on the edge, and this, in turn threw Doireann head first in after them.

The huntsman and gaffers rode furiously on, trying to gain control of the pack. The loud, slopping sound of the horses hooves as they sank into the creamy mud, galloped after them. Stumbling, Doireann tried desperately to scramble up the wet steep side of the ditch. Then the fieldmaster rode up to the edge and stopped briefly. Looking down at her, he shouted angrily from his saddle;

'You stupid woman, do you not know how to ride? Don't you realize that you've ruined the hunt.'

Then he quickly rode off again. Now it was Lady Gowne's turn. Stopping her horse, she dismounted quickly. Reaching out with her riding crop she helped pull Doireann out of the ditch. With eyes flashing she said angrily:

'I'm so embarrassed, you've ruined the hunt.'

Almost in tears, Doireann tried to apologize, but Lady Gowne was not having any of it, she mounted her horse and went to catch Firefly.

Leading the horse back to Doireann, she advised her to return to the pub and get cleaned up.

Alone now, Doireann's wet, sore body was nothing to the feelings of shame and rejection that were churning inside her. Hearing the huntsman's horn in the distance only added to her anguish and sense of loss.

Heading home, her stubborn nature suddenly united with her defiant spirit and, mounting her horse, she turned back quickly.

'I'll show them I can ride,' she said aloud as she took an extra strong hold on Firefly's reins.

Catching up with the field a little while later, she felt it would be easier to control firefly if she stayed among the riders. Also, she would be safely out of sight of both Lady Gowne and the fieldmaster.

The hunt continued on until dusk, ending when the huntsman blowing his horn, signifying a kill. Calling the hounds to heel, horses and riders then trudged tiredly back to 'The Royal Oak'.

That evening most of the riders were assembled in the pub. Manoeuvring her way through the boisterous crowd, Lady Gowne went looking for Doireann. She found her sitting alone in the 'snug' feeling a bit sorry for herself. Reassuring her that all was forgiven she asked her and to come and join the party.

Walking back towards the bar with her clothes all mud stained, Doireann was immediately handed a glass of whisky by the huntsman, who hoped she had recovered.

'Its not all red jackets and mulled wine, you know,' he said, smiling.

Thanking him, she returned his smile but still felt a bit awkward. Sitting on a stool beside her, the fieldmaster reached for a jug. Pouring some water into her glass he looked at her with a twinkle in his eye.

'You'll get it down better with a drop of this,' he said smiling 'and by the way, my name is Harry. I'm sorry I gave you such a bollakin out there.'

Doireann accepted his apology and began to feel accepted again. She relaxed and enjoyed the rest of the evening. As the night wore on, the rounds of drink kept coming. Looking around she noticed some people getting a little amorous. She found this very amusing. However, catching sight of Major Tim playfully slapping Lady Gowne on the behind angered and annoyed Doireann. Had the man no respect.

While Listening to Harry and his friends telling stories of previous hunts, Doireann began to realize that these were real friendly people. They did not let the seriousness of their sport interfere with the warmth of their social graces.

Climbing into bed that night, she pressed her sore tired back on to the warm soft mattress. Looking up at the ceiling she could not help but say with a relieved sigh, 'Oh God what a day!'

CHAPTER 14.

Two years later in the summer of 1970 the building of the new church in Laois was completed. Everyone was looking forward to the grand opening and Fr. William was very busy in preparation for the Bishop's visit. All week his car had given him endless trouble. Then out of the blue, his mother rang to say she wanted to meet him in Gorey. As his old Wolseley car rattled along the road, he could not help wondering what she could be up to now.

Driving into Gorey, he spotted her car outside 'Doggett Motors Ltd'. Then he saw her inside the main door deep in conversation with a tall young man. Noticing William drive in, Hattie walked excitedly out to her son and proceeded to tell him that she was about to buy him a new car.

'While Jim here checks out your old one, we'll go inside and have a look at some new ones,' she whispered, 'and I won't hear any arguments. I gave your brother the house and now its time to do for you. I made my decision after that trouble you had with your car, the last time you visited.'

'Mother this is a great surprise and I am very grateful,' he said thankfully as he followed her into the showroom

'I've already been in and had a look round. This one over here is beautiful,' she said, walking excitedly over to a Ford Granada. It was maroon in colour with a black vinyl roof.

'Imagine me driving around in a car like that.' he humbly protested.

Thinking for a moment, Hattie reluctantly agreed.

Then, after a little discussion about it, they finally settled for a 4-door brown Cortina. Graciously accepting it, Hattie handed him the keys and he kissed her cheek affectionately.

Driving home in his first new car, Fr. William began to think of all the use he got from his old one. Although it was ten years ago, and the car was second hand when he got it, he was still sorry to see it go.

A car was a real necessity to him. All the times he had brought some of the football teams home, rushed to accidents, sick beds, attended mass and the schools, not to mention amateur dramatics, weddings and funerals.

Holding the wheel tightly in his hands, a big smile spread across his face. Then he switched on the radio.

'Yes,' he thought, 'Isn't it great to have something reliable at last.'

However, as he drove around the parish in the next few days, he noticed a coolness among some of his parishioners. Only a few had wished him well with the car. Then he heard an odd remark as he was leaving a shop. The ould collection must be goin' well Father, but at the time he had ignored it.

However, one hot afternoon it eventually came to a head, when Mrs. Stapleton removed his dinner plate before he had quite finished. Sensing something was up he did not hesitate in asking her straight out.

'Is something the matter Orla?'

'It's the car father,' she said worriedly.

'What about it?' he asked puzzled.

'People are sayin' you bought it out of the church funds. The money that was collected for to build the new church Father.'

Unable to believe his ears he asked:

'Who is saying this?'

'Well,' she answered reluctantly, 'it's a rumour that's goin' round'

'But you know that my Mother bought that car for me.'

'Yes father, I know ... but I think ya should tell them.'

Fr. William was stunned.

He suddenly felt a strange hurt inside his heart. Could the people really think that he would help himself to the church fund?

By the time Mrs. Stapleton returned with the tea a quiet anger had built up inside him. Noticing this, she put the tray down beside him and left the room quietly.

As soon as she was gone, he got up from the table and walked over to the window. For the first time a feeling like clinging mud began to creep up his flesh and he shivered slightly. He stood for quite awhile wondering what would be the best way to deal with this harmful gossip.

For the next three days he kept to himself and spent most of his time catching up with his correspondence. He strolled in his garden amidst the scented roses and flowering shrubs. Sitting under the shade of the large chestnut tree, he was lost in thought and prayer. But in spite of his tolerance and patience, he found the whole situation unbearable. He knew deep down that he would have to do something about it.

It was a glorious Sunday morning as he strolled across the yard towards the church. Then, dressed in his vestments, he walked out on the altar in his usual quiet, reverend way. The church was packed with families and summer visitors home on holidays. As he walked up the four steps onto the pulpit, the people sat up in their seats quietly, waiting to hear his sermon.

He read the usual births, deaths, and marriage notices, together with the news of the parish and then he paused a while.

Leaning his elbows on the pulpit, he looked intensely down at his flock.

'I believe there are some people in this parish, who think I took some money out of the building fund, to buy myself a new car,' he began. Someone coughed at the back of the church and others moved uncomfortably in their seats.

'My new car,' he continued in a more serious tone 'was a present from my mother, as was the old one before, as indeed was the money for my education to become a priest. However, I am not here to defend my honour, Instead, I want to talk about evil thoughts behind vicious words that in turn hurt people so deeply. Tongues are double-edged swords and they must be kept under control. I believe it to be a minority that started this dreadful rumour, but one bad apple can turn a whole basket rotten. I want you to know that I am hurt and very disappointed.'

He paused, and a humble quietness descended on the congregation. Some people hung their heads in shame and embarrassment. Others looked up at their curate with sad eyes.

'However,' he continued in a more hopeful voice, 'I do not intend to let this spoil the relationship we have built down through the years. I like what we have achieved together. I hope things will go back to the way they were. Apologies won't be necessary, as I prefer mischievous thoughts to be changed for more constructive ones. Our new church is about to be opened. Our Bishop will come to officiate and I want us to enjoy and be proud of our labours over the last ten years.'

Then he raised his right hand and he blessed his people with an extra feeling of sincerity.

'May God bless and keep you always.'

Picking up his papers he turned, walked back down the steps, and continued with the Mass.

Afterwards, some of the parishioners went home quickly while others lingered to shake his hand and to thank him.

A little while later, while sitting down to dinner, he felt a great weight lift from his shoulders.

'Well Orla,' he said cheerfully as she put a tasty salad on the table in front of him 'I don't think we should have any more trouble about the car.'

'Maybe so Father,' she replied worriedly, 'but what about me new bike?'

CHAPTER 15.

On Monday morning Walter Furlong was up and about as usual bright and early. Walking into the dairy, he thought he heard giggling coming from inside. Noticing it was Frank and Biddy messing about, he picked up his jug of milk and left them to it.

Walking back to the house, he found himself thinking about his dairymaid, come housekeeper Biddy.

It was twelve years ago now since she came to work for him. She was thirteen then, a slip of a girl.

'Where does the time go?' he asked himself.

It was only like yesterday when her mother, the Widow Brown, came to see him.

Having lost her husband, she was unable to cope with life and had taken to drink. She was a big woman with arms that could wrestle a bear. Her hair tied up in a ponytail, always seemed to be escaping from its band. Holding her only child tightly by the arm, she had walked, businesslike into the yard at 'Riversdale House' and asked Walter for a job for Biddy.

'She's a good strong one, Mr. Furlong,' she said through her broken black teeth. Then she held Biddy's arm out for him to feel her muscle, 'and what's more, she'll give no cheek but will do as she's told.'

'I'll take your word for it Mrs. Brown, if ya don't mind,' said Walter, smiling down at the child.

Big green eyes looked up shyly at him from a face that was older than her years. Flaming red hair framed her chubby freckled face, and it was not long before he realized she had a temper to match.

Walter took her on at Aggie's say so, and from then on it was Aggie who took her under her wing and trained her.

Following Aggie around the big farmhouse Biddy found she had a love for her surroundings. There was many an evening when she just did not want to go home. She was a nice enough girl with a simple dedication to the Furlong family. She knew her place and accepted it. The Furlong children were ten years older than she but they all got on pretty well together. She especially liked Doireann, even though she could be a bit bossy at times.

Two years later, the widow took to her sick bed. Like so many other people in that year of the bad flu, she died. Poor Biddy was orphaned. After that Biddy remained living alone in her house at the end of a row of council houses.

Over the years there were rumours of one or two admirers calling to see her after the local hops. But nobody in the local community was ever aware of any romance. Everyone said she was married to her job. What they did not know was that Biddy was one of those unfortunate people who get caught between two worlds.

Not brought up to live with the wealth of the Furlongs, she found she was unable to accept her own background either. The local boys did not interest her and her house was just somewhere to sleep. She never felt it was home.

The house stood beside the field the local's called 'The Long Meadow'. An old stone style built on the opposite side led the way to a worn path. It was up this narrow winding path, that Biddy Brown walked every morning. Picking her way through the odd cow pat she went across the meadow, to do her work as maid at 'Riversdale House'.

One Monday afternoon Walter Furlong drove into the top field. Stopping the engine of his jeep, he climbed out and looked out across the hayfields. He never tired of seeing the same wonderful scene repeat itself year after year. The hot July sun was high in the blue cloudless sky. A slight warm breeze teased his brown flesh, but could give no real relief from the summer sun. Taking his handkerchief from his pocket, he removed his cap and wiped the sweat from his brow. Then, replacing it, he raised his hand to shield his eyes from the bright sunlight.

Looking down across the meadow, he could see David in the distance rowing the hay with the new haybob. A small fog of fine dust followed him as he sped up and down the large meadow. Over on the other side, Frank had started to bale with the new round baler. Walter watched in amazement as the baler stopped every few minutes, opened its big mechanical jaws, and dropping a large round bale accurately on the ground. In the hard earth, short strong blades of hay remained, like stubble on a giant's face.

Leaning back against the bonnet of the jeep, Walter folded his arms and began thinking. This was the first time in sixty-eight years that the Furlong's had not cocked the hay. Once again he found it hard to believe how easily one machine could do the work of twelve men.

With the introduction of the combine harvester some years back, the journeymen were only needed once a year. Now, however, with the further invention of the round baler, they were not needed at all. But Walter found he had mixed feelings about this too. It was sad to think that a whole chapter of country life could almost disappear overnight.

With the metal of the jeep getting uncomfortably hot behind him, he stood up quickly and walked slowly around the field.

He had always tried to carry out his late father's wishes.

'Hold on to the old ways as long as possible son,' he had said earnestly.

Then he remembered how as a boy he would walk around the farm listening to his father. The farm was more than land to him it was a way of life. Thinking about it now, both his parents had taught him to appreciate and safeguard the traditions of the Furlong family.

Kneeling down on his hunkers, he picked up a strand of hay lying on the ground. In that moment he felt a strange closeness to his dead parents. Standing up again, he began sucking on the traneen. Looking down across the field, it was only now he could see the real benefits of what his own sons had accomplished. Because of their hard work and planning, their 400 acre farm was running quite smoothly just by itself. Suddenly he felt a great awareness that he had instilled in them what his father had bred in him, respect and love of the land.

Continuing to watch David and Frank at work Walter knew he had kept his promise. Then he smiled, for in his heart he could not help feeling extremely proud.

Chapter sixteen

As Doireann mucked out the stable, she kept thinking back to her humiliating experience with the hunt. Her confidence and pride had been shaken. Cutting the twine from a fresh bale of straw she slipped it into her pocket. Then taking a clump of the golden straw she began spreading it around the stable floor.

'Maybe,' she thought seriously 'It **is** time I went back on the showjumping circuit.'

Having done quite a bit of it when she was in her teens, she remembered how much Pacha and herself had achieved. Hoping to add to the medals, rosettes, and trophies she had already collected, she decided she needed a greater challenge.

Leading Pacha back into the clean stable, she hugged and patted her affectionately.

'Yes,' she thought to herself, 'It's time I went up a grade and entered some of the big competitions like the Waterford Show. Why, was it not only last week she had discussed the matter with Lady Gowne and she had encouraged her'.

'You will need a good horse to get anywhere in that event,' her friend had advised, 'I may be wrong, but I think Pacha's age might be against her.'

Then she went on to offer her Firefly. Doireann graciously declined. She did not want a repeat performance of the day at the hunt.

As Doireann continued patting Pacha on the neck, she thought back to the time Walter had bought the mare for her. Even though it was a very young horse, it was strong and had a good mouth. Then a bold idea came into Doireann's head. She knew David had forbidden her to ride Cuiteog. He was convinced that only he could handle the stallion's high spirit. However she would show him.

So like a naughty child, she began scheming. She remembered that David went away most weekends.

'That's when the coast will be clear, and I will ride Cuitteog.'

By the time David would find out she would be able to prove to him that she could control his horse.

So rising very early on Saturday mornings long before anyone else would get up, Doireann began to go quietly to the stables.

Being familiar with her, Cuiteog showed no resistance when she went to saddle him up. He actually seemed to enjoy these early morning gallops. Racing across the fields, she found the speed and power of the stallion exhilarating.

One morning on returning to the stable, Frank suddenly appeared around the corner. With a scowl on his cross face he said sternly:

'You shouldn't be riding that horse, you're not able to handle it.'

Recognizing the grumpy mood he was in, Doireann stopped for a moment and cheekily replied:

'So, its none of your business,' and continued walking the horse on.

Following behind her he stopped and leaned against the wall.

'I won't tell Dave, but you're not as good a horse woman as ya think.'

Fed up with his negative remarks, Doireann snapped back:

'Ah ya thick ould farmer, sur, what would you know anyway?'

Later, while resting on her bed, Frank's hurtful words came back to haunt her. She would show him. She would show them all that she was a real horsewoman. But then, on further reflection, she realized the seriousness of it all and what it really meant to her. So she decided to come clean. On David's return she would tell her big brother, and get him to agree.

The following Monday evening she approached him in the stable as he was saddling up Cuiteog.

'Did yerself and Alishe have a good weekend Dave?' she inquired nervously.

'I must say we did thanks,' he replied with a very satisfied grin on his face.

'Where did ya go?'

'We went to Dingle it was lovely.'

'Great,' she thought,' he's in good humour.' Then aloud she said cheerfully:

'I was thinking I might compete in the Waterford show this year.'

'That's great you were always good at that.'

'This time I think I might move up a grade, and I thought …ahem…if you'd let me, I might ride Cuiteog.'

'No,' came a definite reply.

Raising her voice a little Doireann made a great plea:

'But Dave, I've never asked you for anythin' before. I've worked really hard in this place, I've scrubbed and I've mucked out. I've played second fiddle to you and Frank all my life. Now I want to do somethin' for me. What happened at the hunt was not my fault. I can handle your horse. I know I can ride him,' then in a quieter tone she continued, 'I've been exercising him at weekends while yer away.'

Giving the leather a hard pull, he said angrily:

'You mean you've been taking him out behind my back?'

'Well yeah, But only to prove something. Your life has changed and I'm happy for you, but I'm stuck here with Frank, and you know what he's like. I only come alive when I'm ridin' and winnin'.'

'That's grand but you're not doing it on Cuitteog.'

Then she pleaded again.

'But Dave, I can ride him. Nobody believes me, maybe it's because I'm a woman. I don't know. The only one on my side is Lady Gowne. She believes in me and thinks I'm right.'

Then taking hold of the reins she begged,

'Please Dave this is important. Come on let me show you I can ride him.'

David looked down into his sister's pleading brown eyes. It was almost like they were children again and she wanted to play. He remembered how she would try to prove that she was able to keep up with her brothers. He had felt pity for her then and now he felt it happening again. He had just come back from a wonderful weekend with Alishe, and poor Doireann had nobody.

'Well,' he thought to himself, 'if she wants this so bad I'm not going to stop her.

Reluctantly he gave in.

With Cuiteog saddled up, he gave her a leg up. Coming across the yard with a bucket, Frank could not help grinning when he saw David leading her on the horse. Doireann smiled smugly down at him.

Over the next few months, she spent four days a week schooling the black stallion. Newer and higher jumps were set up in the paddock. At first she found it difficult to get him to take the short turns and deal with different jumps. She also found he had difficulty changing his pace. He was so used to galloping fast across the fields. However, as time passed, she felt she was at last getting somewhere.

One morning she woke earlier than usual. She thought about all the intricate work she had been doing with Cuiteog. Then deciding to treat him to a bloody good gallop like he was used to, she jumped out of bed and dressed quickly. After saddling up, she mounted him, and headed out the gate.

Galloping across the countryside, she thought about the events of the last months. The humiliation she suffered at the hunt, Frank's hurtful remarks, and David's lack of confidence in her.

'Come on Cuiteog,' she shouted 'We'll show them, we'll show them all.'

As if resenting the crack of the whip, Cuitteog put his ears down and surged forward. The horse did not frighten her she felt so familiar with him. With her blood up, she thought she could do anything. Being in great physical shape, her strong thighs squeezed harder on the saddle as her gloved hands held tightly to the reins. The fresh morning air blew cold on her face as she raced across the fields.

'I'll never give up this feelin' of excitement and freedom,' she thought determinedly.

Steering the horse to the left, she galloped down the long field and jumped over a hedge. As they cleared it, she suddenly felt something tug at the foot of her left boot. Looking down she shouted angrily:

'Oh damn barbed wire.'

Quickly pulling up the horse, she jumped down to examine him.

To her horror, she saw his four legs were badly torn. The back ones being the worst, with deep cuts bleeding profusely. After tying him to a nearby tree, she quickly whipped off her jumper and blouse. Standing in the open fields with the cold morning air blowing though her vest she tried to calm the injured stallion,

'Don't worry boy,' she whispered, 'you'll be alright, steady now, steady,'

Tearing her blouse into strips she approached his legs slowly and gently. Binding the wounds up tightly she hoped the bleeding would stop. Then, replacing her jumper, she began to walk the horse home. Feeling humiliated and fearfully angry every so often, she would stop and hit out with closed fists at the air saying:

'Damn, damn, damn. Why didn't I see the wire? Who put it there anyway?' Then looking for someone to blame she said angrily, 'I bet it was Frank.'

In spite of hurrying she was reluctant to get home. When Frank saw the sorry pair coming slowly through the gate he ran over.

'What happened Doireann?'

'Just phone for the vet and quick,' she replied angrily, 'and they next time be careful where ya put your bloody barbed wire.'

'Now don't go blamin' me for this, I have to fence the cattle, its you that should have seen it,' he called back as he raced towards the house.

A half an hour later Robert Stafford, the young vet, pulled into the yard. He quickly set about cleaning and bandaging the wounds on the animal's legs and then commenced a thorough examination of the rest of the horse.

Suddenly he noticed a tear in the left testicle. Brushing his long fringe from his dark eyes he looked up at Doireann and said worriedly,

'Oh this looks bad… I'm afraid we may have to geld him.'

Suddenly a dreadful heavy feeling came over Doireann. What would David say when he heard this? Bad enough his stallion was injured but to render him incapable of breeding would be disastrous. Now she was in real trouble.

A little while later the vet scrubbed up for the operation, Doireann biting her thumb nail looked on sadly. Under local anaesthetic, Cuiteog had his spermatic cord tied off and the incision sewn up.

When it was all over Doireann inquired how long it might take for him to recover.

'The front wounds not so long,' the vet replied, removing his plastic gloves, 'but I'm afraid the back ones are more serious. Of course now he's gelded he should be calmer during convalescence. I would expect him to make a full recovery.'

Walking the vet back to his car Doireann thanked him gratefully for his help.

Not being able to contact David, she needed to talk to somebody about the accident so she went indoors and rang Lady Gowne.

'Oh such rotten bad luck,' said Lady Gowne sadly, on hearing the news. 'Thank God I have Propeller. Oh, dear it is such a shame. One has to be so careful with barbed wire where horses are concerned. Still it could have been worse. Now don't go worrying yourself over this, I'm sure David will understand that these things happen.'

But Doireann was worried, so worried that she spent all night in the stable with him. Waking up with the dawn, she felt cold and miserable.

When she heard Alishe dropping David off in the yard a lump rose up in her stomach. The thoughts of telling him weighed heavily on her mind. Trembling she gathered up all her courage and walked out of the stable into the yard. But when she reached him her courage failed her and she just broke down and cried. The tiredness and strain of it all was just too much to cope with. With her head bowed low, she kept repeating:

'Oh Dave I'm sorry, I'm so sorry.'

David tried to raise her chin but she buried it deeper into his chest.

'What is it Doireann? Is it Molly? Is the Boss? What is it?' he asked taking her by the shoulders. With tears rolling down her face, she blurted out her sad story.

David immediately left her standing and ran towards the stables. Hurrying behind him Doireann, in between sobs kept saying sorry.

'Don't keep saying that, you'll only start crying again.'

Entering the stable he noticed Cuiteog's eyes rolling around in his head. Stroking his neck, he turned to his sister and anxiously said:

'He's in pain run in quick and ring for the vet again.'

When Robert Stafford arrived out to the stable he inspected and dressed the wounds once more.

Turning to David he reassured him saying:

'I started him on antibiotics last night so they will start working soon. I've given him a painkiller so hopefully he will settle down now.'

Then taking David to one side he continued in a low voice:

'By the way, don't be too hard on Doireann she was in a right state yesterday. You know there is always a risk of gelding with these animals.'

Deep down David knew the vet was right. But he felt so disappointed. There would be no more foals from Cuiteog. It was such a pity because he had come from a great bloodline.

'Yeah, I know, thanks for all your help,' he sighed sadly.

'I'll fix up with you later.'

Over the next couple of weeks the horse was box rested. Doireann spent all her time caring for him. Feeling very low, she avoided any conversation with David, and he did not push it. He knew her remorse was genuine. She was hurting.

A few weeks later only hairline scars on Cuiteog's legs showed any evidence of injury as he went on to make a full recovery,

David decided that in future nobody would ride Cuiteog but him.

But as the weeks passed, it seemed as if Cuiteog was not the only one who lost his wild spirit that day. To anyone who cared to notice, it looked like a little flame had died inside Doireann as well.

CHAPTER 17.

Sometimes in our lives somebody we love will take us to a place. This place can be visited a thousand times but we only remember the day we spent with that person. There are special people with us who can see magic and wonder in everything. They never tire of the world, and they never tire of the seasons. But their greatest gift is when they open our minds by sharing their unique thoughts with us. Only then do we begin to appreciate our surroundings and try never again to take them for granted. It was on such a day that Aggie Cullen took Molly for a stroll in the woods.

Having set off early that morning, Molly carried a small picnic basket while Aggie carried a piece of light rope. Aggie walked slowly and steadily while Molly kept skipping ahead. Now and again Aggie would pause and look out across the countryside. She would then point out and name an isolated house or farm in the distance.

The morning was hot, with the July sun already high in the sky. A deep dry dike bordered the woods, while an overgrown laurel hedge surrounded it. Finding a gap in the hedge, Aggie pushed through and made her way slowly down the dike. The roots sticking out of the dry clay, she used as steps, while Molly impatiently jumped in after her.

'Ya must be more careful child,' said Aggie worriedly, 'If ya land on a stone ya'll break your ankle, and I can't carry ya home.'

On either side of the wood, and stretching far out in front of them, were larch, beech, and ash trees.

These trees made up the wonderful wood called Paradise. On entering the wood, Molly found the atmosphere different from that of the open fields. A mysterious quietness seemed to come over the place. She felt tiny walking under the tall trees each one having great prescence. Excitedly, she drew Aggie's attention to the little bushy tailed squirrels that skipped playfully out from behind the trees and darted in again.

Onwards they walked carefully on the uneven ground, past the old ruins of a monastery with thick undergrowth protruding from its walls and crevices. Looking up, a gothic-style stone arch was still visible in the crumbling walls. Holding hands, they made their way deeper into the dense wood, with the high trees blotting out the daylight, and the cool air giving welcome relief from the hot sun. Then, stepping over a small dry ditch, Aggie announced that they had arrived.

Molly could not believe what lay before her eyes. Underneath her feet was a soft green carpet of mossy earth. All around, tall trees stood rigidly upright, while the large twisting roots spread out across the ground like alien fingers. In the sky above the sun watched for its chance to break through the thick branches. The gentle breeze rustled the leaves, adding to the timelessness of the moment. In the distance, shafts of light streamed down from heaven, and this, combined with the singing of the birds, gave the woods a beautiful magic all of its own.

Then Molly noticed that growing among the green ferns were the splendid colours of violets bluebells and primroses, while the bushes nearby were laden with berries. The beautiful flowers and plants seemed to have made this spot their home, and here they were sheltered equally from the sun and frost alike. The hazel bush with its shiny bark reached straight up, and, clinging to it, were clumps of nuts not quite ripe. The branches of the sloe bush bowed low under the sheer weight of its berries.

Aggie stopped and bent down to look at the plants and flowers. Molly went over and picked one and tasted it, but quickly spat its sourness from her mouth.

'They're far from ripe yet child,' said Aggie laughing. 'Now do ya see the white thorn bush over there?' she said, pointing to her right, 'The one with the green berries on? Well they turn a lovely red colour in the autumn.'

Leaving Aggie to find her plants, Molly ran in and out between the trees. Shouting her name loudly, she was thrilled when the woods echoed it right back. Then she spotted some acorns scattered around, and began to gather them up in her summer dress. Big or small she only chose the ones that were perfect.

'I'll paint these when I get home,' she thought happily, 'and I'll hang them on the tree at Christmas.'

After some time, Aggie's old back felt stiff so she sat down to rest on the bark of a dead elm tree. Hearing Molly singing in the distance, she called out to her. The child came walking back carefully holding out the hem of her summer dress. It was laden down with acorns.

'What have ya got there child? ' asked Aggie curiously.

'I found all these Aggie, and there's lots more too.'

'Aye the woods are full of them, but don't forget ya'll have to carry them home. Put them down now, and we'll have our picnic.'

Molly dropped awkwardly to her bare knees and the acorns spilled out onto the ground. Then she went over and opened the picnic basket. Julie had packed wonderful ham sandwiches and some tea brack. There was a flask of tea for Aggie and a bottle of milk for Molly. Out in the fresh Wexford air, the food tasted delicious and Molly found she was very hungry. While they ate they were surrounded by an eerie silence.

'Look around ya child and tell me what ya see?' said Aggie, putting her cup down.

'I see trees, leaves, flowers and everything,' she replied happily.

'Aye ya do, but yer only seen the cover of the book child. Mother Nature has a quiet simplicity. She only reveals her secrets to them that search. To anyone with a proud heart an a cold eye, she will appear as dead as this elm.'

'But how do you search for her secrets Aggie?' asked Molly wondering.

Picking up a small three- cornered seed from under a beech tree, she held it in the palm of her hand. Breaking it open, it revealed a grey, white substance inside. Looking at it for a moment, she then replied:

'See this child? To understand nature, compare yerself to this seed. It can feed the squirrels and the birds, or it can hide in the undergrowth. But wherever it is, Mother Earth will coax it into the soil. There it'll sleep in the warm earth, welcome the rain and yearn towards the sun. It can't live without Mother Nature and so it doesn't fight her. Instead it yields and waits for its day to grow.'

'And it always does, doesn't it Aggie?' said Molly, biting into a sandwich.

'Aye it does. One day this seed will grow into a beautiful tree. Just like the seed of curiosity I've planted in yer head will make yer mind grow, and help ya search for the truth.'

'How do you know all these things Aggie?' asked Molly curiously.

Aggie rose from her seat and walked a few steps away. Turning back to the child she stretched out her arms excitedly.

'Look around ya,' she said with great enthusiasm, 'Look closely at God's earth. Bend down and take it in yer hands. Feel the life in the clay. The soil grows plants that can kill or cure. Eat enough and yer dancin, too much and yer sick. It's been here since God made the world. The further folk go away from the soil the more they are lost.'

Then bending down she picked up a nettle.

'Watch out!' said Molly worriedly, 'that'll sting.'

Chuckling to herself, Aggie ignored her cry and picked up a dockleaf that was growing nearby. Walking back to Molly she held them out one at a time

'One to sting, and one to cool,' she said knowingly, 'When I was a wee girl like yerself, me mother, God rest 'er, would boil these nettles in a big pot.' Their great for cleanin the blood and makin it strong,' she would say. She taught me everythin' I know, and these are the secrets ya must search for too Molly. But ya must search with a humble heart. The earth gives and the earth takes away, but to be part of it is the greatest gift of all.'

'But do we always have to search to find her secrets?' asked Molly, jumping up and running towards her. Bending forward, Aggie caught Molly gently by the shoulders. Then, whispering in her ear, she said mysteriously:

'No, child there's another way. Stay very still, so still that your breath sounds like a drum. Don't move a muscle or a hair on yer head.'

With great difficulty Molly froze on the spot. She strained her ears to listen. After a few moments it seemed as if the sounds of the woods were not just around her but had entered into her very being. Before, she had heard an orchestra of sounds, but now, by concentrating, she could pick out individual ones. Her hearing had grown more intense and her senses were heightened.

'I can hear it,' she whispered excitedly to Aggie. 'I can hear it.'

'Aye child, never be afraid of the silence, for in it ya'll find yerself.'

That afternoon Aggie continued to show Molly the wonders of the plants, flowers and trees. She opened up worlds within worlds and filled her with wonder. The childishness with which Molly had previously approached the countryside was now disappearing.

Slowly it was being replaced, by a reverent respect for the hidden life within. Walking on further, they came to a dreaded briar.

Strangely though it carried the juiciest fruit of all, the blackberry. This time they both ate heartily from it.

But like any day of happiness it went too soon, and the evening shadows began to close in. They had entered the woods from one end, and having walked a long way, came out the other on to the sloblands. Emerging from under the heavy shade of the trees, the evening sun felt warm on their faces. Small pools of water, surrounded by velvet bull rushes, appeared covered with frog spawn.

'Ugh!' said Molly indignantly, 'that reminds me of Aunt Hattie's tapioca.'

Then while water hens, calling their chicks, skimmed quickly across the water, white fronted geese flew overhead.

Further on, Aggie waded in a little, and pulled some watercress. Then, with their picnic basket full of flowers and plants, there was just enough room for a little wild mint that she found growing near the road.

As they made their way home down the dusty narrow road, Danny McGuiness pulled up alongside them in his ass and cart.

'Hello Mizz Cullen, hop up and I'll give yerself and the child a jont home. Since I got the rubber wheels on me cart's, she's fit for a queen.'

He jumped down awkwardly, released the metal clips that held the tailboard and helped them up. Then tightening the belly band, he hopped back up on the front again. Before moving off he rooted in his pockets and took out a packet of Silvermints. Carefully picking out three, he popped one in his mouth and held the other two in the palm of his open brown skin-cracked hand. Turning around he said cheerfully:

'Here Mizz Cullen one for you and one for the child.'

Then they set off.

Molly was delighted with the ride, for her legs were getting a little tired. As she sucked the sweet she thought that she would have preferred a little chocolate instead.

Rattling along in the old cart, the woods got further and further out of sight. With the sun going down behind them, the looked almost frightening. As if she knew what Molly was thinking, Aggie squeezed her hand in a comforting way. Now they both understood that only the people who searched would know the wood's true secrets.

Suddenly Aggie reached into her pocket and pulled out the small piece of rope.

'Look child,' she said laughing 'didn't I forget to gather me sticks.'

CHAPTER 18.

Every weekend, Alishe Furlong would drive the long road from Dublin to Wexford. Walter had grown accustomed to seeing his daughter -in- law speeding up the avenue towards 'Riversdale House'. With David's financial help, Alishe had bought out the old law practice of 'Wilkinson and Rice Solicitors'. Established since 1926, its offices were in the most impressive building in Bray. Standing three stories high, it overshadowed the bank, and insurance offices on either side. Speckled with silver, three wide granite steps led the way up to a black Georgian door. Overhead, a canopy of sheer rock was supported on either side by two tall granite pillars. Down through the years many a troubled citizen had come through that black door looking for help, compensation and justice.

Alishe had become completely wrapped up in the business and was somewhat pleased and relieved, when old Rice suggested staying on in an advisory capacity

The third floor of the building they had turned into a fashionable apartment. Alishe's taste in décor meant lots of space and muted colours. The paintings hanging on the high walls were colourful impressionist prints and only furniture that was necessary was bought. The large apartment had an old feel about it, and this added to its relaxing atmosphere. It was here that on many an evening she entertained her fellow solicitors and friends. Here also she could be found burning the midnight oil as she pondered and studied her cases for court next morning.

Alishe's father, John, was a shop steward in 'Clondalkin Paper Mills'. A fanatical trade union official, (who was decorated with not only a pioneer pin, but a fainne` as well.) He revered the politician James Connolly, and was adamant about educating his children. The family lived close to his work in a nearby village called Tallaght. Being a conscientious worker he found no real need to take any holidays.

His wife, Minnie, was a small timid person living under the shadow of her husband. She never exerted her own personality, but attended quietly to the domestic running of the household. Having reared five children, only two remained in Ireland. Malcolm and Alishe.

Malcolm, an after thought and the youngest of the family, had just entered the Garda Siocana. A tall striking young man, his air of confidence made him stand out from the other guards training at Templemore.

As for Alishe, to have a daughter a solicitor was beyond her mothers wildest dreams. While going about her chores, she would secretly smile at the thoughts of Alishe in court confidently speaking out before all those men.

Over the years, John had constantly instilled in his children the evils of drink. Now being adults, they still would not dare drink any alcohol in his presence. The freedom that Alishe experienced away from her domineering and strict father only heightened her enjoyment at parties. Raising her glasses of light Martini, she would regularly toast his good health.

Since their honeymoon in Rome, David and Alishe's marriage had settled down to a less heady affair. Their passion was confined not only in their own home, but also in different hotels when they got together at weekends. However the rest of the week they lived separate lives.

David worked full time on the farm in Wexford and in the evening he usually visited with Molly at the Rectory.

Remembering the heartfelt vow he made at her mother's grave, he continued to lavish his time and love on their daughter. With her babyhood behind her, each passing year brought father and daughter closer together. Reading her bedtime stories had given way to teaching her how to ride ponies. Watching her grow brought him great satisfaction and happiness. He loved when they could sit together and talk quietly about her mother. Then he relived that magical time and would tell their daughter how he had loved her.

Molly would look at him a certain way, or say something funny and he would have to catch his breath. It brought back to him what he saw the night she was born, his wife's very soul shining out in her two beautiful eyes.

On Friday evening, Alishe would pull down the white venetian blinds on the office window and drive down to Wexford. Speeding up the avenue, she would make a great entrance, honk the horn loudly and wait for David to join her. Sometimes she would visit her in-laws for awhile, but more often than not David would hop in the car and they would disappear for the weekend. Walter never really knew what to make of his new daughter-in-law, but he had to admit he admired her independence. Sometimes Frank and himself would tease David about his career woman.

But it was all done in great fun.

The young couple both had a love of the cinema. Sometimes David would suggest that they bring Hattie along. Whenever Alishe agreed she would insist that Fr. William come as well.

Feeling a slight coldness from Hattie, Alishe thought it best to stay away from Molly as much as possible. She would not interfere. Anyway with her busy career she would not have much time for a child. Maybe in the future when her practice was more established.

Driving along the road, she looked over at David and smiled excitedly. Just then David spotted Aggie Cullen's bent figure walking along the road in the distance. Carrying a bundle of sticks on her back it looked like she was heading home. He asked Alishe to slow down. Aggie was surprised when they pulled up and stopped the car alongside her.

'Ah its yerself Master David,' she said, wiping her runny nose with her hanky.

'Do you want a lift Aggie?' he enquired. Alishe moved uncomfortably in her seat but still smiled.

'Ah no, sur, I'd only dirty yer lovely car with me sticks,' she replied caringly.

'Not at all,' insisted David, 'we can put the sticks in the boot.'

'Ah don't go to the bother, sur, I'm nearly home now anyway.'

Alishe breathed a sigh of relief.

'Well if you're sure we'll be off so,' he said 'See ya next week, look after yourself Aggie.'

'Aye, Master David, you to, and yer young Missus.'

Driving on a little Alishe said quietly:

'I know she reared you, but don't you think you have outgrown her now?'

David did not reply. Instead he sat thinking for a moment. He tried to see Aggie through Alishe's eyes. He realized that she could see nothing attractive or smart about her. Aggie's humble qualities and country ways would not be admired in the circles his wife moved in. And although he understood and admired his new wife's ambition, it was starting to worry him a bit. He was now aware that she was beginning to resent the people who were most important to him.

CHAPTER 19.

After Doireann's unfortunate accident with Cuiteog, Lady Gowne decided to take a hand in bullying her back on the show jumping circuit. Walking around the indoor stables at 'Mount Benedict', Doireann was deep in thought and only half listening.

Suddenly Lady Gowne smiled to herself. She would try a different tactic. Stopping outside Propeller's stable she leaned over the half door and said casually,

'I was thinking…Propeller is three years old now and it's time to break him in. could you recommend anyone for the job?'

Doireann's face lit up with enthusiasm. Know anyone? Why there was no one else herself! Hadn't she saved his life? Did she not have a bond with this horse like no other? Lord how she wanted to break him in.

Walking over beside Lady Gowne she replied calmly, trying to suppress her excitement.

'I could do it if you want.'

With a mischievous twinkle in her eye she replied quite seriously:

'Oh but Doireann, I couldn't impose, you have enough to do.'

'No trouble at all,' said Doireann, looking in affectionately at the horse, 'I would love it.'

'Well if you're sure,' she said trying to hide a smile, 'then I would be rather grateful.'

In the months that followed, Doireann spent most of her time at 'Mount Benedict '

'Ya ought ta go live there altogether,' Frank would say as he scowled after her as she hurried out the door.

'You're just jealous,' she would reply smugly as she grabbed her coat.

But Doireann was so happy she did not care what anyone said. For the next year she dedicated herself to training Propeller.

Being raised with the other horses at 'Mount Benedict' and having the opportunity to canter from an early age, she found him easy to school. She was pleased that he already had some discipline as this was necessary to his potential as a jumper. It was not long before he got used to her putting the bit in his mouth and driven in long reins.

Over the next couple of weeks he learned to trot in an orderly fashion on the lunge. He also became used to wearing a rug and having a strap tightened around his belly.

Because she needed him to grow into an athlete strong and powerful, Doireann supervised all Propeller's feeding. Sometimes, if he showed signs of getting a little heavy, she would change his diet to include more protein, vitamins and less fat.

Exercising him round and round the ring, she listened intently to Lady Gowne's instructions and applied them to the letter. By the end of the year both horse and rider were ready to start competing in the novice competitions.

Over the next couple of months they travelled around to all the different shows. Doireann felt even more confident with Charlie, her groom, as back up. He could do everything, from driving a lorry to dressing a wound.

Unfortunately Propeller's first outing at 'The Strokestown Chrysler Cup' did not go according to plan. On entering the arena he was so surprised by it all that he gave up halfway through the competition. However, on his second attempt, the excitement of the crowd seemed to encourage him and he got into gear. They were quite pleased when they finished in second place.

The following year Lady Gowne decided to jump him up a Grade and compete in the 'National Class' in Dublin. By now Doireann had a great feel for the horse. The more time they spent together, the more his movements became second nature to her.

Before the competitions she would walk around the course getting to know the jumps. Then just before it officially began she would whisper the same secret words of encouragement into Propeller's ear:

'Come on boy it's just you and me.'

Round and round they would go taking each jump with great precision and skill. Then, as each rider succumbed to the wide water jump, Doireann knew by the tremendous applause that they had cleared it and won.

A week later she could be found, as usual, grooming the horse in the stables at 'Mount Benedict.' Waving a sheet of paper excitedly, Lady Gowne ran into the stable and announced that they had qualified for 'The Boomerang Competition' in Millstreet.

'Oh God!' exclaimed Doireann on hearing the news

'If only I could win that.'

For the next two months they put more effort into their training. Doireann stuck to a routine of early nights and early rises. Her own fitness improved and she glowed with health and determination.

On the morning of the competition she found that 24 horses had been entered. She was particularly nervous. Lady Gowne took her aside and advised her to hold Propeller back a little and to take her time over the jumps. She listened to the good advice and kept her head. She found that the skill in jumping this horse was not to let go but to hold with discipline. At the end she was rewarded. Out of the 24 entries only nine had clear rounds and Doireann was one of them.

Because the next round was against the clock, Doireann began biting her bottom lip nervously and tightening up. On hearing her name called over the loudspeaker, she adjusted her hat, mounted Propeller and entered the arena. Dressed in her smart black fitted riding jacket and despite her nerves, she sat confidently erect on her horse. The applause of the crowd suddenly filled her with ambition and encouragement.

'Good,' thought Lady Gowne, watching from the wings,' she needed that.'

The horse jumped superbly as if he too was excited by the crowd's reaction. Sailing effortlessly over each fence his feet seemed to have wings. Once or twice his back hooves touched the bars, but to everyone's relief the bars managed to stay in position. Then he cleared the final jump, having the first clear round. But Doireann's smile waned a little when she realized that Garret O Loughlin qualified too.

'Oh no,' she thought to herself, 'how can I compete against him with all his experience?'

Knowing how important it was to both of them, Lady Gowne ran over and encouraged her on.

Doireann was the first competitor into the arena and to her delight she had a clear round. Some of the crowd rose to their feet with excitement. Then it was Garrett OLoughlin's turn. Doireann grew worried when he reached the half way mark, realising that he was up on her time. But she could not help feeling relieved when his horse refused the big treble, giving him three faults.

Doireann had won.

Putting her hands up to her face with sheer joy, she reached up and hugged and patted Propellor.

Standing in line with the runners-up and their horses, she shook hands warmly with the Judges.

'Propeller is a fabulous horse in tremendous self carriage,' said Judge Fleming smiling happily 'He shows lots of expression and has everything I look for in a horse at this level.'

Then he proudly presented Doireann with a large silver cup for first prize. Next he reached up and pinned a red rosette on the horse's bridle. Doireann beamed with happiness and shook the judge's hands again. Standing in second place beside her, Garrett also congratulated her and shook her hand too.

'Well done,' he said sincerely, 'You did jolly good out there.'

'What a marvellous way to end the season,' said Lady Gowne, clapping her hands together as she kissed and slipped her winning cheque of £20,000 into her pocket.

A little while later, Doireann watched anxiously as some foreigners came up to Lady Gowne and offered her big money to buy Propeller. But she was thankful and relieved when their offers were kindly refused.

On the journey back to Wexford Lady Gowne turned to Doireann and said thoughtfully:

'Now I think I will rest Propeller and then we will put him in the higher class next year.'

Doireann felt relief in the security of that suggestion. For another whole year she could be with Propeller and the thought of that made her extremely happy.

CHAPTER 20.

Having been away on retreat for a week, Fr. William missed his usual first Friday visit with the Berminghams.

It was a cold, wet, miserable damp day when he arrived at their cottage. When he knocked on the door it took Jack a few moments to open it.

'Won't ya come in father,' he said, looking a bit flustered. Noticing he had a bandage on his right hand, William enquired as to what happened.

'I cut meself with the bread knife father, they can be horrid sharp ya know.'

The kitchen felt cold and there was only a small fire smoking in the hearth.

'Excuse the state of the place, but herself's not well, it's the oul ulcers, they've broken out again.'

As he proceeded to tidy some dishes away Fr. William noticed Jack's appearance was unusually grubby and untidy. The collar of his shirt was worn and his jacket was crumpled and torn. William put his hand gently on his shoulder and said in a concerned way:

'I'm sorry to hear that now, did you get the doctor?'

Getting more flustered Jack replied:

'Yeah Father, he was here a couple of days ago."

'How many days?'

Scratching his head he thought for a few moments,

'Could be three...or maybe four.'

Quickly sizing up the seriousness of the situation William said worriedly:

'Look Jack I'm going out to ring the doctor.'

Getting a little more confused, Jack replied: 'But what about the prayers?'

'Listen Jack, we'll get Annie fixed up first, then I'll be back and we'll have the prayers this evening.'

William left the cottage quickly.

Driving down the lane he got it hard to suppress his anger. This was typical example of the way old people were treated. Having worked hard and lived right all their lives, they now seemed to be left to their own devices.

By the time he returned that evening the Doctor had been and Jack was looking a lot happier. He had the kitchen tidy and a good fire burning in the hearth. The little table was set up complete with candles and crucifix and it looked like he had had a good wash too.

'I'll just get herself up,' he said cheerfully as he turned for the bedroom.

'No wait,' said William, walking over and carefully picking up the small table, 'Tonight we will bring the prayers to Annie.'

In the bedroom the old woman was sitting up in bed, her rosary beads slipping silently through her fingers. On seeing Father William she finished praying and blessed herself quickly.

'Hello Annie,' he said kindly as he took her hand 'I hear you're not well.'

'I could be worse Father,' she said, coughing to clear her throat.

'The ould ulcers are sore but sure God is good.'

'Now you rest there and Jack and I will say the prayers with you.'

A quiet holiness that only praying can bring descended on the little room. Towards the end William raised his hand to give his blessing and Annie let out a little gasp of pain. Leaning down towards her William asked worriedly:

'Are you alright?'

Pulling hard on her dry lips, she winced as she nodded. Knowing the type of pain she must be enduring, William felt a great compassion for her, not just in his heart but also with his feelings. He removed the sacred stole from around his neck and slipped his prayer book into his pocket. Then he drew up a chair beside the bed. Jack rose from his knees and began clearing the table away.

'I'll leave yez to chat for a while and I'll go make the tea.'

'Thank you,' said William as he took Annie's hand. 'You know you're a very brave lady,' he said tenderly.

'Well I try not to complain,' Then she whispered: 'ya see poor Jack has enough on his plate.'

William was moved by the sincerity of her words as in her discomfort she thought only of her husband. Then leaning over she whispered:

'These ulcers are awful things, they look terrible.'

'Yes I can imagine,' he replied sadly.

'Tell me, what is the sense of it all Father?'

William knew he would have to try and explain suffering to her. Moving his chair a little closer to the bed he began;

'Well Annie, to understand suffering we must look towards the Cross. Jesus a King in Heaven came down to earth and let himself be insulted and killed by his own creatures. Now by doing this he put a great dignity before us. A dignity he would not have had if he had not suffered.'

'Maybe so,' she replied, wincing her face, 'but suffering is a dreadful thing.'

'Yes it is Annie but it is also part of our nature. We all have to suffer.'

Thinking for a few moments, she asked more seriously:

'But Father, you take Jesus… now He chose to suffer because He was God, where as I didn't.'

William smiled at her childlike remark.

'All the more reason we should look at what happened on the Cross. Innocent suffering redeems the world. He loves you Annie and He will come to your help.'

Tears welled up in the old woman's eyes and she wiped them away with her handkerchief.

'Oh I know He does,' she said quietly, 'That is why I keep prayin'.'

As they chatted Annie accepted all Fr. William told her with a quiet reservation. Then she reached over and touched his hand.

'You make everything sound so simple,' she said smiling up at him.

'Well Annie,' he said smiling back, 'love is simple and if you can't love, you will not know God.'

Just then Jack appeared at the bedroom door with a small tray of tea and sandwiches. Placing it carefully in front of Annie, he kindly requested William to join him in the kitchen.

Looking at Annie for her approval the old lady said cheerfully,

' I'm alright now, you go out and warm yerself by the fire.'

A little later the two men were very comfortable sitting down on the big armchairs on each side of the hearth. William found the mug of tea very refreshing. Leaning over to a large wicker basket, Jack picked up a black sod of turf and threw it into the fire.

'Have another sandwich will ya Father?'

Then just as quickly he leaned over to him and whispered:

'Well what do ya think? she's not well is she?'

'Well she seems to be coping Jack, why she looked very peaceful when I left the room.'

'Maybe, Father but its not fair, seems to me that the ones who suffer the most are the good. You take my Annie, she never did anythin' only give to others all her life. Now look what she gets. I tell ya watchin' her suffer makes me that I can't pray anymore.'

Seeing the helplessness in the old man's face William suddenly felt worried about him.

'You can't pray Jack?'

'No every time I try me heart grows cold.'

William thought deeply for a few moments. 'Well then Jack you must try another way. The ordinary things you do each day, no matter how small, take them and offer them up as prayers. When you bring Annie in a cup of tea to the bed let that be your prayer. Whenever you make her comfortable, let that be your prayer also. Then you may find your heart growing softer and you may let God in again.'

'But I'm so angry with Him for makin' her suffer like that.'

William noticed an expression of confusion coming into his old face.

'Maybe it's not God you're angry with Jack, maybe it's your situation.'

Jack lowered his gaze and stared into the fire.

'How's that?'

'Well all these years Annie has been cooking and washing and been there for you. But now you have none of these comforts. You have to look after yourself.' Then leaning over to him he whispered,

'Could there is a little bit of self pity in there somewhere?'

A silence descended on the room for a few moments as Jack thought about what Fr. William had said.

'But that was always Annie's way,' he said, defending himself, 'she wanted to look after everybody.' Then quietly he added,

'ya know yer right maybe I am feelin' sorry for meself.'

'Well that's only natural,' replied William, 'but you have turned inwards, into your own feelings of unhappiness. There you will find nothing only more misery and complaining. There is nothing in you to comfort you. Now Annie on the other hand, she has done the opposite, she has turned outwards towards Heaven. Who will she find there to give her courage? Who knows the pain she is bearing? Who will console her and ease that pain? '

'Tell me Father?'

'The answer is Jesus. when God gave us His son He gave us everything.'

Leaning over towards William with an almost desperate look on his wrinkled face, Jack asked:

'But will He help her? Will Jesus stop the pain?'

William thought for a moment and looked deep into his eyes, 'Sometimes,' he replied quietly, 'we must have the humility to bow our heads and realize that we don't know all the answers.'

CHAPTER 21.

It was now 1973 and five years since Molly had come to live in Wexford. The freedom that the countryside brought to her had become part of her life. She felt safe in her surroundings and she loved her family dearly. Her granddad's constancy, Doireann's fiery spirit, Frank's boring sense of humour, her daddy's love, Hattie's fussiness, Julie's homemaking and Aggie's wisdom all helped form her young character.

Being an only child, she found herself often in the company of adults. This gave her a feeling of great security and love. They became the living toys that she studied and played with. Watching their faces, she learned how to read their expressions. Every frown and smile, every tension revealed to her what their words did not. She was like a sponge soaking up their stories, their joys and their sorrows. She became a good listener and would ponder over their advice in her mind.

On the outside she appeared a carefree and sometimes giddy young girl. But hidden beneath that frivolous surface, was a personality with a depth and sincerity unusual for her age. Physically she was quite strong and any fat was kindly put down as 'big bones.' Having just turned thirteen, she was blossoming with good health. The beauty that was to come in later years lay discreetly hidden behind a teenage awkwardness

It was the fourth of September when Molly set off to boarding school. Hattie had chosen a convent in Kildare run by the Cross and Passion Sisters.

'A girl is not properly educated unless she goes to boarding school,' she would say, 'you can't beat the nuns for that.'

She had spoken of nothing else that year. Whenever Molly had doubts Aunt Hattie would expel them telling her how much fun she would have making new friends. Then she would begin reminiscing about her days boarding in a school in Eccles Street in Dublin. 'That was during the last war you know. Why I remember the night in May 1941 when the Germans dropped their bombs on Dublin City.

We were all terrified and took shelter under our beds. But we were lucky. I believe 28 people died that terrible night. Luckily there was no damage done to the school.'

The next day Hattie drove Molly to town and purchased her new uniform. It was a little bigger than her actual size, as Hattie knew from previous experience with her boys that Molly would grow into it. Two grey skirts, one with small pleats for weekdays and one with large pleats for Sunday. A blue blazer with the school crest embroidered on the pocket and a long grey gabardine coat for the winter.

Adjusting the blue beret on her head, Molly looked unimpressed at her reflection in the mirror and decided that the uniform did nothing to enhance her appearance. In fact it made her look even more plump and childish. Despite her reservations about going to boarding school, Molly accepted the inevitable and in her own way looked forward to growing up.

The morning of her departure from the 'Rectory' was a sad one. Julie hugged her tightly and having presented Molly with a little diary as a going away present, she kept telling her not to forget to write.

'This house will be very quiet without you,' she said tearfully.

On their journey Molly took a short detour to visit Aggie and say goodbye. After all she would not be home again until Halloween and that seemed like a very long time indeed.

'Now don't take too long dear,' said Hattie, sitting in the car and anxiously looking at her watch, 'we have to make good time.'

As usual the door of the cottage was open and Aggie was sitting by the fire smoking her dudeen. Molly went over and stood beside her.

'I'm off to boarding school now and I've come to say goodbye.' she said sadly.

Rising from her chair Aggie quenched the pipe and walked over towards the door.

'So yer off are ya child,' she said, looking out and waving at the occupants in the car. Then she closed the door a little.

'Yes Aggie,' replied Molly, 'Fr. William is driving us to Kildare. He knows one of the priests attached to the convent.'

'And I see herself in the car as well,' she said smiling. Then walking back to the fire she enquired.

'Tell me are ya lookin' forward to it child?'

'I am and I'm not. I'll miss you and all the fun we've had.'

'But sure in no time at all ya'll be home on holidays.'

'Not for eight weeks,' she said as if it was a lifetime. Aggie patted her shoulder affectionately.

'Wait now,' she said grabbing Molly's arm lightly, 'I have somethin; for ya lass.'

She went over to a small dresser and pulled out a drawer. It seemed like she would never find it. Molly waved reassuringly through the small window at Hattie and Fr. William waiting patiently in the car. Eventually after much rummaging Aggie found it.

Walking slowly back to Molly, she held out her hand and in her palm lay a very old brooch. In the center of the brooch behind the glass was a tiny dried flower-a bluebell.

'Take this child and remember the days we had in the woods.'

'Oh its beautiful,' said Molly reaching over and hugging her tightly.

Looking a bit flustered Aggie continued: 'Aye, it was me Mother's, the only thing she left me.'

Then taking Molly's hands in hers she looked into her eyes.

'From now on child yer days of freedom will be less. You will be closed in behind cold walls of learnin'. Guard yer heart and thoughts if ya want to keep them. Carry with ya memories of your childhood and don't let things disturb them.'

Molly kept looking down at the brooch and turning it over in her hand. In that moment she felt such love and tenderness towards Aggie.

'No matter how far away I go I will never forget those times Aggie, and when I come back we will have them again.' she said as she swallowed hard.

'Now that would be nice. Off with ya and don't keep them people waitin'. God bless ya child.'

Molly leaned over and kissed her cheek and then she turned to leave. Aggie waved until they were out of sight.

Bending down, she picked up Blackie in her arms. The large cat purred contently with each stroke of her hand. Turning to go indoors, Aggie looked back up at the autumn sky. As she thought about Molly leaving a little shiver of gloom came over her.

'Well Blackie,' she said, sadly, it looks like you an me's in for a long winter.'

CHAPTER 22.

Hattie Thornton emerged from Joe Kenny's small grocery shop. Joe junior followed behind carrying the usual large cardboard box of groceries. Opening the lid of the boot, Hattie thanked him as he placed the box in the car. Then, closing it down, she walked up to the front of the car and went to get in. Suddenly a deep voice with an English accent came from behind.

'Harriet Furlong is it really you?'

Surprised, Hattie turned around and looked up with a dazed look on her face. The large frame of a tall gentleman was blocking the sun.

'Well you haven't changed a bit,' he said smiling. 'There's no doubt, but you must have the secret of perpetual youth.'

Harriet looked on, desperately trying to cover up the fact that she did not recognize him.

Across the road to the right of the man, a red Jaguar car with English number plates caught her eye. But this was no help, she already knew by his accent that he was English.

Getting a little agitated she inquired crossly: 'Do I know you?'

Removing his tweed hat he gave a little bow and said: 'Nick Robinson at your service.'

Then he smiled a big smile with even white teeth.

Closing the door of the car, Hattie stepped back a little. He was a striking man indeed, very tall with a straight sharp nose. But Hattie still failed to recognize him. Noticing this, the stranger smiled amusedly,

'We went to school together remember? We got our confirmation together.'

Hattie could not believe her eyes. Now she suddenly remembered. But this could not be the little chap that sat behind her in 'The Presentation Convent.' Why that was so long ago. The images flashing into her mind could not have grown into this big handsome man.

'But your accent...' she said confusedly,

'Well, when you went away to school I caught the boat to England. I've worked over there for the last forty years. Then Dad died last year and he left me the home place. Me Mum went to live with my sister Margaret.'

Hattie thought for a moment.

'Margaret Robinson. Yes, I remember her,' said Hattie putting her hand up to her face, 'but she would have been in a class above me.'

'That's right, she was married a chap from Cork she did. They run a little guest- house in Dingle. I'm thinking of retiring myself and coming home to live in the old homestead.'

Not really listening to what he was saying, Hattie was still trying to place the family.

'I've seen Walter from time to time but I never got the chance to speak to him.'

'And did you marry?' asked Hattie, trying to sound casual.

'I'm a widower actually,' he said, with a mischievous twinkle in his eye.

'Did you have any children?'

'One son,' then sadly he added 'I had two, but the youngest chap got killed in the same accident as his mother.'

A concerned look came across Hattie's face

'Oh I am sorry,' she said sincerely, 'was it long ago?'

'Nearly 20 years now, and yourself, did you marry Hattie?'

'Oh yes, I married a wonderful man called James Thornton from Dublin, he too died suddenly, it was his heart so I am also widowed. I have two sons and you could say in a way I have a daughter.'

'You what? come now Harriet you either have or you haven't.'

'Well she is actually my nephew's little girl. Her mother died in childbirth and I am rearing her.'

'Oh I see, but you're single aren't you?'

'Oh yes,' she said, getting annoyed with herself for saying it so quickly.

'That's great, we must go out for dinner some night and catch up on old times.'

'Oh I don't know, I'm quite busy,' replied Hattie as she fumbled with her car keys.

'Oh come on, we would have so much to talk about. Where do you live now?'

'Not too far from 'Riversdale House' in the old 'Rectory.''

'I suppose I could ring you?'

'Bless your life no,' said Hattie chuckling to herself, 'It would be better if I rang you?'

Taking out a small piece of paper and pen from his pocket, he proceeded to write his number down.

This was Hattie's chance to look at him closely. Her quick eyes took in his expensive brown tweed suit. Covering quite a paunch, was a matching waistcoat and gold pocket watch. His thick grey hair shone like silver in the sunlight. On the fourth finger of his right hand he wore a gold signet ring.

'Okay,' he said as he folded the piece of paper. 'There you have it, that's my number. Would the middle of next week be okay?'

Hattie diverted her eyes away quickly and replied,

'Yes that would be fine.'

'Well listen, its great to see you looking so well, and I look forward to that.'

Hattie held out her hand.

'It's been nice meeting you again Nicholas,' she said sincerely.

His handshake was warm and strong as his big hand closed around hers. Then he turned and went into the shop.

Driving home, Hattie could not help thinking about her encounter. It brought her pleasantly back to her school days.

It was as if she was in the old Presentation Convent of years ago. Images of a skinny little boy in short trousers and knobbly knees flashed into her mind. She smiled as she continued to feel funny, exciting girlish feelings. Suddenly it was as if the last forty years had never existed. She felt more like 16 than 63 as her fantasies began to run wild. Then catching sight of her reflection in the mirror she scolded herself saying;

'You want to get a hold on yourself woman.'

But in the next moment she thought excitedly:

'God, How did that awkward boy ever grow into such a fine man?'

CHAPTER 23.

Young Jason O' Brien could not get his little bike to go fast enough. His heart was beating loudly in his young chest and his legs ached from peddling. But none of that mattered because he knew he just had to get to 'Riversdale House.'

On reaching the yard, he dropped his bike on the ground and ran breathlessly into the kitchen.

'Mr. Furlong, Mr. Furlong,' he shouted.

Walter Furlong was sitting at the table quietly reading his Sunday paper.

'Mr. Furlong, Mr Furlong, its Aggie… Aggie Cullen. There's trouble, there's trouble,' said Jamie clutching his chest as he tried to take a deep breath.

'What is it, what's wrong with her?' asked Walter rising to his feet.

Too worried to wait for the boy's reply, he ran to his jeep and, scattering the hens, he drove quickly out the gate.

On the way over to Aggie's cottage, he kept hoping she was not hurt or, worse still, dead. In his terrible fear he knew deep down how he loved that old woman.

Driving up the lane he stopped the jeep, jumped out and hurried up the path. He could see Aggie sitting on the bench outside the door. A feeling of relief swept through him, but then, as he got closer his relief was quickly replaced by shock. He began to fear for her as a strange sorrow was spread over her form.

With one frail arm holding the other, she sat gently rocking her body. The skin on her eyelids were purple and swollen, and he knew by the way she was holding her head that she was finding it difficult to see. Her long white hair, protruding wildly from her head, was matted with dried blood. Her jumper was torn and her apron was hanging loosely around her waist. The cries of the cats gathering around her bruised bare feet only added to the horror of the moment. She was in a terrible state and needed desperately to be comforted.

Walter went to put his arms around her, but he drew back afraid he might cause her further pain.

'It's alright Aggie,' he said gently, 'It's me Walter, I'm going to take you straight to the hospital.'

'No,' she cried out, 'leave me in me own place. If I go there I'll die.'

Walter sat down on the bench beside her and put his arm gently around her shoulder. It took a while for him to persuade her, but only after he reassured her that he would stay with her until she was allowed home. Then he went into the cottage to fetch her coat.

The sight that met him only confirmed his dreadful fear. The whole place was strewn with upturned furniture, broken crockery and scattered clothes.

As he grabbed the coat and returned to help her up, Frank, Doireann and Biddy came running up the lane towards them. Seeing a wave of shock and revulsion coming over their faces, he signalled to them not to speak.

Then he nodded at Frank to help him carry her. Frank immediately bent down and lifted Aggie carefully up into his strong arms. She cried out painfully, his every step to the jeep being sheer agony. Frank was amazed at how frail and light she was as she trembled in his arms. Then once he had eased her carefully in the front seat of the jeep Walter straightened up and gave his instructions:

'Doireann you come with us. Frank ring the Guards then see if yerself and Biddy can get the cottage fixed up. I don't know how long we'll be, but I'll tell ya now, if I ever find out who did this, I will kill them.' With his eyes darkening and his lips trembling he repeated, 'I'll kill them with me bare hands.'

Frank had never seen the boss so angry and he became really worried as he watched him drive down the road.

Biddy and Frank walked slowly into the cottage, picking their way carefully over the debris on the floor. Seeing a trail of Aggie's blood on the flagstones, Biddy started to cry. Frank touched her shoulder clumsily in an effort to comfort her. Shrugging him away, she held her hands up to her ears. With her eyes flashing in angry confusion she shouted:

'Will ya go and do something with those bloody cats.'

They then spent all afternoon tidying the cottage. The broken crockery could not be saved so they threw it out. Aggie's old coats were walked into the floor with black turf mixed through them. Biddy shook them out and hung them back up in the corner. In the bedroom, the mattress and bedding were upturned, and pictures and clothes thrown everywhere. Back in the kitchen Biddy picked up the soldier's picture. The brown glass and frame shattered. Suddenly she remembered the locket and wedding ring. She started frantically searching for them but could only find the ring.

It was almost dark that night when Walter and Aggie returned from the hospital. Frank and Biddy had the fire burning brightly in the hearth.

With Walter and Doireann supporting her on either side, Aggie walked slowly into the cottage. Her broken arm was set in plaster tied up in a sling. Her hair had been brushed and a large plaster covered the wound on her ear.

She had a new pair of slippers on her feet. Looking around she started to cry. The cottage was so neat and tidy. The kindness of all the family had lifted some of the sorrow from her heart. Resting her tired head on Walter's chest, her tears flowed down her cheeks. In the safety of his arms, she cried like a baby.

Feeling weary from her ordeal and a little groggy from medicine she received, she sat down tiredly in her own chair. A little while later she was dozing peacefully at the fire. Walter kept a watchful eye on her from the settlebed in the corner. Frank, Doireann and Biddy had returned to Riversdale House.

On hearing a tap on the door, Walter stood up nervously and was relieved when it was Sergeant McGarry who walked in.

'Good evening Walter,' he said in a friendly way.

'Hello Peter,' whispered Walter.

'Well,' continued the Sergeant, looking around 'you've certainly got this place cleaned up since this morning.'

Walter just nodded.

Aggie woke up with a nervous start on hearing their voices.

Walking over to her, the Sergeant bent down and asked in a very sincere way:

'Are ya alright, Miss Cullen?'

'Aye,' she replied sleepily as she kept her swollen eyes down and stared into the fire.

'Do you think you'd be up to answering a few questions?' he asked, pulling up a stool beside her and opening his notebook.

Aggie did not reply, she just turned her head away and looked very downcast. Feeling awkward the sergeant looked over at Walter.

Walter stood up and nodded discreetly towards the door,

'Leave her Peter,' he whispered, 'I think you may leave it till mornin', she's very upset.'

'Yes Walter, but I need to know before this happens to somebody else. Did she say anything to you?'

'No, she didn't. She's on oul' tablets she got in the hospital, so it's better to wait until she has a sleep. Did your men find any clues today?'

'No, I'm afraid they didn't, so you see it's very important we talk to her as soon as possible.'

'But sur, ya saw the state she's in, ya may come back tomorrow Peter.'

Reluctantly the troubled Sergeant replaced his notebook in his pocket said goodbye, and left.

Just then Doireann drove up in the jeep. As she entered the kitchen she carried with her a basket filled with food. Aggie tried to eat some scrambled egg, but with only her left hand in use, most of it ended up on the floor.

'She's goin' to need some lookin' after for awhile Doireann,' said Walter. 'You and Biddy may take it in turn. I'll stay here tonight in case there's any more trouble.'

An hour later, with Aggie tucked up safely in bed, Doireann went to leave. Outside, Walter opened the door of the jeep and asked her to tell Frank to bring back his top coat.

'Aye and tell him to bring the shotgun, he'll find the cartridges on top of the dresser.'

Returning back indoors, Walter put on a good fire and sat back in the old settle bed. All night long he sat there, with his coat over his shoulders, and his cap pulled down on his face. He was too angry to sleep. He could not stop thinking about what Aggie had been through the night before, while they were all safe in their beds.

A chill evening and a very cold night proceeded to the warmth bright sunshine of a pleasant morning. As dawn broke Walter got up from the bed quietly and wandered outside. As if on patrol, he paced up and down with his shotgun across his arm. Then it suddenly dawned on him that Aggie had been very quiet all night.

Going back inside, he gently opened the door of her bedroom and peeped in. He was surprised to see her already awake and staring up at the ceiling. He walked over to the side of the bed. Her battered face looked a lot worse than yesterday. The reddy purple on her eyes had turned to ugly big black bruises.

Feeling upset he asked awkwardly: 'Are ya alright Aggie?'

'There was two of them,' she said nervously, 'they were only young fellas.'

Walter could feel his blood beginning to boil. He sat down carefully on the side of the bed.

'Did ya know them?' he asked cautiously.

'No,' she said, trying to recall, 'they were strangers. They talked rough, they kept shoutin at me 'where's the money?' and then they started pullin' everythin' around.'

'What time was this?'

'I think it was about ten. I had just fed me cats and was gettin' ready for bed when the knock came to the door.'

'What did they want?' asked Walter crossly.

'They wanted ta know if I had any furniture to sell. Not a stick I said, then they pushed past me into the kitchen.'

Successfully hiding his real anger, Walter's stomach tightened at the thoughts of Aggie being alone at this time.

'We'll see for ourselves,' they said, 'ya never know what we might buy off ya old woman.' and before I could stop them they just walked in. They had big hard boots and started firein' me things around.'

Her voice became anxious and she started to tremble.

'Its alright now Aggie,' said Walter as he took her hand, 'your safe now.'

Then she continued,

'The smaller of the two, an evil lookin' bugger said: 'where's the money?' when I said I'd none he reached out and started hittin' me... hittin me on me face.'

Tears trickled silently down her cheeks.

They searched the two rooms and threw all me things around. I was shakin' with fear. They kept shoutin' at me 'Where's the effin money,' then they came at me again. One of them grabbed me neck from behind and held a knife to me throat. Oh! Boss a terror came into me stomach and I thought I was done for.'

Walter patted her hand caringly.

'Hush now you're okay,' he said quietly.

More tears flowed and crumpling up her handkerchief in her hand she continued talking, horrible memories bringing fear into her eyes.

'Ya must have your funeral money hidden somewhere,' said one of 'em as I felt the sting of the blade on me neck. When I told him I had none he cut me ear. Oh! Boss it was terrible I was covered in blood. Then they threw me on the hard cold floor.'

She unfolded her hanky and, with a shaking hand, she tried wipe the tears from her eyes with her left hand.

'What happened then Aggie?' asked Walter, hoping this would be the only time she would have to tell.

'It seemed to be ages while they were searchin'. Then they got fed up and went to leave. One of them got really mad, the big lad with the strength of the devil. He turned back and kicked me with his big boot. 'Ya stubborn ould bitch' he said. Oh! the pain of that Boss. Then they ran away out. That must have been when they broke me arm.'

Walter leapt up off the bed with fury. He clenched his fists and felt his stomach sick with temper.

'I crawled to the door but hadn't the strength to go further. I lay there all night, Oh the cold was terrible. That's where young Jamie found me, God bless 'im.'

'Yes,' thought Walter, 'If Jamie hadn't taken the short cut to Mass who knows what might have happened.'

Hearing Doireann and Biddy arrive with the breakfast, Walter quickly left the room. He suddenly needed some fresh air.

Outside in the morning sun he paced angrily up and down in front of the cottage. Picturing everything Aggie had told him in his mind, he tried to justify what they had done. Running his big hands through his thick white hair he ran it over and over in his head. But no, there was no justification for this. Two strong rough men going up against a defenceless old woman. Aggie had never harmed anyone in her life.

'Oh God!' he prayed fearfully as he clasped his hands together: 'What is this country coming too?'

CHAPTER 24.

Molly had settled well into her new school, which stood impressively behind high black iron gates. From the top of the hill the tall grey building domineered all others in the small country town. Surrounding the school on both sides were high walls that gave it a timeless air of mystery. Opposite the school at the crossroads was a popular public house and behind it was a very busy little cattle mart.

To Molly Wexford seemed far away but then to her surprise she found out that some of the other girls had travelled even further. From places like Cork, Kerry and even the North of Ireland.

On her first night in boarding school the senior girls put on a disco for the newcomers. Not that there were any boys allowed mind you, instead Molly found herself dancing with girls. It was a nice gesture on the senior girl's behalf, and it helped the 'first years' feel welcome. As Molly and her classmates rocked to the strains of 'Moly Moly' coming from the old record player she really felt that she had arrived and it was fun.

Her dormitory, St. Anne's, was a very long room with ten beds on each side and a narrow corridor down the middle. A curtain divided each one and lent some privacy to the occupier. A small sink was provided in each cubicle for washing and the floors had shiny bright-coloured linoleum on them. Sometimes the girls slid playfully up and down on them in their stocking feet.

From now on Molly's movements would revolve around a bell. There was a bell to get up at 7 and a bell to go to bed at 9, lights out at 9.30 sharp. There was a bell to attended class and a bell for recreation, a bell for mealtimes and a bell for prayers.

Dressed in long black tunics with short black and white veils on their heads, the nuns seemed quite cheerful. They would smile pleasantly as they glided airlessly among the noisy sea of blue uniform which noisily thronged the corridors daily.

However it was the Revered Mother, Sr. Amelia Mary that everyone was in awe of. Small in statue and slight of build, her movements were light and swift. She was a gracious approachable woman, cultured and deeply spiritual.

Without as much as raising an eyelid she could by just entering a room command complete respect and silence.

Most of Molly's days were now taken up with studying. With one of the Sisters supervising from a rostrum, Molly would sit in the classroom in the evening with the other students and study the subjects on the school curriculum. However, these were lonely times. She would find herself staring out the large windows into the blackness of the winter night. She would think about Aunt Hattie and Julie far away at home in the sitting room.

The small busy town outside the convent walls was strictly out of bounds to the students, except on Saturdays when the girls were trusted to go out to the parish church and have their confessions heard between the hour of one and two.

How Molly missed the freedom and idleness of her young days. Oh how she constantly thought and reminisced about the times with Aggie in the woods, and running wildly around the farm.

However, she was becoming aware that her mind was now learning knowledge while her spirituality was being nurtured as well.

In the little convent chapel a wonderful atmosphere of peace was sensed by all and also in every room and corridor of the school. This peace and the reverend respect that everyone derived from it, seemed to naturally come from the graceful conduct of the nuns.

Having had Hattie, Julie, Doireann and Aggie as previous role models, Molly found herself unknowingly studying these women she had now come to live with. Their ages ranged from late twenties to early eighties. Not comprehending them as ordinary beings it seemed to her their world was extraordinary good.

Although some of the girls complained about the strictness of the school, others found it pleasant to be in the company of other young females, at a time when they were discovering and getting to know themselves.

Friendships were formed that were to last a lifetime and one of these was between Molly and her friend Kate and with Molly not having a sister Kate became even more special.

Kate Kearney came from a large town in Co. Offaly. The daughter of a school teacher, she almost bounced into Molly's affections. Standing five foot nine in her stocking feet, her figure was slim with the longest legs Molly had ever seen. Her brown hair was shoulder length and her thick glasses made her blue eyes appear quite large and full of wonder. She was a homely girl with a gentle ladylike nature.

Late at night when everyone was sleeping, Molly and Kate could be found sneaking into each other's cubicles. There they would sit crossed-legged on the bed whispering their dreams to each other or giggling about daytime events in the classrooms.

Other times they could be found walking around the hockey pitch discussing life's serious problems like how to go to a feast in the main hall at midnight without being caught by the nuns. Whatever happened from day to day, they gave each other a great feeling of sharing and security. They also got a lot of happiness from their close friendship because they cared deeply about each other.

So it was only natural that it was Kate Molly ran to one sad Wednesday morning. She had just received a most disturbing letter from home. Kate put her arm comfortingly around her shoulder and re-read the letter.

Tears ran down Molly's face as she listened to the scanty details of how Aggie had been attacked. Molly could not even imagine it happening. Violence like that was so far removed from the protected world she was now living in.

'But your Aunt says Aggie is out of hospital and home again, and that she will bring you down on Saturday to visit her. Cheer up Moll, Aggie seems to be okay,' said Kate reassuringly.

'But you don't understand Kate,' said Molly, wiping her tears with a tissue, 'she is old and frail and so gentle and kind. How could those men do that to her?'

'I don't know,' said Kate angrily as she looked at her young friend's tear-stained face, 'but they will never ever have any luck for it.'

CHAPTER 25.

It was one of those depressing dark drizzly days in Wexford and Hattie Thornton was feeling fed up and lonely. With Julie gone to Dublin to visit her sister in Dalkey, and Molly away in school, the Rectory seemed very quiet indeed.

Hattie wandered aimlessly from room to room. She began thinking about Nicholas, the man who had been occupying a lot of her thoughts lately. Impulsively she picked up the receiver of the telephone and dialled numbers from a scrap of paper. Then, unsure of herself, she quickly replaced the receiver again.

However, in the next moment regained her confidence and picking it up quickly, she proceeded to dial the numbers, but once again she replaced the receiver without finishing the sequence. Walking over to the window she stared out at the greyness of the day. Then feeling very uncomfortable with her own dithering she went back to the phone and confidently dialled again.

This time she held on as she listened to a ringing tone at the other end. Despite her nervousness when the gentleman spoke Hattie immediately took control of the situation.

'Hello Nicholas,' she began, 'this is Harriet here. I'm ringing to tell you about 'The Wexford Festival Opera' on the 25th of this month. I was wondering if you would like to come?'

'Yes indeed Harriett I would love to go.'

'Oh good, it's the first performance of the season.'

'Yes I saw that advertised on the paper.'

'It's in 'The Theatre Royal" and one of the singers happens to be a favourite of mine, James O'Driscoll. Have you heard him sing?' she said, getting quite excited.

'No, but I've heard of him. I believe he has a powerful voice.'

Hattie went on to tell him that she would meet him in Enniscorthy. But Nicholas would have none of it. He had decided that he was going to make this a very special evening. He insisted that he would pick her up at the house and eventually she agreed.

'Oh Nicholas there is just one more thing, I'm afraid we must be in our seats at 8.30. p.m. sharp otherwise we will not be admitted until after the first act.'

'Not to worry,' he said humourlessly 'don't you know that punctuality is one of my endearing qualities?'

Having said their good-byes she replaced the receiver on the phone and felt a funny excited feeling running through her. She began thinking about Nicholas coming to pick her up in his beautiful red Jaguar car.

But Hattie had learnt to keep her excitement to herself. Her housekeeper did not approve. From the moment she had told Julie about meeting Nicholas she had been surprised at her reaction. Hattie thought she would have been delighted for her but it seemed as if it was quite the opposite. Then to her further annoyance Julie kept reminding Hattie of her age.

Despite the strained atmosphere in the house, Hattie excitedly set about choosing her outfit for the evening. Having changed her mind almost everyday as to what she would wear she finally settled on a black lace evening dress. Laying it out on the bed she added a marquisette necklace and matching earrings to it.

'Yes,' she thought clasping her hands together, 'perfect.'

The following evening she took extra time and great care getting ready for her big night out. Julie showed her objection to the date by staying well out of the way. By 6.45p.m, Hattie was dressed and ready to leave.

Standing in front of the cheval mirror in her bedroom her eyes sparkled with approval as she took in her appearance.

Then she went downstairs into the dining room. Not wanting to turn on the light, she stood in the semi darkness, her expensive perfume lingering in the air. Looking out through the lace curtains on the bay window she kept watch.

Up in the sky the full vibrant moon dimmed the stars near to it as its soft light illuminated the avenue. The shadows of the big trees reaching across the lawn gave the night an air of magical mystery.

Too nervous to sit down and not daring to have a cigarette, she kept checking her gold watch. She hoped he would be punctual. Then as if on cue, car lights swung around the bend and Nicholas drove up the avenue to the front door.

Smiling at him as he held the door for her, Hattie sat happily into his car. Suddenly noticing a movement in the upstairs window she looked up. She smiled when behind the curtain she saw Julie peeping out.

On the journey to the theatre Nicholas chatted on about the weather, her house, and the opera. Not being able to resist any longer, Hattie opened her handbag and took out her Craven A's. She offered one to Nicholas.

' Oh yes would you light it for me please?' he said smiling.

Hattie tried to light the cigarette without getting her deep red lipstick on it. Then she handed it to him. As she took deep satisfying pulls she suddenly felt more relaxed

'I would rather you call me Hattie if you don't mind Nicholas. The only one who calls me Harriet is my auditor and he's a pompous old thing, always giving out to me.'

Nicholas laughed and they started to relax a little more in each other's company.

As usual 'The Wexford Operatic Society' lived up to its high standard with the fine performance of 'Ivan Susanin' by S.M. Gorodetsky. Accompanied by 'The Radio Telefis Eireann Symphony Orchestra', the harmony of mixed voices rang out and filled the auditorium. The traditional dances, choreographed by Heidi Cooke, transported the audience back to what life was like in cold Russia.

In the glow of the theatre lights Hattie found it hard to concentrate on the show as she kept watching Nicholas out of the corner of her eye.

As the story unfolded on the stage, the Polish officers interrupted the engagement party of the lovers Antonida and Sobinin. Then they took her beloved father away by force to show them the shortest way through the thick forest.

Hattie noticed Nicholas was following the performance intensely.

At the short interval he met up with some old friends he had not seen for a long time and this added to the surprise and enjoyment of the evening.

However, later at the longer interval Hattie linked Nicholas as she moved excitedly through the patrons and proudly introduced him to her friends.

Resuming their seats for the final act Hattie would have liked to sit closer to her companion but became slightly agitated with the armrest between them. Resting her elbow on it she hoped that by the time the hero Susain was shot, Nicholas might reach out and hold the hand she dangled in emotional anticipation. But unfortunately Nicholas, being so engrossed in the opera was completely unaware of her gesture.

With the finale and the dropping of the final curtain, the applause rang out loudly in appreciation of the talent of the performers. Then the audience stood up to leave.

Nicholas picked up Hattie's coat and draped it around her shoulders. Turning to thank him, her heart soared as they glanced deeply into each other's eyes.

'I hope you don't mind Hattie,' he whispered, 'but I've taken the liberty of booking a table for dinner in 'Whites Hotel.'

A lovely comforting feeling came over her as he put his arm caringly around her and escorted her towards the hotel.

As Hattie entered the restaurant the splendour of the room and the perfection of the table setting pleased her eye immensely. She was quite in awe of this huge handsome man sitting opposite her. As he read his menu card, she studied him from behind hers and took in every detail of his attire, from the darkness of his blazer and the immaculate white of his shirt to the expensive silk of his cravat set off by a gold stud.

Having finished with the menu and chosen the wine, his fingers interlocked confidently as sparks of light caught his gold cufflinks and signet ring.

His thick grey wavy hair and heavy dark eyebrows gave his face a striking seriousness. But as he talked about the different operas he had enjoyed, this seriousness and gave way to an endearing relaxed boyish look.

Towards the end of the meal as they sipped their wine he reached over and took her hand in his.

'I don't mean to sound corny or anything Hattie but you really are a beautiful woman.'

The sincerity in his eyes suddenly caused a wave of emotion to stir inside Hattie and her swelling heart fluttered more than usual. For the first time in years she knew that she was feeling what a real woman should feel. Smiling up radiantly at him she relaxed and the night took on a Cinderella type feel to it.

It was quite late when they eventually returned back home. Stopping outside 'The Rectory' Nicholas got out, walked around the car and opened the door for her. Then arm in arm they strolled towards the house.

'Thank you for a lovely evening,' said Hattie smiling up at him, 'it's been a long time since I've had such fun.'

Then she reached up tippy toe to kiss him on the cheek.

Unexpectedly two strong arms came around her and held her in a tight grip. His lips came down on hers and sharp hairs from his moustache pricked her tender soft skin. For a moment she felt breathless and completely overpowered. Not being held in such a masterful grip for many years, she suddenly realized how strong he was and she was quite taken aback.

Releasing her from his embrace he said quite casually:

'Right I'll pick you up next Wednesday night for that comic opera,'L'ajo nell imbarazzo'. I'm really looking forward to it. Good night Hattie and thank you for a lovely evening.'

Then with a wave he got into his car and was gone.

Hattie stood on the doorstep for a few moments. The night breeze cooling her hot flushed cheeks.'

In a thrilling way she was worried about the effect he had on her. But this was madness. Her head told her so. But then her feelings were saying the opposite. Turning, she opened the door and went inside.

Later she sat up in bed smoking a cigarette, unable to sleep. She began thinking about his kiss.

It must be forty years since she had been kissed like that, and in a strange way she felt a little disloyal to James's memory. But that was silly too. Because deep in her heart she knew that James would have wanted her to be happy.

Extinguishing her cigarette in the ashtray she snuggled down between the bedclothes and looked up at the ceiling.

She started thinking about her life, her marriage to James, her pregnancies and her babies. All that had happened with Molly's mother and her own return to Wexford. All those years were like a moment now. Then she smiled to herself.

Thinking back to his kiss she was surprised to find that at her age she could still feel like a full-blooded woman. At last having twisted and turned most of the night sleep finally found her.

Coming down late to breakfast the next morning she felt tired and groggy from her restless sleep. Julie sat quietly reading behind the morning newspaper, and for once Hattie was glad of her silence.

CHAPTER TWENTY six

Seamus Thornton rang his mother very early one morning. He broke the sad news to her that Jessie McDermott had been taken to the Mater Hospital the previous night following a massive stroke.

Feeling quite upset, Hattie drove over to 'Riversdale House' to tell her brother Walter.

'She's had a stroke ya say,' said Walter shocked at the news, 'God help us.'

Then he went over to the cooker to put the kettle on.

'Seamus says it does not look too good and there's no hope of a recovery,' said Hattie anxiously as she pulled out a chair from the table.

'Be kinder if God took her,' replied Walter as he took two cups down from the shelf.

'Yes,' replied Hattie thoughtfully, 'then she wouldn't have to put up with that horrible little man looking after her.'

'I suppose you're right,' he replied as he wiped a saucer and put it under her cup. 'but there again he's all she's got at the end of the day. Tell me Hattie how old is Jessie?'

'She's in her late seventies, but sure J.J. would have be eighty if he was alive now.'

'You're right too,' said Walter looking a little puzzled. 'Where does the time go?'

Hattie lifted the black kettle and poured the water into the old brown teapot.

As they chatted over the cup of tea, Walter decided that they would both go visit Jessie early the next morning.

'I'll have to let David know,' he said anxiously as he rose from the table.

'This would have to happen the week he's away. I think he'll be quite upset. Now he left a phone number around here somewhere…'

Rising from the table, he began rummaging in a sideboard drawer until he found it.

On the drive to Dublin the next morning Walter seemed concerned about the effect Jessie's illness might have on Molly.

'I'm afraid they were never as close as Jessie and her mother were,' replied Hattie, 'But you know something Walter? It was almost as if that time Molly died so did a little piece of Jessie. She really loved her you know.'

A far away look came into Walter's eyes, 'I think I know what you mean,' he replied sadly as he thought about his Doris.

Arriving at the main door of the hospital, they were met in the hall by a worried looking Mick McCoy. To her relief Hattie was glad to see he was appropriately dressed this time in dark slacks and blue blazer. His brow was wrinkled with worry, and each wrinkle seemed to have its own problem. Shaking both their hands, he said thankfully:

'I'm glad you've come.'

'How is she?' asked Hattie.

'I don't know, sure...er... she can't talk,' said Mick crossly.

Quickly realising that Mick was not in control of the situation, Hattie immediately went over to the desk porter to enquire if her son, Dr. Thornton, was on duty. On hearing he was, she then proceeded to lead the way towards the ward.

When they eventually reached Jessie's bedside, they found the poor woman unconscious, with her life depending on a ventilating machine. A young nurse, checking a drip in Jessie's left arm, smiled kindly at them as they approached the bed. Inquiring if they were all family, Mick quickly replied,

'Sur we're even closer than family, nurse.'

Walter smiled amusedly as he noticed his sister's sudden change of expression.

Jessie looked a dreadful sight.

With her teeth out and the right side of her face fallen in, she appeared only a shadow of her former self.

Realizing now what Mick had to cope with in the last few days, Hattie looked over at him with a little more compassion. Admittedly she had no time for the man, but he had redeemed himself a little in her eyes by the care he had shown to Jessie.

Nobody spoke, they were too nervous in case Jessie could hear them. Hattie sat down on the only available chair beside the bed. Taking Jessie's thin hand in hers, she held it gently. Her old friend did not respond.

Only the whishing sound of the ventilator machine filled the silence in the room. Walter wandered over to look out the window. Mick followed him and began talking in a whisper. Hattie began thinking back to that Sunday when she first met Jessie. Up to then she had only seen her a few times at 'McDermotts Fish Shop.'

Jessie had jealously forbidden Molly's mother to visit with Hattie. But the previous Saturday night Molly had come clean and told Jessie about sneaking off behind her back. So it was a pleasant surprise when Jessie had walked over to Hattie after Mass and extended her hand in friendship.

'Good mornin' Mrs. Thornton,' she had said.

'Good morning Mrs. McDermott, isn't it a lovely day?'

'Yes it is … em I've come to say somethin' to you Mrs. Thornton and I'll say it quickly before Molly comes over. I want to thank you for for being so good to my girl. She's fond of you, but I'd hate to see her get hurt,' replied Jessie as she looked worriedly across the churchyard at Molly standing beside William.

'Why thank you Jessie, may I call you that? And you must please call me Hattie. It is a pleasure to do anything for Molly. Why! she is so full of life. You must be very proud to have brought up such a fine girl.'

'Oh indeed I am,' she said, smiling.

As the two women stood chatting, Hattie, being a mother herself, kept reassuring Jessie that she was not taking Molly's affection away from her. And by the time they parted, a new friendship and trust had built up between them.

Hattie could smile now, fifteen years later, at Jessie's unnecessary words of warning.

Just then her thoughts were interrupted when Seamus entered the room. With one hand in the pocket of his white coat, he walked over to his mother, and placed the other one on her shoulder.

'I'm glad to see you mother and you too Uncle Walter. Let's all step outside for a moment shall we,' he whispered.

In the corridor and safely out of Jessie's hearing, he told them that her condition had deteriorated and that in fact she was clinically dead.

'But she can't be dead,' said Mick pointing to the door and looking a bit confused. 'She's breathin' away in there.'

'Yes, but that's only the machine, it's breathing for her. If we were to switch it off then…' shrugging his shoulders, Seamus looked hopelessly over at his mother.

'Who will decide that Seamus?' asked Walter moving closer to him.

'It's usually between the doctor and the next- of- kin Uncle Walter. In this case that would be up to you Mick,' he said, looking seriously at him, 'I believe there is just the two of you now.'

Realizing the seriousness of what the doctor had just said, Mick took a step backwards. 'I can't decide that on me own,' he replied in a shocked voice as he reached his shaking hand into his pocket and pulled out a packet of cigarettes.

Then looking at everybody gathered in the little group he said worriedly,

'We'd all have to make it.'

Seamus led the way to an unoccupied waiting room, and there, for a little while, they discussed what had to be done. The proper forms were produced and signed and then Seamus went to leave the room.

'Will there be a priest there?' asked Mick with tear filled eyes.

Seamus stepped back and touched his arm,

'I'll arrange that with the hospital chaplain, don't worry,' he said, giving him a reassuring pat on the shoulder. Then he turned and quietly left the room.

Suddenly Mick looked all in. Hattie suggested that they might go somewhere for a cup of coffee and Walter agreed.

By the time they returned the machine was switched off, and Jessie McDermott was dead.

Looking down at her lying peacefully still at last, Hattie remarked that it was a happy release.

'Yes mm,' replied Mick affectionately, taking hold of his dead sister's hand. Then he added quietly 'but for who?'

Walter returned to Wexford the same day to break the news to his family and organise the travelling arrangements.

Hattie stayed on in Dublin with Eithne and Seamus to help Mick with the funeral.

On the morning of the burial the rain lashed down from the dark skies as a small crowd of mourners gathered in the cemetery. Old customers, friends and neighbours came to pay their respects to a woman who had always been there to serve them.

Underneath a large black umbrella the parish priest recited the prayers for the dead. Molly shared another umbrella with her dad. His thoughtful gaze would wander thoughtfully from time to time to her mother's name engraved on the headstone nearby.

Mick McCoy stood red-eyed at the grave as people came up, hook his hand, and then hurried away. One of these introduced himself as a solicitor from the firm of 'Gratten and Fitzsimons'. He asked Mick if he could come to the house that evening around four o clock to read the will. Mick nodded his approval.

Back at McDermotts, a small black wreath pinned to the front door of the red-brick house brought an air of sadness to the street. It was also a sad reminder that with Jessie's passing, it was the end of an era. 'McDermotts Fish Shop' would be no more.

Not attending the funeral Eithne and Julie decided to stay back in McDermotts. They cleaned the house and prepared some tea and sandwiches for the family and some friends when they returned from the graveyard.

Everybody complained about the dreadful weather when they returned, and so a warm fire and hot beverages were welcomed by all. Pretty soon the little house was crowded with people coming and going. As they all sat around reminiscing about old times, Fr. William decided to take Molly away from the sad atmosphere and show her the fish shop. He found the key with a shabby label attached hanging on a hook in the kitchen.

The heavy door of the shop gave a funny little screech as if rejoicing that it was being opened after all those years. A strange salty smell hung in the heavy cold damp air. Fr. William went over and opened one of the shutters. Shafts of light poured in through dusty windows and across the old blue tiles now covered in dust.

'Gosh I can't remember it being this small,' he said looking around in amazement. The counter seems much lower too. You know Molly this is where I have the best memories of your mother. We were always popping in here after school. Of course Seamus would mess about with the fish and she would scold him. It was so funny. She always spoke so plainly you know. She would stand right there, in behind the counter, and with her hands on her hips she would say: 'Put them down right now Seamus.'

As Molly listened to Fr. William reminiscing, she wandered in behind the counter idly touching things lightly, as heavy dust was everywhere. She began playing about with the different sized brass weights and placing them on the old heavy weighing scales.

By now Fr. William was peering through small slits in the shutters, as he watched the traffic pass by on the street.

Suddenly underneath the counter a small drawer with a brass handle caught Molly's eye. Curiously she tried to open it but it was quite stiff. Not being able to resist she pulled even harder. Suddenly it broke free from its slot and crashed to the floor. Old bills and receipts scattered everywhere.

Fr. William jumped at the noise and was a little annoyed because it had broken into his thoughts.

'Oops sorry,' said Molly as she bent down to retrieve it. Putting all the papers back she struggled to replace the drawer but found it just would not fit in. Lifting it up, she looked closer and found a piece of old paper taped to the wood underneath.

Molly put the drawer on the counter. Carefully she peeled the paper away and started to read the writing on it. But before she finished, she walked over and handed it to Fr.William.

'I think this could be for you,' she said as she looked confusedly at him. Then she left the shop quietly and went back into the house. Fr. William looked down at the poem. It began:

To William.
Those few moments.
Was it the everyday things we did separately uniting them at the end of the day?
Could it have been our love of music, that heavenly rhytmn reaching out and stirring our deepest emotions?
Who was the Creator?
Just two souls, two minds, two bodies reaching out, oblivious of all, but that touch, look, and held.
Oh! How tender was that first embrace, born of a need deeply rooted in our souls.
Always it will be with me.
Those moments were so rare, so tender, so unholy holy.
Take them with you dear William and hide them deep in your heart,

In times of loneliness and despair, summon them to the corner of
your mind and behold them, for they are yours
From one, who for a brief time in life, held you in her arms for
Those few moments.

William stared in disbelief at the paper. It was as if Molly's mother had reached out to him across the vast silence of the grave. Reading again the meaningful words, he held the paper tightly as if it too might disappear. Fearing he had missed something very important, his mind went back to that magical night on the bridge.

A happy smile broke out on his face as he remembered the painful innocence of that embrace. Stunned by the wonder of it all he turned from the window.

In his mind's eye he could see Molly standing behind the counter smiling at him. In that moment he remembered her extraordinary loveliness. Then as if caught in a timeless fantasy he tenderly sighed:

'Oh Molly.'

CHAPTER 27.

When the bell rang on McDermotts door at exactly four p.m. in the afternoon it was Eithne Thornton that opened it. She found a tall slim gentleman standing on the step. He wore a dark pin striped suit and very thick glasses. Carrying an old brown leather briefcase and a walking stick, he introduced himself as the Mr. Grattan, the solicitor.

Having invited him in, Ethine then showed him into the sitting room.When he entered, Hattie rose from her armchair and offered him her hand. With a slight bow of his head, he shook it politely.

Resuming her seat, she raised an eyebrow when she noticed how out of place his brown suede shoes were. Then she asked Eithne to go and quickly call the others.

Remaining seated, Hattie watched closely as Mr.Gratten sat down at the oak table and proceeded with the meticulousness of an eccentric old schoolmaster, to take some papers from his briefcase. Then he laid them out neatly before him.

As the other members of the family quietly entered the room, Hattie took it upon herself to introduce them. Nodding in the direction of each one, Mr. Grattan only rose from his seat once, and that was to shake hands with Fr. William. As everyone found a place to sit down, he then enquired if they were all present.

'I think there is one more to come,' replied Hattie, looking around in an agitated way.

Then leaning over to Seamus she whispered impatiently:

'Where is that wretched little man?'

'He's gone to the jacks mother,' replied Seamus, trying hard not to laugh.

Just at that moment Mick McCoy could be heard coughing loudly in the hall. When he walked into the room the solicitor leaned across the table, extended his hand and offered his condolences. Mick grabbed it and with both hands shook it sincerely.

'I'm so sorry for your trouble Mr. McCoy, your sister was a fine woman.' Mick grabbed it and with both hands, shook it sincerely and replied:

'Aye that she was, that she was.'

Peering out from over his thick glasses Mr. Gratten looked around the room and announced in a serious tone:

'If everybody is present we will now begin.'

Perching himself upright on his chair, he gave a sharp cough as if to command attention. Then he picked up a sheet of paper lying in front of him. Everyone sat in a patient silence and it seemed forever until he eventually spoke.

'The last will and testament of Jessica Ann Mc Dermott.

I, Jessica Ann, being of sound mind do hereby bequeath all my possessions as follows:

To Molly Furlong, I leave the sum of five thousand pounds.' Then the solicitor reached over to his right, took up another sheet of paper and continued:

'Mrs. McDermott hopes this money will be used for Molly Furlong's education, and that it would not cause any offence to both her father David, or her guardian Mrs. Hattie Thornton.'

Slowly replacing the piece of paper, he picked up the first one and continued:

'The two properties, that is, the building that was formerly 'McDermotts Fish Shop', and the dwelling house next door I bequeath to ...' he paused, lifted his glasses, squeezed the bridge of his nose and then replaced them again. Mick leaned forward eagerly in his chair,' ...Mr. David Furlong.'

Mick swallowed hard as he found it difficult to hide his disappointment.

Then reaching over once again, Mr. Grattan picked up another piece of paper from his right.

'It was Mrs. McDermott's late husband's wish that these properties would, on their deaths, pass to their niece Molly Malone. Unfortunately, due to the untimely death of Miss Malone, and the sudden tragic death of Mr. McDermott, this will was never changed. However, Mrs. McDermott hopes, that by leaving the properties to Molly's husband, David, she is complying with her late husband's wishes. Mrs. McDermott goes on to say, that for the love and happiness that David Furlong brought to their niece, and the way they both felt themselves about him, she hopes that he would keep these properties and eventually pass them on to his daughter Miss Molly Furlong, Jessica's grand-niece.'

Carefully replacing these two pieces of paper he returned his gaze to the will. Then looking straight up at Mick McCoy he said,

'I leave the following to my dear brother Michael the money remaining in the current account after Molly Furlong's £5,000 and £200 for a headstone for myself and J.J. is deducted. I leave also to Michael, a savings account, which I opened in 1948, with the sum of ten shillings.'

Mr. Grattan picked up a smaller piece of paper and continued.

'Lodgements were made on a regular basis until February 1966. So between the principle and the interest accumulated on the principle, and even with the change over to decimalization, this money comes to the sizeable sum of £15,100,12p'

Then, looking back at the will, he continued reading,

'I leave also to Michael, the money which came from J.J.'s life policy which has been lodged in an account in 'The Hibernian Bank.' This comes to...' and as he checked his small paper again, Mick McCoy sat up quickly in his chair.

...The sum of £10,000. Now with interest, this figure is now...£15,401,50p and the current account with the requests taken out of it leaves the sum of £2,300.

Mick McCoy looked on as if he had been stung. Lighting up a cigarette, he started doing rough calculations in his head, but in his excitement he just got more confused.

Then the solicitor announced calmly that all this money came to the grand total of £27.701.50p.

Mick never had 27,000 shillings much less 27,000 pounds.

He always knew Jessie and old J.J. were a bit tight, but he never dreamt that they would have saved so much. Not that he was not grateful mind you, he was. After all, he had looked after poor Jess as best he could and made her last years comfortable.

With the reading of the will over, David offered Mr. Grattan a drink. Putting his papers back in his briefcase, he graciously declined. He had one last stop to make before finishing up his business of the day.

Mick walked over and shook Mr. Grattan's hand vigorously.

'We must arrange a day for you, Mr. Furlong and the little girl to come to my office. I will need you to sign some papers.'

'Name it sir, name yer day and we'll be there,' said Mick smiling.

Before anyone had time to congratulate him on his new fortune Mick slipped quietly out the back door.

Then with a new spring in his step, he went down the road towards his local pub.

'Imagine,' he said rubbing his hands gleefully together, 'an old sea dog like me havin' all that money.'

CHAPTER 28.

Two weeks later Molly sat in the front of Hattie's car with a large box of Black Magic chocolates on her lap. She had saved up most of her pocket money to buy them for Aggie. When the car pulled up outside the gate of the cottage Hattie told her she would call back for her in an hour or so.

'Aren't you coming in?' asked Molly curiously.

'No dear I think she'd rather talk to you on your own. I'll call in when I come back to collect you.'

Molly often sensed a strange coldness between Aggie and Hattie but never questioned it.

When she entered the kitchen she saw Aggie sitting in her usual chair. Carefully leaving the box of chocolates down on the table, she ran over and gave her a big hug.

'Ah me girl yer back at last,' Aggie said as she reached out trembling with emotion.

Molly picked up the chocolates and placed them carefully on her lap.

'These are for you,' she said affectionately.

'Well bless me heart but you'll have me spoiled,' she replied bashfully as she ran her hand slowly over the large red ribbon tied at the side.

Molly noticed the ugly marks of the fading bruises on her face and hands and her right arm still in plaster. But with her hair tied up neatly in a bun instead of her usual headscarf she looked well

'Put the kettle on child and you and me will sit here and eat some of these lovely sweeties.'

Molly took off her coat and draped it on the back of the settle-bed. While she was waiting for the kettle to boil she noticed how clean and tidy the cottage was. Aunt Doireann and Biddy were certainly looking after Aggie well.

When the tea was ready Molly poured it into two big mugs, walked over and handed one to Aggie. Then she sat down opposite her on a stool. After she helped open the box they both examined the little card carefully to find their favourite chocolates.

'So tell me child how's school?' asked Aggie as she popped a strawberry one into her mouth. 'Have ya made new friends at all?'

Molly told Aggie all about Kate and that she would bring her to visit during the summer holidays.

'Aye I'd like ta meet yer young friend. She sounds a nice wee girl.'

Then Molly went on to tell her all about her teachers and the new things she was learning. As she talked, she suddenly felt a little embarrassed in case Aggie might think she was showing off. Worse still, she might think she knew better than the old woman. So in consideration of these feelings she began to change the subject.

Sensing this Aggie would have none of it.

'I want to hear it all Molly, ya have been given a great chance in life, ya should be very proud.'

'Did you ever want to go to boarding school Aggie?' asked Molly.

'Gosh child no, that was far above me. Why, we were lucky to have the little bit of learnin' we got. Most children went on to find work. People were poor then and there were large families to be fed and dressed.'

'Did you ever regret not getting the chance Aggie?'

Aggie's eyes looked thoughtfully into the fire.

'Sur what is readin' child? What are books? Why, in a way I've learnt from the hard book of life, things you'd never learn in a classroom. Some sad, and others passed as if all was one.' she paused for a moment and looked over at the soldier's picture.

'Then there were ones of great love and happiness,' she continued 'these live on in me mind and give me hope.'

Molly rose from her chair and walked over to the picture. Picking it up, she brought it back to Aggie.

'Who is he Aggie?'

Aggie took the picture from her hand and looked lovingly at it. Her eyes lit up and she smiled.

'That was Tommie Foster and I was his girl, he told me so time and time again. He came to work on your great grandfather's farm up at the house. It was a great summer. I was only seventeen and he was two years older. I used to work in the kitchen like young Biddy does now. Anyway, I was bringing the tay down to the hayfield and I noticed him among the other men. He was very tall, with the cheekiest wink I ever saw. That evenin' he came into the dairy where I was milkin' the cows. Lord me heart lifted when I saw him but I didn't let him know,' she said, breaking out into a mischievous laugh.

'But how come he's in a soldier's uniform?' asked Molly curiously.

Aggie's eyes darkened and suddenly she became very sad.

'The great war came child, and Tommie signed up with the Royal Irish Fusiliers. He was all fired up about killin' the Germans and defendin' the world. The night before he left he called to this cottage and gave me that weddin' ring. It had been his mothers he told me we would marry as soon as he got back."

'Did he ever come back?'

'No child, he never did. I've waited for news all me life. I don't know if he's dead or found another, all I know is he brought me more happiness. Not a day goes by that I don't think of him. And funny thing, the older I get the more I think of him.'

Then shrugging her shoulders she said shyly,

'Oh listen to me goin' on, put that picture back child you don't want to hear all that.'

'Oh but I do Aggie, I have learned more from you than anyone else,' said Molly sincerely.

A silence fell on the room. Then Molly just had to ask,

'Was it awful Aggie?'

'Was what awful child?'

'Getting beatin' up like that. Were you scared?'

Aggie began rubbing her arm nervously, 'I've thought about it a lot since. It was like being punished for somethin' I didn't do. Lord child, you know me I'd never hurt another livin' thing. I was afraid they'd kill me.'

'Oh! I would have died if it had been me,' said Molly in a frightened voice.

'No child you wouldn't. Inside all of us is a great will to live.'

'You must really hate them though, I know I would.'

'Funny 'twas them that was full of hate, you see they had no life in their cold eyes. All they knew was puttin' out their hand and takin' all they could get. When I came back here from the hospital I didn't feel this was home anymore. I could see them and hear their rough voices everywhere. They had been through all me things. Me mind was fillin' up with hate for them and what they done. That was what frightened me child. Their evil was castin' a great shadow over me."

'But you had been through a terrible time,' said Molly, making excuses.

'Its hard not to hate but nothin' should be so terrible that it would kill the good spirit inside ya. Evil makes ya become strong in yer mind. It made me use wisdom to choose.'

Molly walked over to the table and replaced the picture. Then as she picked up the wedding ring, a small surge of anger rose up inside her as she thought about the locket that was missing. But not wanting to upset Aggie further, she replaced it and talked some more about her school.

After a while Aggie began to doze off in her chair. Molly put on her coat and wandered outside to look at the cats.

Sitting down on the bench she tried hard not to think about the men attacking Aggie. She stood up again and went back indoors. Tip-toeing to the small cupboard she quietly took out the jug of milk then returned to the yard. She began pouring some into the old saucers lying around. As the cats drank thirstily from the dishes Molly wandered around the garden thinking about the first time she came to Aggie's cottage.

Suddenly something glittering in the withered grass caught her eye.

Walking over to the path she bent down and pushed the dry strands back with her hand. A gold chain glittered in the sunshine. Untangling it carefully, she managed to get it free from the strong weeds. Then she could not believe what she saw. At the end of the chain, was the locket locket. She felt her heart would burst with excitement as she ran back into the cottage.

'Aggie Aggie,' she whispered shaking her gently by the shoulder.

The old woman woke quickly and looked up at her with glazed eyes.

'What's the matter child?' she said anxiously.

'Look! the locket, **your** locket I found it.'

Aggie stared at the precious locket dangling from the young girl's fingers. Quickly reaching her old hand out Molly placed the locket in the palm of Aggie's hand. Aggie closed her fingers on it tightly and held the precious jewellery up to her lips. Lowering it again, she opened it slowly to check it was still there.

Looking up at Molly she said delightedly:

'God bless ya child, and bless the eyes of youth. This was my present to Tommie. I wanted him to wear it. But he said no, I was to keep it until he returned.'

Then she stopped and looked over excitedly at the small table.

Pulling back the rug from around her knees she said happily:

'Quick child help me up.'

Molly reached out, and supporting her left arm, helped her get up from the chair.

With the aid of her blackthorn stick Aggie made her way hurriedly across the floor. Molly walked beside her in case she might fall.

The old woman fumbled with the jewellery until eventually she got the chain through the ring. Then she moved them around as if there was a particular spot that they had to be put in. She stared at them for a second as she tried to bless herself with her left hand.

'Thanks be to God,' she prayed gratefully.

Just then Hattie's car could be heard pulling up at the gate. Molly helped the old lady back to her chair.

Hattie breezed into the cottage in her usual busy way carrying a large bunch of colourful flowers.

'Oh,' said Molly reaching out, 'let me put them in water.'

'Why thank you dear,' said Hattie, then turning to Aggie she inquired,

'Well how are we today?'

'Ah sur' I'm grand,' came the quiet reply.

'Well I hope Biddy and Doireann are looking after you. Come along now Molly we must hurry, Julie will have our tea waiting.'

Molly placed the flowers in a bowl in the centre of the table. Going over, she put her arm around Aggie and kissed her forehead.

'I'll see you again soon.' she whispered.

Aggie looked up at her with tears trickling down her face. 'Thank you,' she said gratefully 'Thank you both.'

Looking slightly puzzled at the old woman's reaction Hattie said cheerfully,

'Come come my dear their only a few flowers.'

CHAPTER 29.

It was a bright, crisp, sunny spring morning.

Walking across the yard at 'Riversdale House', Doireann was surprised to see Lady Gowne drive in. The jeep pulled up alongside her and shuddered to a noisy stop. Lady Gowne opened the window and peered out.

'Good mornin' Maureen,' said Doireann smiling. 'What brings you here so early?'

Lady Gowne found it hard to return her smile.

'There is no easy way to say this… she began seriously, but I may have to sell Propeller.'

Doireann was stuck to the ground. She tried to swallow a lump in her throat but it just would not go down. Her whole world came crashing in around her.

'But why?' she said, unable to comprehend this news.

'I don't want to but I'm afraid it's a question of finance,' replied Lady Gowne as she awkwardly rubbed the steering wheel with her hand.

'You see I've been made a fantastic offer.'

'By who?'

Bracing herself for a shocked reaction Lady Gowne replied,

'Em … Garrett O'Loughlin.'

'I don't believe it. Well of all the lousers, and all the encouragement he gave me last year. Every show we were at he'd come over to me, remember. With all his gaddin' about, could he not have found some other horse besides Propeller,' she said, scuffling the gravel with her boot.

Seeing the disappointed look on her friends face Lady Gowne said concernedly

'I hope you're not angry.'

'Of course I'm bloody angry,' she said with her eyes flashing, 'when did this happen anyway?'

'He rang me last night and came over first thing this morning. He is getting a team together for the Olympics.'

Thinking for a moment Doireann asked hopefully:

'Well if you don't mind me askin' how much are you gettin' for him? Could I afford to buy him?' she asked hopefully.

'Oh gosh I don't think so anyway it's too late. The deal has already been made. Garrett does not want the price disclosed because he still needs to buy some more horses."

Looking a bit puzzled, Doireann bit her lip anxiously as the finality of the sale hit her .

'When is he comin' to collect him?' she inquired curiously.

'Sometime this afternoon.'

'So soon?'

'I'm afraid so.'

A sudden panic welled up inside Doireann. She had a great urge to go to what she would always considered it to be, her horse. Trying to control her temper she asked in a quiet voice:

'Will I have time to see Propeller before he goes?'

'Of course you will my dear,' replied Lady Gowne in a comforting way.

'Listen Doireann, I really feel awful about this. I know how much the horse means to you and I have not forgotten all you've done. I wish I didn't have to sell him, not for my sake, but for yours. I love to see you ride him, he responds to you. But it is still a question of finance."

Her words rang empty on Doireann ears, as feelings of betrayal and disappointment kept increasing inside her.

Sensing her friend's distress, Lady Gowne immediately made a kind offer.

'Why don't you come over now, I can drop you back later.'

'No I've a few things to do first,' she said, looking back over her shoulder. 'I'll be over meself after. You go ahead.'

Wanting to be alone for a while Doireann, stood watching as the jeep bounced out the gate. Then she walked across the yard to the stables and Pacha.

Once inside she shut and bolted the door. Walking over to the corner she hit out at the air with her fists.

'Damn it, why the hell did he want to do this to me,' she thought angrily to herself.

Pacha, sensing her anger moved, nervously in the stall. Doireann reached out and patted her neck.

'It's alright girl,' she said reassuringly, 'steady now, its not you I'm angry with.'

Thinking back, she could see in her mind's eye Garrett's face as he chatted to her at the various shows. He was a tall muscular man with incredible blue glassy eyes and a most attractive smile. She thought he liked her. Now she knew why he was always so friendly. He wanted to get his hands on her horse.

Tears began to hurt her eyes. She walked over to the corner and sat on her hunkers. Placing her head in her hands, she remembered how much she had looked forward to him coming over. How easily she would smile and chat back to him. Thinking about it now Doireann felt embarrassed. Oh! what a silly fool he must have thought she was.

From the night Propeller was born, she always had such high hopes and ambitions for him. She thought of everything that they had achieved together. Unable to comprehend the betrayal and injustice of it all, she suddenly thought back to Cuiteog being gelded.

How she had wanted to make up for that unfortunate accident. She needed desperately to prove herself and ride this horse to victory. She wanted to bring honour to 'Mount Benedict' and the Furlong family.

As she sobbed bitter salt tears, she thought that he, of all people, should know how important a horse becomes to you.

A little while later, driving over to 'Mount Benedict', she started to calm down. She began to admit stubbornly to herself that Garrett was after all a very professional horseman. Maybe with Propeller, they could win a gold medal in the Olympics and bring fame to Ireland.

Garrett's lovely eyes flashed into her mind. Thinking about him again she said aloud as she switched on the radio:

'I don't care he's still a louse.'

As she pulled into the yard at Mount Benedict she saw Charlie standing with Propeller already saddled. On hearing her drive in, Lady Gowne walked out of the stables. Taking the reins from Charlie she offered them to Doireann.

'We hoped you would take him out for one last gallop,' she said kindly.

'Thanks Maureen,' she replied.

Charlie gave her an encouraging smile and a leg up.

Doireann leaned forward and patted the horse on the neck and stroked his lovely velvety ears. Then they turned and cantered out to the paddock.

Once on the grass she gave the horse an encouraging squeeze. It responded immediately.

'Come on Propeller,' she whispered, 'we'll show them that you really are my horse.'

Soon she forgot all about Garrett and the sale as she relaxed and enjoyed the ride. Gliding effortlessly over the jumps, Doireann knew that he was a superb animal. She felt that the oneness she had achieved with him was of her own making, and this made her feel particularly proud.

After a while she headed towards the gate, leaned forward and hugged his neck.

'I'll never forget you Propeller,' she said, tears smarting her eyes. Then, sitting back up in the saddle, she was annoyed to suddenly see Garrett O Loughlin, standing a little way off and holding the gate open for her. Quickly she straightened her back and brushed her tears away with the back of her gloved hand.

As she drew nearer to him a rather stern look came over her face. Completely ignoring him, she rode by, her chin proudly up and in total silence. Returning to the yard she dismounted slowly.

Charlie began unsaddling the horse.

Doireann stood very close to Propeller, possessively rubbing the horse's nose. From the corner of her eye she watched Garrett as he approached.

'Doireann I'll be sorry to see the like of him go,' said Charlie sincerely. 'You were certainly a powerful combination.'

'Thanks,' she replied as she kept watching Garrett draw closer.

Then loudly she replied to Charlie's compliment but her words were meant for Garrett's ears alone,

'Yes Charlie, and that is something money can't buy.'

CHAPTER: 30.

With Hattie and Nicholas enjoying each other's company, the long dark winter months seemed to fly. She found his conversation interesting, his manners becoming, and she took great comfort in his physical presence. In fact she often wondered how in heaven's name, she had put up with her own company for so long. However she still knew very little about him. Nicholas was not one to talk about himself.

One particular night they arrived home quite late to the Rectory from the festival ball in 'The Talbot Hotel'.' It had been a marvellous night's dancing and Hattie looked flushed and radiant.

Nicholas, seated comfortably in an armchair, could not help but admire her as she poured out a nightcap into two glasses. She looked so elegant and sophisticated in her ball gown of red taffeta and sequins.

As he watched, her graceful feminine movements caused an excitement to build up inside him. Then with eyes sparkling, she walked confidently towards him, the material of her dress rustling as she moved. Extending her hand she offered him a drink.

When reaching for his brandy the tops of his fingers accidentally brushed against hers. They giggled simultaneously and smiled into each other's eyes. Suddenly for a moment he saw the girl in her again. Her soft red lips and her flirtatious smile arousing him further. He wanted so much to reach out and just gently touch her beautiful long legs through the slit in her gown. But afraid of frightening her he let the moment pass.

As she sank graciously into the comfort of her armchair, they sipped their drinks and kept glancing at one another in a manner, unusual for their age.

'Remember when I met you first Hattie,' said Nicholas as his finger seductively rubbed the rim of his glass.

'I said I was thinking of retiring and coming home to Wexford to live? Well I've made up my mind. I'm going to fix up things in England and move home. I should be over there for about a week. Maybe you would like to come with me?'

Thinking for a moment she replied: 'But you would be working? I could only be a distraction,' she said with a rather mischievous smile

'Not at all,' he protested. 'I would love you to come.'

After a small silence she asked seriously

"Why do you want me to go Nicholas?"

Leaning forward, he put his glass down on the small table and clasping his hands together, he said sincerely:

'Because you're the very reason I want to move home.'

Hattie was flattered.

'These last few months have been just so good you know. Has it been the same for you Hattie?'

'Oh yes Nicholas,' she replied earnestly.

'Well that's what we'll do then, I'll make the necessary arrangements and I'll let you know when we sail.'

Standing up, he began buttoning up his jacket.

'I better go now,' he whispered, 'before Miss Clancy comes down after me with the brush.'

They both giggled quietly behind their hands.

The next day Hattie walked cheerfully into her kitchen. Pulling up a chair beside the table she watched as Julie rolled out the dough for some apple tarts. Lighting up a cigarette, she announced excitedly that she would be going away for a few days.

'Oh to where?' came the sudden cold reply,

'Nicholas has asked me to go to England with him.'

On hearing this latest news, an unhappy scowl came over Julie's face as she drew her dark heavy eyebrows together.

'What does he want you to go for? Why would you want to do that? Let him off on his own, he's big enough to take care of himself.'

'Well I'd like to go, I need a little holiday.'

'But what will people say? I mean a woman of your age and standing in the community going away to England with a man.'

'I don't care what people say, it's none of their business,' replied Hattie defiantly exhaling the smoke from her cigarette.

'Well if you won't think of them maybe you might remember you have a son a priest.'

'Well I have another one a doctor and I don't see what that has to do with anything,' said Hattie, trying to bring some humour into the conversation.

'This is not funny,' replied Julie, lowering her voice.

Hattie sat with her eyes turned upwards to the ceiling listening to Julie going on and on. Then she watched amusedly as she went from the table to the press taking out things she did not even need.

Standing at the kitchen table with her hands covered in flour, Julie began rolling out the dough aggressively.

Hattie found herself puzzled as to why Julie was reacting like this. She was getting unusually upset. Why was she not happy for her having found a friend?

Then she began to sense the undertones of feelings that lay beneath her frustration. It seemed to Hattie as if Julie was frightened of something. Surely it could not be change. Why down through the years they both had their fair share of that.

'I don't think its me,' she thought to herself, 'so it must be Nicholas. But she could not really dislike him or could she? But he never did anything to offend Julie. Then it dawned on her what was wrong.

The only reason Julie could be feeling like this was, that she was afraid that they might get married. Then Nicholas would move in to and Julie might have to leave.

Hattie stubbed her cigarette out in the ashtray and stood up from the table.

'Now Julie lets not quarrel,' she said, walking over to her. 'We've shared too much in the past for that. Look I'm only going away for a few days, it's not like there is a question of marriage or anything.' Then placing her hand on Julie's shoulder she added: 'and even if there was, you know you will always have a home here with me.'

'Yeah I know that, but **he** might think different.' said Julie sadly, her eyes filling up with tears.

In that moment a great affection came over Hattie for the vulnerability she was only now seeing in her housekeeper.

Over the years it was always Julie who had been a rock of strength for them. Turning her around gently Hattie put her other hand on her shoulder.

'Julie dear, it goes without saying that this house is your home for as long as you want. And please don't worry about Nicholas, as the song says, 'God help the mister who comes between me and my sister, for that is what you are like to me.'

Slowly a smile broke out on Julie's unhappy face, she reached over and the two women embraced affectionately. Then Julie burst out laughing when she noticed that Hattie was covered in flour.

From then on, with Julie's place in the family was secure, she was able to relax a little and become more pleasant towards Nicholas. She managed to keep her misgivings on the matter to herself. This in turn caused a lovely peaceful atmosphere and Hattie began to look forward to her trip to England.

Three weeks later as the happy couple drove on to the ferry Dun Laoghaire, Hattie's spirit of adventure had begun to take over. She could not help thinking that maybe now she might find out more about Nicholas. The crossing on the Irish Sea was calm and they even ventured up onto the top deck together. Then early next morning they began their journey to Cornwall.

Hattie yawned tiredly as Nicholas looked over at her and smiled. These were the times she felt very close to him.

Not having any motorways in Ireland, Hattie found the English ones amazing. Nicholas zoomed along them with such ease.

It was late evening when they arrived at what looked like a small hotel.

'Listen darling' suggested Nicholas as he turned the key in the door. 'You sit there and I'll go and put the heating on.'

Hattie declined to sit on the hard oak chair after the long journey. She was glad to get out of the car at last and stretch her legs. Instead she walked around the large hall and admired the old paintings. Lifelike scenes of the beautiful English countryside were captured forever in oils and watercolours.

When Nicholas returned to the hall he crept up quietly behind her, and put his arm around her shoulder.

' Now,' he said apologetically, 'I'm not much of a cook and anyway there's no food here, but I know a nice little pub down the road where we can eat. The house should be warm by the time we get back. What do you say?'

Hattie had absolutely no objections.

A little while later they were sitting in Doran's pub tucking into a lovely meal of roast beef, Yorkshire pudding and fresh vegetables. The red wine was served just at the right temperature, and as they raised their glasses to their little holiday Wexford seemed a world away.

Returning back to the house around midnight, they found that the central heating had the rooms heated up nicely and everywhere had a cosier atmosphere. Entering the sitting room, Nicholas opened a rather unusual Chinese drink's cabinet and poured out two large brandies. Hattie wandered tiredly to the couch and kicked off her shoes.

Sitting down beside her he tipped his glass against hers and said with a twinkle in his eye:

'Here's to us.'

Hattie settled back into the deep soft couch and relaxed. Even though the house was situated near a busy road it was so quiet.

Laying her head back she began taking in her surrounding's. She could not help thinking of the little boy in the classroom all those years ago and all he had achieved. Unable to resist she turned to him and asked:

'Nicholas is this all yours?'

'Sure is, and what's more its ready to go on the market.'

'You mean you're going to sell it?'

'Well unless you'd like to live here.'

Then, stretching his arm out on the back of the couch above her head, he turned to her and said curiously,

'Tell me Hattie, would you leave Ireland?'

'Well, I hadn't thought about it,' she replied honestly.

Looking around the room, Nicholas cupped the brandy glass in the palm of his hand and said sadly

'I've never really settled in any of these houses you know. They mean nothing to me. I always think of Wexford as home.'

Hattie's drink suddenly went with her breath.

'Why, have you more than one?' she gasped.

'Yes, I have four more houses just like this one.'

'What exactly do you do?'

'They call me a property developer, but really I'm only your average wheeler dealer,' he said modestly. 'I buy up big old houses like this, do them up, then dispose of them for a handsome profit. I've had this one for ten years now but it's never been home.'

Hattie suddenly began to realise how lonely he must be and she felt a great affection for him.

As they snuggled closer together she listened as he chatted on about his life. However, when the subject turned to religon she thought he was a little cynical in his views on the 'Roman Catholic Church'. Even though it hurt a little, she ignored it as she felt he was entitled to his opinion.

After a while the brandy took effect and Hattie felt very sleepy. Noticing her yawning a few times Nicholas reached over, took her empty glass from her hand, and placed it on the coffee table.

'Look at you my dear your all in. That's enough talk for now let's go to bed.'

Taking her hand, he led her to the hall and switched off the light. Then he carried the cases up the stairs after her. Opening a heavy oak door, they stepped into a huge bedroom. Nicholas dropped the heavy suitcases on the floor and whispered with a wink:

'I shan't be a jiffy.'

Then he left her alone in the room.

Feeling very tired, Hattie sat down on the edge of the bed and lay back. Closing her eyes, she sighed contentedly. Suddenly she realized that she did not know what the sleeping arrangements were. Opening her eyes widely, she sat up abruptly and reached for her cigarettes.

Nicholas returned a little while later in a blue pjyamas and said casually:

'Aren't you in bed yet?'

Hattie immediately got up off the bed.

'Em where are you sleeping?' she asked curiously.

Walking over, he held the tops of her arms and said hopefully:

'Oh Hattie, I thought we could snuggle in here together.'

Taking a step back from him she replied seriously,

'Oh no Nicholas, I'm not ready for anything like that just yet.'

'Well nothing like that need happen, don't you trust me? Come come now Hattie, we're both adults. It's not like we're children.'

'No, I'm sorry Nicholas, I would not feel comfortable. Look this is your bed, I can sleep somewhere else.'

Then she bent down to pick up her case.

'No, I wouldn't hear tell of it,' he said disappointedly, taking the case from her hand, 'there is another bed made up in the guest room, I'll take that one.'

Hattie looked at him and suddenly he seemed rather boyish. She put her two hands up to his face and kissed his cheek.

'Nicholas you're a sweet man but lets just take things a little slower.'

'I'm sorry Hattie,' he said humbly taking her hands in his, 'I had forgotten just how much of a lady you are.'

Then he kissed her on both hands, turned and quietly left the room.

With the tiredness suddenly gone, Hattie paced up and down the room. Her mind became confused. Maybe she was a little too hasty. After all he did not force himself on her, on the contrary he had accepted her decision. But he was a man after all with male hormones racing through him and God help her, but wasn't she only a woman.

'Oh flip it,' she thought frustratingly, 'I need love too.' But she knew she could only give herself to a deeper commitment.

Opening her suitcase, she took out her nightdress got undressed and climbed into the big double bed. Looking around the strange room she began to feel lonely. Then, reaching for her handbag, she rooted in it until she found her bottle of 4711 cologne. Putting a little dab behind both ears she smiled as she thought of Nicholas, then she whispered:

'Just in case he happens to change his mind.'

CHAPTER 31.

Eithne Thornton woke drowsily from a heavy sleep. She could hear her six-month-old baby crying in the nursery. She got out of bed quickly, and went to comfort him before he woke his daddy too.

Hurrying into the room, she took him out of his cot and up into her arms. Reaching for the bottle of gripe water she awkwardly poured some onto a teaspoon. The baby coughed and spluttered as he tried between heavy sobs, to swallow the cool liquid, his little cheeks red from teething.

Eithne held him close to her. Then, picking up his feed from the bottle warmer, she sat down in the rocking chair. In a few moments the baby lay contentedly sucking on the teat.

She wondered, as she strained her ears to listen, if any of her other children had been disturbed by his crying. But the 5-year old twins, 4-year old Susan, and little Celine who was only 2, all seemed quiet. Ethine breathed a deep sigh of relief.

The clock on the wall said two a.m. and she relaxed as she stroked her little son's head. In the quiet of the early morning she laid her head back and began thinking.

Being a mother, she spent all day giving to others. But at this hour when everything was quiet she found peace and space for herself.

When she married Seamus a few years ago they had both wanted children. Like most couples, they had a romantic picture in their minds of them being be a joy and a blessing. However, neither of them realized that children also meant commitment. It was hard work rearing them, but it was also very rewarding and Eithne took it in her stride.

Then she began thinking back to the brief time when there was just the two of them, her and Seamus, that magical time before the twins came.

They were madly in love and spent most of their free time together. Their lovemaking was so passionate, so frequent, and Eithne had found this wonderful.

Noticing how quickly the baby was drinking she decided it was time to get his wind up. Taking the bottle from his mouth, she placed it on the locker, sat him forward on her lap and began rubbing his little back gently.

Then a fear built up inside her as she began thinking again. She was very fertile and seemed to conceive so easily.

This month, her period was three weeks late, that could only mean one thing, she was pregnant again. Oh but she wanted her babies too. Each one filled her arms with love. They were all so different and yet each one had some small characteristic of their parents.

Seamus often joked about it saying they were coming out of the woodwork. But behind his jokes Eithne sensed a frustration. She knew he loved their children but yet there was something wrong.

Suddenly the baby brought up a forceful bout of wind from his little stomach.

'Good boy,' she said smiling with relief.

Then kissing the top of his soft head, she resumed his feeding.

Ten minutes later, with his nappy changed, she kissed and laid the sleeping contented baby back in his cot. Covering him with his small blanket, she tiptoed out of the room. Then she climbed wearily back into her own bed, to try and get some much needed sleep.

She was just nodding off when Seamus turned in the bed and snuggled in close to her. As she felt his hand move on her body his nose nestled into her hair. She knew her husband's advances so well. But tonight she was all played out and still deeply worried about her condition. She lay very still.

Slowly, Seamus lifted up on his elbow and leaned his body over hers. Eithne turned around and kissed him for a few moments then went to turn back. Seamus gently pulled her towards him and began to make love.

Suddenly a serious tension built up inside her and she began pushing him away. Even though she loved him she knew tonight that she could not respond to him.

Seamus rolled over on his back, and let out a disappointed sigh. A deafening silence descended on the room.

'I'm sorry honey,' she whispered, 'but I'm just too tired.'

'I see,' he said in a tense way.

She immediately felt she had let him down. She knew his needs so well. Again she apologised.

'Its okay, just go to sleep,' he said as he turned his back to her.

The space between their bodies became as vast as the ocean. Still the silence continued. Eithne knew she would not sleep unless she felt he really did understand. Reaching out to him with her hand, she said lovingly:

'I won't be so tired in the morning...' but before she could finish Seamus jumped out of the bed.

'Yeah sure, that's what you always say,' he said angrily, 'but in the morning it will be something else. One of the kids will want you.'

Hearing the hurt in his voice Eithne now became upset too.

'I won't go to them, I'll let them cry.'

'Yeah right, that would be the day. Look forget it, go back to sleep its okay,' he said as he went out of the room and into the bathroom.

The tiredness suddenly left Eithne as she watched the light from the hall stream into the bedroom. She turned over on her side and hugged the pillow. Tears were building up in her eyes. Nothing had turned out the way she had expected.

She always thought she would be able to juggle being a mother and being a lover. But with the birth of each child her body had changed and her energy was sapped.

'Oh,' she thought, 'it's all so unfair. Seamus is as strong as the day I met him.'

His body had not been invaded by a foetus and tightly stretched, nor had his pelvic bones been opened. His most intimate privacy has not been looked on by strangers, who, to bring new life into the world, took sharp painful instruments to it.

Not only through birth had she lost her girlishness, but also her slim body so favoured by the world of fashion. Then, with the responsibility of each child, her own sense of self-worth had faded slowly into the background.

Eithne ran her hand gently over her stomach. Now it was to happen again. Already inside her new life had taken root.

Just then Seamus returned from the bathroom. As he lay quietly beside her she said in a soft voice:

'I think I'm pregnant.'

'Right, that's it. We will have to do something about this,' he said, sitting up and turning on the bedside lamp.

'What do you mean?' asked Eithne, so afraid that he did not want the child.

Seamus put his arm caringly around her shoulder and pulled her close. After thinking for a few moments he said seriously,

'I can't have you getting pregnant every time we make love. I am going to refer you to one of my colleagues. He will advise you on contraception.'

As he went on to talk about the subject, Eithne snuggled in close to him. She was pleased that he cared, but unfortunately, the tiredness took over and she fell asleep.

The next morning Seamus was up and gone on his rounds at the hospital before she awoke.

It was not until the children were fed and dressed that she remembered the conversation of the previous night. Making herself a cup of coffee, she sat at the window watching the children playing in the garden. The baby lay gurgling contently in the Silver Cross pram.

As she sat looking out she was deep in thought. She began thinking back to her childhood. She remembered how her parents and teachers had told her that everyone was special.

That she was a being never to be created again.

It was with this knowledge that she had passed into her teenage years. She remembered going to dances and having fun, but always keeping in mind the dignity of her personal femininity. Then she fell deeply in love with Seamus. He was the one whom she knew she could make a life long commitment too.

She felt he respected her, and that he would always protect her vulnerability as a woman.

Suddenly she was annoyed as she remembered how she agreed to what he had said about contraceptives last night. She was tired then, she was not thinking straight. She had read a few years back about a new pill on the market and the excitement it caused.

What was it they were saying? Yes, now she remembered.

There would be no need for abortions. No more unwanted pregnancies.

It would give women of the future a sexual freedom equal to men. Thinking about the implications of it all, a threatening fear started to creep into her mind. She did not want to be like a man, she was a woman.

Slowly she rose from her chair and rinsing out her cup, she looked out the window at her children playing on the grass. Suddenly she had an overwhelming need to hold them close.

That night, as Seamus was undressing, he reached into his pocket and pulled out a slip of paper. Sitting down on the bedside he handed it to Ethine.

'There's the man to go and see about our little problem,' he said happily. 'He's married himself and is very understanding."

Eithne did not pick up the paper.

'I've thought about nothing else all day,' she replied coldly,' and… I've decided I'm not going.'

'Maybe you will change your mind after you talk to him. He is one of the best doctors in the country.'

'No I won't,' she repeated stubbornly, as she turned away and pulled the blanket over her head.

Seamus said nothing, he just sat down on the bed. He felt deeply hurt.

It was seemed to him as if Eithne did not care, or worse still, she did not want him sexually anymore.

Standing up, he walked around to the other side of the bed. Taking his two pillows up in his arms he walked out the door towards the spare room. Suddenly he stopped

'Other women do it,' he said disappointedly 'I don't understand why you can't?'

CHAPTER 32.

From the corner of Aggie Cullen's cottage the ghostly form of a handsome solider stood watching from the shadows. Silently and patiently he waited. Aggie sat up in her sick bed with her breathing shallow and fast.

Doireann puffed up the pillows behind her, and settled her comfortably. Aggie felt a little better today, she had not coughed as much as previous nights. But her chest was tender and sore. Doireann reached for a black woollen shawl and pulled it warmly around the old lady's shoulders. Then, placing a breakfast tray in front of her, she left the bedroom and walked into the kitchen. Having lit the fire and tidied up quickly she returned a little while later for the tray.

'We're off to that wedding in 'Courtown' today Aggie,' she said excitedly, 'but the boss will look in on you around four. I've left sandwiches on the table, and when I come back I'll bring you the dinner. Will you be alright till then?'

'Of course I will child, ya go and enjoy yerself.'

As she removed the tray, Aggie tugged gently on the end of her jumper.

'Before ya go child, will ya do one more thing for me? Will ya bring me the ring and locket that's lyin' in front of Tommie's picture?'

Returning a few moments later, Doireann hurriedly dropped them on the bedcovers. Aggie reached out urgently and caught Doireann by the wrist. Picking up the ring, she turned her hand over and placed it in her palm. Doireann looked curiously at Aggie.

'You've always been like a daughter ta me. The way ya've turned out, I know your mother would be proud. Over the years ya made me very happy watchin ya grow.'

Looking deep into Doireann's eyes she continued,

'This is the most precious thing I own and I want ya to have it.'

'But Aggie, I…,'

'No child listen ta me now, this is the only way I know how to thank ya properly for all ya done for me. Please take it. Put as much value on it as I have. Now off with ya to your weddin' or they'll go without ya'

Doireann looked down at the plain gold ring. She knew how precious it was to Aggie. Feeling very moved by her gesture, she said affectionately:

'Thanks, not just for the ring, but for what you said.'

Crumpling up the locket in her hand, Aggie whispered softly:

'This I'm keepin' for David's child.'

Doireann leaned over put her arms around Aggie's shoulders, kissed her lovingly on the forehead and quickly hurried from the room.

Aggie sat up in bed and smiled happily to herself. After a while she got up slowly from the bed and the help of her old blackthorn stick she walked into the kitchen.

The morning sun shone brightly through the small window. Moving slowly through it, her small bent figure broke its shaft of light. Then after filling the kettle with fresh water, she wandered over to the picture on the table. From the corner the soldier smiled tenderly as he watched her. Picking up the frame she ran her fingers over the glass.

'Oh Tommie darlin',' she said sadly 'I wonder have ya forgotten me?'

In one quick movement, the form of the solider glided across the room. She continued to stare at the photograph and looked down at his lips. Then she held the picture close to her breast. In her mind she could still feel his kisses, his skin against her cheek.

She was unaware that his spirit was standing behind her, as she was not in that world yet

Suddenly the cat jumped down from the settle bed and knocked over the broom. Aggie jumped nervously. Turning around she scolded the cat for frightening her.

'You're a bad cat Blackie to go frighten' me like that,' she said breathlessly.

The soldier glided back to the corner and continued watching.

Finding she was still weak after her time in bed, Aggie walked slowly over to her chair. Sitting down wearily, her gaze wandered to the fire. Taking her dudeen from her pocket, she leaned over and tapped it against the chimney-breast. The ash fell into the hearth. Then she refilled the bowl with some fresh tobacco, lit the dudeen and settled back for a nice relaxing smoke.

'I'll just catch me breath,' she said quietly to herself, 'Then I'll put some more sticks on the fire.'

But in her weakness she dozed off and the fire was forgotten.

The form of the soldier glided out from the shadows again and stood watching while she slept. Unable to touch her, his eyes wandered over her wrinkled face and white hair. She had been his girl, the love of his life. All those years ago she had filled him with happiness.

'It won't be long now, Aggie darling,' he whispered, 'It won't be long now.'

In her peaceful slumber she was still unaware of his presence, as she was not in his world yet.

After a while she woke up feeling chilled. The fire had died down. Shivering and shaking, she rose quickly from her chair to get some sticks. Reaching over to the basket, a sudden dizziness came over her and she tripped. Falling heavily against the chimney, her stick gave way and she fell down. Her head landed with a great thud on the cement floor, while thin red blood gushed from a deep gash in her forehead.

'Ah God no,' she cried out as she felt the warm blood on her fingers.

'I'm just a stupid ould woman.'

The solider came closer, kneeling down, his hand gently caressed her cheek. Aware now of a presence, Aggie cried out:

'Ah, Blackie, will ya go away, can't ya see I'm hurt?'

His hand continued to caresses her, as she moved hers to brush the cat away. Trying to rise up from the floor, she found she was in great pain. Her hip was broken. The cold of the stone came creeping into her bones, and as time went by she became quite fearful.

'Boss,' she called out weakly, 'Boss are ya there? Doireann, Biddy, somebody help me.' But there was only silence.

'Oh God,' she cried, 'I've lived alone all me life, don't let me die alone.'

Time went slowly by. Sometimes it would seem as if she was a little girl again living in the safe loving time with her parents. Then that image would fade, and she would dream she was running through a wood picking wild flowers with her dead mother. Each dream got more vivid and Aggie grew colder.

Eventually it seemed that she woke from her dreams and all her pain had gone.

The floor felt soft and warm. In her hour of need she looked up and saw Tommie.

'Ah my darlin', if only ya were real,' she said, tears filling her eyes. Now she was almost in his world. Her hand appeared translucent as she tried to reach out to him.

'But I am real Aggie,' he said, smiling.

Aggie looked down at his hand but could not feel it.

'No,' she cried fearfully, 'It's the evil one playin' tricks with me mind.'

'No Aggie, this time you're wrong. There is only peace and goodness now.'

Touching his beautiful young face, tears of joy mixed with sadness rolled down her cheeks.

'But ya've never changed Tommie, ya're still young, and I'm an old woman.'

'No Aggie,' he said smiling, 'You will never be old again. Look, see how beautiful you are.'

He reached out and stroked her hair and this time she could feel his touch. Her limp body shook as a strong current of fear and excitement passed through her.

'Oh Tommie, ya are real. I can feel ya,' she said, her eyes opening up with joy.

'Oh keep touchin' me, it's been such a long time.'

Continuing to stroke her he kept encouraging her saying:

'Let it go Aggie, let this life go. Come, come with me into the real world.'

Suddenly as he bent down and raised her up, Aggie body became weightless as she beheld her own vision of Heaven.

Looking down at her feet and back up again, she could hardly believe her eyes.

Her form became as a young girl again. Her breasts were firm, her long golden hair was hanging waist length to her hips, her thighs had strength and her legs were straight. But the greatest change of all was inside her emotions. Aggie felt young again. Turning around she looked down at her old heavy body lying useless on the floor.

Tommie stepped closer to her and said softly,

'It's over Aggie, that life is finished.'

In one movement, he turned her back to him and held her close. Love joined love, and a great happiness filled their souls. In that moment a bright light illuminated them from above.

'You are mine Aggie,' he said, 'and this time nothing on earth will separate us.'

Aggie rested her head on his chest. At last she had come home. The lovers walked out of the dark room into the bright sunshine, The cottage faded into the background.

They stopped for a moment to embrace with one long lingering kiss, and then they were gone.

An eerie stillness entered the kitchen. The cat wandered over and nestled down beside its dead mistress.

A little while later Walter Furlong walked across his field towards Aggie's cottage.

He thought about all that happened since that dreadful night she was attacked. Funny, she was never quite the same again. Her front door, which was always open to everyone, now had to be not just closed but locked as well. Her nerves were a little jumpy when she heard a sudden noise and she always kept a light on in the cottage at night. She never ventured out and Walter had a telephone installed at his own expense to give her a feeling of security.

As he drew nearer the cottage he felt she was recovering from that dreadful bout of bronchitis. He began to think about what he could do for her when she got better. Maybe he could bring her for little drives to get her out in the air. Then he reminded himself that it could not be too far, as Aggie liked to be near home.

Opening the door of the cottage, he could not believe it, when he saw her body lying in a pool of blood and the paleness of death on her face. His heart almost stopped beating. Immediately, he thought she must have been attacked again and started looking cautiously around. In shock and fear he ran into the other room, then outside and around the back.

Satisfied there was nobody there he went back into the cottage. As he walked over to her body, for, the first time in his life he did not know what to do. He quickly shooed the cat away and knelt down reverently at her side.

Then removing his cap, he leaned over and whispered the act of contrition into her ear. Reaching out, he took her cold hand in his.

Holding it tightly, he began stroking her wispy hair. Walter Furlong, who was always master of his emotions, found he could control them no longer and became over-whelmed in a sea of sorrow. Tears filled his eyes and rolled down his cheeks. In the privacy of the cottage he sobbed bitterly.

'Aggie, I'm quare sorry,' he cried, 'I'm sorry I wasn't here for you, like you were always there for me.'

But there were no comforting words from Aggie this time, only a dead silence filled the room.

After a while he took his handkerchief from his pocket and dried his eyes. He thought of lifting her off the cold floor but was reluctant to in case she had been beaten up again. The guards would need evidence. Instead he took the rug from her chair and covered her. An eerie feeling crept up his spine. Death was so final.

Standing up, he picked Blackie up in his arms. Walking out of the cottage to get some help, he paused to look fondly back one more time.

Aggie Cullen lay dead on the floor.

In her hand a golden locket and on her face a smile of peace.

CHAPTER 33.

Arriving home after her little holiday, Hattie was glad to be sleeping in her own bed again. She never thought she would miss the squawking sounds of the black crows in the trees.

Because of Nicholas's impeccable behaviour in England, she now felt that she could not only trust him but that their relationship was moving up a gear. She knew she was falling deeply in love but she still wondered what he could be thinking sometimes.

Driving home one night, he suddenly pulled into the gateway of a field and stopped the car.

They were returning from Alishe Furlong's 30th birthday party in Bray. Although the music at the party had been a little too loud, they still found that they had enjoyed it.

Alishe was in high spirits as she welcomed her guests and opened her gifts. The large sitting room filled up quite quickly with friends and family. The buffet of delicious meats and salads followed by very rich desserts went down a treat. Champagne and Martinis flowed quite freely. Hattie was delighted to meet up with the sons and daughters of old acquaintances and was very interested to hear what they were doing now. But as the evening wore on more young people came and Hattie decided it was a little too noisy for her. Having eventually found David in the kitchen pouring drinks, she pulled him one side and asked him to make their excuses for them. Then they slipped quietly away.

An hour later and weary from driving, they pulled off the main road and into a gateway. With the engine switched off, they sat in the blissful quiet of the car surrounded by the open fields. Settling back in their seats, they enjoyed a nice quiet smoke and Nicholas became very romantic and talkative.

'Hattie, there is something I want to say to you,' he began seriously, 'now please don't interrupt until I'm finished as this is very important to me.' Then taking her hand in his he continued:

'Hattie darling, I love you very dearly. Since we came back from England I've been thinking about a lot of things. For some time now the challenge of my work has gone and I'm making money that I don't need. I want to retire and enjoy life. I feel I want to share everything with you. Oh Hattie, I know I have found in you someone very special. We could have such a great life together. We could go to theatres all over the world. We could have racehorses, holidays, anything you like. What I suppose I'm really trying to say is…I love you Hattie would you consider marrying me?'

As Nicholas spoke, a dream of enchantment rose up in Hattie's mind. She had not felt like this for a long time. Now it seemed she was being given a second chance. Everything she ever dreamed and read about as a young girl now seemed possible. It was true she had found love with James all those years ago and wealth too. But, because of their youth and commitment to work and rearing a family, they had no real freedom to enjoy it.

But what she had now with Nicholas was different. It was more mature, adult, relaxed and yet very exciting. Here, was this rich handsome gentleman offering her the world. Images of travelling, shopping trips, romantic strolls on the beach, visits to art galleries all flashed before her mind. Julie, Molly, her sons, everybody disappeared.

Her eyes sparkled in anticipation and her excitement built up to and almost orgasmic level.

'Yes,' she thought excitedly, 'I will marry him, I will. 'But before she could reply he continued:

'My divorce should be through pretty soon and…'

'Divorce! It was like a bomb exploding in her ears, but from whom? Suddenly Hattie's dream began to dissolve and disappear. Turning to him she said hoarsely:

'I thought you said your wife Elizabeth was dead, killed in an accident.'

Taken aback by Hattie's sudden change of voice, he stuttered as he replied:

'Oh yes, my first wife, but then I got married again. My second wife Jessica was my secretary. But the marriage only lasted six months, too much of an age gap. We went our separate ways almost ten years ago now. I don't consider myself married.'

'Come come now Nicholas,' said Hattie, getting a little annoyed. 'Either you are or your aren't.'

'Well legally I suppose I am but emotionally I'm not. That marriage meant nothing, nothing I tell you.'

Hattie was stunned. Not only at his shattering news, but the fact that he could say a marriage meant nothing.

As she listened to him trying to explain and reassure her of his position in the marriage stakes, she found she could not take it all in. Suddenly she felt an old familiar tension rise in the back of her neck and sweep upwards towards her temples.

'I'm tired Nicholas, I have one of my headaches coming on,' she announced, as she rubbed her forehead wearily

'Perhaps you might drive me home please, we will talk about this again.'

They drove on in silence, Nicholas not knowing what to say. Now and again it was broken when he inquired as to how her head felt.

When he reached her home she opened the door herself the moment he stopped the car. Stepping out quickly, she paused.

'Thanks for a nice evening I shall ring you tomorrow.'

Leaning over, he looked up at her with pleading eyes.

'Just remember Hattie, it's you I love and want to spend the rest of my life with,' he said sincerely.

'I know,' she replied softly, 'we will talk tomorrow.'

Once inside the house she leaned her back on the closed door and listened to the familiar sound of his car driving down the avenue. In her heart she did not know if she could talk about this tomorrow, the next day or any other day for that matter.

As she climbed the stairs slowly to her bedroom, all Hattie Thornton knew was that she had a blinding headache.

Chapter Thirty Four

It was three weeks to Molly's Intermediate Certificate examinations when Aggie Cullen was laid to rest. Befitting the ceremony for a very special human being, nature seemed to organise her farewell.

As her remains left the church, the summer sun shone like precious gold in the clear blue sky. Perched on individual branches, birds sang hymns of sweet praise. Like a thousand small hands, the leaves on the trees rustled their loving applause. As the small procession walked quietly onwards towards the cemetery the colourful heather's and shrubs swelled proudly in their beds. Tears fell silently from eyes that had loved her.

Then suddenly two sparrows flew upwards with great speed to the heavens. As the prayers for the dead were recited, the perfume from the fresh flowers drifted into the senses of the living and gave them joy. Like a womb waiting to receive its child, Aggie's coffin was gently lowered into a welcoming hole in the ground, while beside it a mound of rich brown clay waited to cover its old friend.

A little while later, with the graveyard deserted, under a large evergreen tree, Aggie Cullen's remains lay sleeping, the sleep of the eternal.

After the funeral a few friends were welcomed for refreshments at 'Riversdale House'.

In the kitchen Walter Furlong took Fr. William gently by the arm and pulled him to one side. He seemed to be a little concerned about something.

'I don't know what to do about Molly,' he whispered.

'Well, I was expecting her to be here,' replied William, looking casually around.

'No your mother said not to tell the child, it might disturb her and she sitting her exams.'

'Well, I can understand that,' said William thoughtfully, 'But somebody should tell her that Aggie is dead.'

Then after thinking for a moment he said concernedly:

'Maybe I will go up to Kilcullen and see her myself.'

'Well that would be great,' said Walter, relieved at the suggestion.

'When would you go?'

'I'll go now,' he said looking at his watch and putting his cup down on the table. Then he whispered in Walter's ear:

'I'll leave you to explain to mother.'

Two hours later when he arrived at the convent the nuns were delighted to see him. Fr. William felt a little unworthy of their reverence to him as they welcomed him into the convent.

In the classroom, Molly was engrossed in her studies, and did not look up when Sister Miriam Gabriel tiptoed into the room. She was one of the younger sisters, quite popular with the girls. A quaff of her brown wavy hair peeped out attractively from under her veil, and her eyes were always lit up with a wonderful childlike expectancy. Walking swiftly over to the rostrum, she whispered words to the sister in charge. Then waited patiently while the older nun announced loudly:

'Molly Furlong, you are wanted in the parlour.'

Whenever the girls heard the word parlour a great excitement came over them. It usually meant somebody from home had come to visit.

The parlour was a large long room with a high ceiling. A dining table stood in the centre with eight chairs to match. Two armchairs sat beside a white marble fireplace, while all around the walls hung prints of religious scenes from the bible.

Molly was not expecting visitors and she was rather puzzled as she rose quickly from her desk. Wishing they had been called, the other girls looked up longingly at her.

Out in the corridor Sister Miriam told Molly that her uncle, the priest, had come to visit. An instant surge of excitement that the girls always got from a contact with home, rose up inside her. Walking respectfully behind Sister Miriam, Molly's shoes seemed more squeaky than usual and the corridor longer. As there were two parlours each side of the entrance hall, the young nun indicated with her hand as to which door Molly should enter. Then quietly, with one of her warm smiles, she took her leave.

When Molly opened the door she saw Father William standing with his back to her, looking pensively out the window. Turning around, he walked forward to greet her but despite his smile, she noticed a troubled look in his eyes.

'Is there something wrong ?' she asked worriedly.

'Well yes in a way,' he replied quietly, trying not to alarm her. Walking towards the fireplace, he signalled to her to sit down. Then, taking the chair opposite he began:

'It's Aggie... I'm afraid... she died two days ago.'

Molly's bottom lip began to tremble and then the tears started.

Father William stood up and kindly offered her his handkerchief. He stood awkwardly in front of her for a moment and then stepped back to the fireplace. Eventually she looked up through heavy sobs and muttered: 'Why didn't they tell me?'

'Well, I'm afraid that was mothers idea. She didn't want your exams interrupted. Anyway, there was nothing anyone could do. When your granddad called to the cottage last Tuesday evening he found her dead.'

'What happened to her?' asked Molly fearfully.

'Well it seems she may have fallen from her chair and hit her head on the floor.'

Trying to picture the awful event in her mind Molly asked worriedly: 'Would she have been in pain?'

'No, not at all, ' he replied reassuringly, 'apparently when you bang your head like that Molly you are knocked out immediately. Your granddad says she had the loveliest smile on her face, and, of course, the cats were minding her.'

'Oh!' said Molly concernedly, 'who's going to mind the cats now?' William was caught with this question.

'I'd imagine Biddy will,' he said smiling.

Then he put his hand into his jacket pocket and took out a gold locket. Reaching down, he took her hand and placed it into her palm. Then closing her fingers, he held them firmly.

'Aggie told your Auntie Doireann that morning that she wanted you to have this and when you grandad found her it was in her hand.'

When Father William took his hand away Molly opened her fingers and looked at the locket.

In her mind's eye she could see the smile on Aggie's face the day she had found it in the garden. More tears flowed as her heart ached.

Trying to lift the sadness in the room William asked cheerfully: 'Do you know the story about Aggie and her solider Molly?'

'Yes,' sniffled Molly.

'Ah it was a shame, so sad.'

Molly was about to explain when she suddenly thought there was no need. It was enough that Aggie and she knew the truth.

'So Molly, tell me, how do you think you are getting on with the exams?'

As she started to tell William, he smiled when he saw some of the Furlong spirit returning to her eyes.

Then a knock came to the door and two nuns entered.

One was carrying a tray and the other a silver teapot.

With great care they transferred the china tea set from the tray and placed it on the table. Delicious sandwiches and a large cream sponge cake followed. After inquiring how Father would like his tea, Sister Teresa poured it out carefully into the china cup. Then, having filled Molly's cup too, they excused themselves and quietly left the room.

Knowing how rare cake was to students in boarding school, William rubbed his hands excitedly together and exclaimed:

'Well now, isn't this wonderful? Come now Molly let's have some tea.'

He cut a large slice of cake, put it on a small plate and offered it to her. She dried her eyes and took it from him. As he watched her enjoy it, he decided that this could be a good time to explain some things.

'You know Molly,' he began, 'I have been meaning to talk to you about that day in the fish shop. Remember the day you found that poem? Well I want you to know that there was never anything in any way improper between your mother and I.'

'When I was sixteen I had a crush on her, as indeed did Seamus,' Then smiling coyly he admitted:

'All I know is that my vocation came so strong just after that.'

This was the first time Molly heard Father William talking intimately and she began to feel a little embarrassed and happy at the same time. Being an absolute romantic, she could just imagine what it must have been like when they were younger. Then she could not help but feel very proud of her mother.

After all, she must have been very special to have two young men in love with her at the same time.

'In a way I'm glad I found that poem,' said Molly sincerely.

'Heaven only knows why she didn't give it to me herself.' replied Father William in a puzzled voice.

'Still, I'm glad it happened this way. You know there was a very spiritual side to your mother, Molly. She had an uncanny way of seeing the future. Why I remember the day when we were only children and she asked Seamus if he would be a doctor. Then a few years later when I told her I was going to be a priest she said she knew it. The way she said it was eerie.'

As they enjoyed their tea, he went on to tell Molly about the night her mother gave birth to her.

'There was no medical reason as to why she died and yet…'

As he told her about the events of the time, Molly began thinking back to what Aggie had said about her mother.

Aggie had a strange spiritual side to her too, and Molly knew that not many girls of her age would have been able to sense it. Then her mind wandered to the first day she asked Aggie if she was a witch. Suddenly she remembered that Aggie was dead.

The cake felt dry and caught in her throat. Trying hard to swallow it down she started crying again. This time her sobs came straight from her very heart. Sitting watching her William found it very hard to control his own feelings.

He could feel a lump building up in his stomach. Wanting to cheer things up, a mischievous thought suddenly came into his head.

Taking the silver cake knife he began cutting the rest of the cake into small slices. Then he packed them tightly into the serviettes on the table and carefully struggled to put them into his jacket pockets.

He was just finished when the Sister Teresa came into the room to collect the tea tray.

'You must think I am awful Sister, but I couldn't resist your lovely cake, it was delicious,' he said, looking sheepishly at the empty plate

'Oh no Father, I'm glad you enjoyed it. I made it myself,' she said proudly, 'maybe you would like some more tea?'

'No thank you Sister, I'm afraid I must be getting back.' he replied as he checked his watch and rose from the table.

Molly dried her eyes and blew her nose loudly.

Noticing that she had been crying, Sister Teresa put her arm around her shoulder.

'Ah ya wee pet,' she said in her sharp northern accent, 'don't be upsetting yourself now.' and she went on to offer more words of comfort. Then she left them to say their good-byes in private.

'I'm sorry to leave so soon but I have to be getting back,' he said regretfully.

'I know,' she said understandingly, 'thanks for coming and telling me.'

Molly awkwardly handed him back a crumpled handkerchief.

'I'm afraid it's a little wet,' she said with an embarrassed smile suddenly breaking out on her sad face.

'And that's what it's for,' he said, putting his hand caringly on her shoulder.

Looking down at his pockets stuffed with cake, he had no option but to put the handkerchief up his sleeve. It felt cold and damp and against his skin.

When they reached the main door Father William put both hands tenderly on her shoulders and said in a most sincere way:

'I'm always here for you Molly, you're like a younger sister to me. Now your daddy and all at home send their love. I'm afraid mother didn't send you anything because…' leaning over he whispered: 'I didn't tell her I was coming.'

Then reaching into his pockets he said happily: 'But I have something for you.'

Then looking up and down the corridor to see if the coast was clear, he took the two serviettes from his pockets and handed them to her. Molly giggled as she shoved them up her jumper.

'Don't forget to return those serviettes to the refectory,' he said with a boyish grin.

Then putting his hand lightly on her cheek he said thoughtfully: 'I'll say a prayer for your exams,' and with a wave he was gone.

Late that night Kate could hardly wait until everyone was asleep to sneak quietly into Molly's cubicle. In their nightdresses and dressing gowns they sat crossed legged on the bed. Molly reached under her pillow and pulled out the serviettes. Handing one to Kate, they opened the cloth carefully and, smiling, looked down at the pieces of squashed cake. Feasting on the creaminess of their treasure, Molly related to Kate all the good times she had shared with Aggie. As she reminisced she suddenly realised that Aggie would always be alive in her memory.

After awhile they grew tired and decided it was time for sleep. As Kate left the cubicle she suddenly turned back and peeped through the closed curtain.

'You have some cream on your cheek,' said Molly giggling. Kate quickly knocked it off with her finger.

Sucking the last of the cake her eyes twinkled as she said sincerely,

'Hey Molly, God bless Father William.'

CHAPTER 35.

David and Alishe Furlong smiled happily at each other. It had been a busy week for them both and they were looking forward to being together for the next couple of days. The weather was not the best however with squally showers falling quite often from the dark skies.

It had been two months since David had inherited 'McDermotts Fish Shop' and house from his mother-in-law Jessie, and as they turned onto the Dublin road it was foremost in his mind.

'I'd like to call to the fish shop before we go home,' he said anxiously.

'Oh but I had arrangements made to meet my friends for drinks this evening,' said Alishe crossly.

'Well I shouldn't be long darling, you see Mick McCoy moved out this morning and I want to check that he locked up the place properly.' he explained.

'Oh where did he go?'

'Well he rang Aunt Hattie during the week and told her he was going back to England. Apparently there were some people over there he was missing.'

'Must be the ones in the white coats,' laughed Alishe.

Later, as they drove through the streets of Dublin, they began discussing Jessie's will. Listening to his wife's views on the subject, David thought she sounded a little cynical about it all. It suddenly became obvious to him that she would have preferred if things had been bequeathed a little differently.

'How do you mean?' he asked sharply.

'Well, Mick could have lived in that house and set the fish shop. Then he would have had a roof over his head for the rest of his life. Now on the other hand, we could have done with the money. We could have extended the practice and paid off our mortgage. Instead we will now have the hassle of selling it all.'

David was getting more upset by the minute at her suggestions but remained quiet.

'I have good friends in auctioneering,' she went on boasting proudly, 'they would be only too pleased to advise and help us dispose of the property.'

Very quietly and with control he replied:

'I'm sure they would, but I'm not selling it.'

Pulling quickly into a parking spot Alishe switched off the engine.

'Well David,' she said loudly, 'if you think I'm going to live in that grotty little house you have another thing coming. Are you mad?'

David found it very hard to control his temper. Slowly he answered her in a firm voice.

'Look Alishe that house is mine. Whether I sell or live in it will be up to me. You have your flat and your practice. God knows I have put enough money into that, so don't take it for granted that I'm going to do everything you say.'

Realising that he was getting vexed and there would be no talking to him, she cunningly leaned over, smiled teasingly up into his eyes, and kissed his cheek. Then fiddling with his tie she whispered,

'I love it when you take control.'

Then she sat straight up in her seat again, fixed her mini skirt and restarted the engine.

David could not help but smile. She could get him all fired up one minute and cool him down again in the next. As the tension between them relaxed a little, it seemed to him that they had just narrowly missed another major row.

When their car turned the corner into the street, the fish shop and house looked so shabby and forlorn that Alishe forgot herself and started protesting again.

'How could anyone live in that dive? ' she said, pulling into the kerb and looking up through the windscreen.

Remembering the love he felt for the people who had, a sudden anger built up in David again. Opening the car door he got out quickly onto the pavement.

'Don't bother collecting me I'll find my own way home,' he said as he slammed the door of the car.

Looking up surprised at him she shouted: 'Don't worry I won't.'

Having watched her take off with great speed David was left standing alone on the pavement. Taking a large bunch of keys from his pocket, his hand trembled with anger as he tried to turn the key in the lock. Opening the door, he suddenly thought back to the first time, years ago now, when Jessie opened the door for him. She had been shocked at the thoughts of Molly going out on the back of his motorbike. Closing the hall door behind him, a musty smell lingered in the air. Tuning left he walked into the sitting room.

Looking around the room he began thinking back to the day he asked J.J. for Molly's hand in marriage. It was in this very room. Then he walked slowly over to the window. In the stillness he could hear, as if it was yesterday, J.J. saying proudly:

'One day this will all be hers.'

He smiled as he thought of the way both J.J. and Jessie had, over the years, wormed their way into his affections.

He stood thinking for several minutes, then slowly turned and went back out through the door. In the kitchen he checked his keys again to find which one would open the door of the fish shop.

Once inside, he did not linger but walked around the back of the counter and up to the flat. Climbing the stairs, he remembered bounding up the same steps the night his Molly died. Being in a terrible panic at the time, the stairs seemed like one gigantic step.

On reaching the door of what had been their bedroom, a familiar old pain came into his heart. Stepping into the room he flicked the light switch but nothing happened. He could just make out the contents of the room with the glow from the street lights.

Nothing had really changed and judging by the dust and cobwebs nobody had been in the room for a long time.

Sitting down on the bed, he reached over to the switch on the bedside lamp. To his surprise Matty's wedding present still worked. He smiled as he remembered the awkward way his best man had handed it to him the night before his wedding.

'We can't have a spark sleepin' in the dark,' he had said jokingly.

David had not seen him for quite some time and he wondered now how he was getting on.

The lamp gave the room a warm feeling, and as David lay back against the headboard his eyes wandered over to the bathroom door.

Suddenly he imagined Molly standing in the doorway. He lay almost paralysed as if she walked towards him.

Her beautiful body, her long strawberry blonde hair and her very own special smile of love filled his memory. As he relived that wonderful night of passion, he quickly sat up again as he also remembered the inevitable consequences of it too.

Unable to hold back his powerful emotions his head dropped forward into his hands and he cried bitter tears of regret. Taking his hands from his face he crossed his arms and caught both his sides. With a deep ache in his chest he rocked to and fro moaning from the depths of his heart:

'Oh I love you Molly.'

After a while he dried his tears, got up from the bed and walked over to the window. As he looked down into the empty street he thought: 'Where is Alishe?'

Disappointed that she did not come back for him, he began thinking about the first time he saw her in the offices of 'Wilkinson and Rice.' He had come to town that day to collect a cheque from Mr. Wilkinson. Matty and him had done a lot of work wiring the old gent's private house.

It was not loneliness that started their relationship, rather it was the sparkle in her dark eyes as she waved the cheque teasingly at him and said:

'How about spending some of this on me?'

She was determined to thoroughly enjoy life, her way, as she never dreamt of any other. He thought back to the wonderful weekends they had shared in the beginning. How she had helped him to snap out of his dark moods. She had such a zest for life, but how quickly all that had changed after they married.

He thought now of her burning ambitions. Most of their weekends were taken up with her friends. Their boring conversations over dinner about the power games they played in court. Her desire for the luxuries that she claimed her position demanded.

Then there was her selfish attitude to not having children.

'She is just so self-centred, so ambitious,' he thought.

He remembered the way she spoke about Aggie Cullen, God rest her, and had scoffed at her appearance.

'Molly was so different,' he thought sadly.

'Oh what I would give just to have her back. All Alishe cares about is her bloody law practice. I think I've made a dreadful mistake.'

Realising Alishe would not be coming back to collect him, he put his hands in his trousers pockets and wandered sadly in and out of the bedroom. Eventually he decided to go back down through the shop and into the adjoining house.

In the kitchen he began to feel hungry. However, on opening the fridge and presses, he found they were quite bare. He was worse to expect Mick McCoy to be domesticated.

An hour later, having returned from the shops, he sat down comfortably in J.J.'s old armchair. A large plate of ham and cheese sandwiches sat on the tray before him. With a good coal fire burning in the hearth he settled in to enjoy his hot mug of tea.

When his hunger was satisfied he got up and removed the tray to the table. Walking over to the sideboard he switched on J.J.'s old wireless. It crackled and banged for a while and then it worked. Settling back in the armchair, he folded his arms and put his feet up on a little stool. The peace of the night gently enfolded him. Eventually he dozed off to the strains of J.Strauss II 'The Nuns Chorus.'

When he awoke the fire had died down and the room was chilly. Looking at the clock on the mantelpiece he knew it was too late to go home, so he decided he would stay the night. Leaving the dishes till morning he went up the stairs to check out Mick's bed.

Pulling back the clothes he sniffed them to see if they smelt clean. Then deciding to stay on the safe side, he removed only his shoes, climbed into bed and fell asleep.

The next morning he was just about to sit down and enjoy a large fry he had prepared himself, when he heard a knock on the door. Opening it, he was surprised and relieved to see Alishe standing there. Kissing his cheek, she breezed past him and made her way towards the kitchen.

Following her down the hall, he asked her if she would like some breakfast.

'No thanks I've already had mine.' she said quite happily.

David sat down to his fry again. Moving slowly towards his chair Alishe stood behind him and leaned over. Putting her two arms around his neck, she brought her soft cheek down to his and said quietly: 'I'm sorry David let's not argue again eh?'

Before he could reply, she had picked up one of the rashers from his plate, walked over and stood with her back to the cooker. Holding it between her fingers and thumbs, she nibbled daintily on it as she flirted with her beautiful brown eyes.

Looking blankly at her, David watched her suggestive movements. What usually excited him he now found rather distasteful.

In that moment he knew that she would never change.

Whatever he had felt for her in the past, it had died in his heart the previous night.

But it was not entirely her fault and deep down he knew that too. After all, he had not been totally honest. It was only now 16 years later that he had finally admitted to himself just how much he was really missing his first wife Molly.

CHAPTER 36.

Doireann Furlong waited patiently for her turn to compete in the ''Hennessy Brandy Stakes International Competition No.1.' The Horse Show attracted competitors from all over the country to Ballsbridge and tensions ran very high.

The course was a big one, and after some accurate riding by the eleven entries, there were only five riders in against the clock. Three of them had Faulted at the final parallel bars and this left only Doireann riding Gadan, and Garrett O'Loughlin on Propeller. She was determined to beat him.

When her turn came she mounted her horse quickly and rode out. From a distance Garrett stood watching.

Her great horsemanship was evident as she urged her horse skillfully around the course. As the minutes went by she was up on the clock and clear to the last fence. But as she jumped the large parallels up hill, her horse could not make the back pole and she had four faults.

Garrett took off his riding hat and shook his head in disappointment for her. Then, as he was replacing it again, he heard his name being announced over the loudspeakers.

This was the first time someone else rode Propeller, and, as Doireann looked on, she wanted so much for the horse to win, but not its rider.

The animal was in great form. His dark groomed coat shone like silk in the sunshine. The dressage was a joy to watch but to see Propeller enjoying his jumping again was the greatest thrill of all.

'Oh he's a lovely horse,' she thought affectionately. Then with a little bit of anger she added 'and unlike his new rider he's honest and genuine.'

While watching them perform on the course, she got lost in the excitement of it all. The fences were bigger than the previous year but this did not put Propeller off. Instead it seemed the bigger the fences the better he jumped.

Maintaining a relentless pace, Garrett took up all the shorter options and managed a good shot at each one.

Moments later all feelings of hurt were forgotten the moment Doireann realised they had won.

Later, as she sat beside Garrett, to receive second prize, she tried hard to muster a smile. Leaning across the saddle, she shook his hand begrudgingly in congratulations. Her horse had tried its best, but it did not have the same spirit as Propeller.

Then, much later when everything had quietened down, Doireann went back out to the stables. Checking that the coast was clear, she sneaked into Propeller's stall. Taking some polo mints from her pocket she reached up and gave him the tasty treat. Hugging and stroking his large neck' she whispered sadly: I miss you old boy.'

Then, not wanting to bump into anybody, she turned to leave. As she lifted the latch on the door she suddenly heard voices at the entrance to the stables.

Peeping out through the door, she saw it was Garrett talking to another rider.

'Damn,' she thought angrily, 'why didn't I leave this till later.'

Crouching down on her hunkers, she hoped they might go away. After a few moments it all seemed quiet so, presuming they had gone, she went to leave. She was so busy sneaking quietly out of the stall she did not see Garrett standing behind the stable door.

'Hello there,' he said cheerfully.

Doireann jumped, and in the embarrassment of the moment just walked coldly past him.

'Doireann wait,' he called as he ran after her, 'This is ridiculous, we have to talk.'

She stopped for a second then continued walking.

'There's nothin' to talk about,' she called back as she hurried away.

Catching up with her, he pulled her arm gently and through the light material of the sleeve of her blouse his hand felt warm.

'Oh but there is, ' he said anxiously, 'let's go somewhere and talk please?'

As he continued to convince her, she could not help but notice once again the piercing attractiveness in his eyes. Eventually she agreed to go to the local pub for just one drink.

Deciding to take her jeep, Doireann leaned over and unlocked the passenger door. As he removed some papers from the seat she said coldly: 'Sorry I wasn't expecting visitors.'

Pulling up outside the 'The Tavern' fifteen minutes later, they noticed it was packed as usual. While some people took their drinks outside to sit at the tables, others perched quite happily on the old stone wall. The atmosphere was cheerful and noisy with the customers enjoying the best pint in town.

'What'll you have Doireann?' shouted Garret above the noise.

'Vodka and orange please,' she said loudly as she pushed her way after him.

While he wrestled his way to the bar, she spotted an elderly couple getting ready to leave and she quickly grabbed their two stools.

When Garrett returned with the drinks she was sitting waiting at a small wooden table. He sat down opposite her and began to explain a few things.

'Look Doireann,' he said as he sipped his stiff whisky, 'I didn't go behind your back when I bought Propeller.'

'Well that's the way it seemed to me,' she replied coldly.

'No, it wasn't like that. You see there were some Germans going round trying to buy up horses. I found out they were very interested in Propeller, so I rang Lady Gowne immediately. The first thing I asked her was would you mind if she sold the horse.'

'Well that's not the way I heard it,' replied Doireann angrily, 'I heard you came in wavin' your big cheque book around.'

'Ah no, please listen,' he protested, 'look if you must know, I rang Lady Gowne and asked her if you would mind her selling Propeller to me, not at all you leave Doireann to me she said; So I made her my best offer and she said she would ring me back. When she rang back almost immediately, I knew we had a deal. You see I thought she was going to discuss it with you. But the day I went to collect him, I noticed you were annoyed with me.'

'Damn right I was, wouldn't you if someone took your horse?'

'Yes I would,' he said, trying hard not to remind her that Propeller was really Lady Gowne's, 'but at the same time I couldn't let a horse like that leave the country and God knows I didn't want to beat you today either but I had to win.'

Doireann took a large swig of her vodka as hurt feelings began to surface again.

'Well,' she said angrily, 'It seems to me maybe it would be better for everybody if I stayed out of your way.'

'That's a bit drastic don't you think? 'he said, raising his dark eyebrows.

'Anyway Garrett,' she continued, with her brown eyes flashing,
'You could at least have made a phone call. My number's in the book.'

Garrett looked a little sheepishly down at the floor and then tried to justify his behaviour.

'I know I should and I'm sorry. But I had to borrow serious money to buy Propeller, and in such a short time.'

Thinking for a moment Doireann asked curiously,

'What did you pay for him?'

'£6,000.'

Doireann raised her eyebrows and looked surprised,

'That much did you buy any other horses?'

'I bought two others. I got one in Longford from a Mr. Costigan and another in Kildare from a lovely old gent at 'Grangeclare Stud.'

'What are they like?'

'Well, they seem promising at the moment, but their nothing like Propeller. They'll need a lot of work.'

Then raising his eyebrow he asked cheekily: 'maybe you might give me a hand there?'

Not knowing if his offer was genuine, Doireann scoffed at the very idea.

As he rose to get two more drinks, he whispered sadly across the table, 'Now all I have to live on is prize money.'

Then noticing an attractive glint in his eye, she replied smiling:

'Well with a horse like Propellor under ya, you shouldn't go hungry.'

She noticed how, with a little hint of sadness he had said that, so unlike his usual cocky way of speaking.

When Garrett came back from the bar he stopped beside her. Reaching his hand out towards her he said humbly.

'Am I forgiven?'

'I'll think about it,' she said smiling coyly.

Surprised at how quickly she grabbed his hand he raised his glass and proposed a toast to their friendship.

Smiling, she clicked hers against it in agreement.

Then he sat down on his stool again.

'Do you like dancing?' he asked curiously trying to get to know her a little better.

'Not really,' she replied, 'I used to go with Frank and David, my brothers. I liked the music but found the men stupid. If they weren't drunk they were all over me. No, horses are my life and the farm too. Anyway I don't think I'd be any good at the housewifey bit, do you?'

'Oh I wouldn't know that,' said Garrett, not wanting to upset her again.

'Are ya married yerself?'

'Yeah, I'm married alright,' he said, sipping his whisky, 'like you to a stable yard of horses.'

Then they both laughed.

Beginning to enjoy the conversation, Doireann regretted the months lost when she tried to avoid him.

The evening wore on and Doireann knew that it was a long time since she had felt so relaxed. She did not protest when he bought round after round of drinks.

Eventually at closing time they were both feeling quite merry as they left the pub. Stepping out into the fresh air, they decided it would be safer to leave the jeep and walk back to the yard. Garrett joked that they should have brought the horses instead.

'Then we wouldn't get pulled for drunk driving,' he laughed.

It was a gorgeous warm bright summer's night. Walking back to the yard, he held her hand protectively against the lights of the oncoming traffic. Doireann suddenly found that for the first time in her life, she felt an exciting closeness towards a man. The feelings welling up inside her were so passionate, that she thought he must aware of them too. But he seemed oblivious to what was happening. Although her ears were listening to him, her whole being was very aware of his physical presence.

When eventually they reached his long trailer, she was just about to say goodnight when he took her by the elbow and said with a strange urgency in his voice:

'Doireann kiss me.'

Those unexpected few words thrilled her to the bone and in one quick movement she joined her lips to his. His warm kiss sent shivers of desire right through her. When it ended they looked a little embarrassed at each other.

Then as if an invisible friend was pushing them together, they fell back into each other's arms. This time there was a hunger not only in the way they kissed, but also in their tight embrace. Arms encircled each other and held their bodies close, while hands roamed freely over their backs, necks, and shoulders.

Realising the depth of his feelings for her Garrett suddenly broke off and took her by the hand. He dared not utter a word. Words did not belong in this scene they might break the magic.

As he opened the door of his trailer and led her inside, Doireann at 29, felt she was woman enough to match his passion and tonight, as she heard the door close behind her she instinctively knew that she wanted him.

Almost as if they had rehearsed their movements they both sat down together, laughing on the edge of the bed with their passion subsiding briefly for a moment.

Then Garrett reached over and encircled her neck gently with his strong hands. Using his thumbs, he tilted her face to look up at him. His blue glassy eyes took on a deep yearning expression as they looked into hers.

Doireann felt she was falling into an endless pit of desire. As he held her head, childlike, but firmly in his hands, she felt for a moment that he was in control.

Slowly, tenderly his mouth came down on hers and they began kissing again. Easing back gently on the bed, his hands slipped under her T shirt and found her soft firm breasts. Hers slipped up under his shirt and she felt the strength of the muscles in his back. Their thighs pressed hard against each other's as they explored all the sensuous hiding places of desire.

Then Garret moved his hand slowly, teasingly, down to the end of her spine. This, to Doireann was like an electric shock. It sent shivers of pleasure right through her.

Suddenly their tight jeans became an unwanted barrier. Like children excited by the rushing tide, they quickly discarded them and threw them onto the floor. The only light was from the full moon outside. It peeped in like a protective mother through the small window in the trailer. But the lovers failed to notice they were in such awe of each other's flesh.

'You are beautiful,' said Garrett sincerely as he pressed his warm body down on hers.

For the first time in her life Doireann felt beautiful. She closed her eyes. In her mind it was as if she was riding once more across the open fields, her strong legs astride a powerful stallion. Her thighs gripped tightly to his body as her hands squeezed hard on his mane.

As he thrust forcefully into her, so she took it, and gave it right back to him. It was so natural, so exhilarating. Faster and faster they went with their human urges driving them on. Then together, as if they grew wings, they flew among the stars with their passionate movements causing their bodies to become one.

Suddenly a physical explosion sent them into a spiritual world higher than the highest heaven. Trembling they moaned as they clung tightly to each other, their passion now reaching the height of its power.

Then with each fading ripple of pleasure they descended slowly, unwillingly back to earth.

Moments later they lay side by side basking in the wonder of it all. With their arms tenderly around each other, Garret was the first one to break the peaceful silence.'

'Doireann,' he whispered, 'you don't know how long I've wanted you,' he said stroking her arm tenderly.

She was unable to reply as a small tear fell silently from her eyes.

'Damn it,' she thought, in her new found vulnerability, 'I bet he says that to all his girls.'

CHAPTER 37.

Julie Clancy sat at the dining room table and angrily watched Hattie's dinner go cold. She had already been upstairs twice to call her for breakfast a couple of hours ago, and now it was a repeat performance for dinner. Hattie wanted to be left alone. This was the second day of this behaviour and Julie was beginning to worry.

Picking up the receiver of the phone, she listened first for any movement from above, and then dialled Fr. William's number.

Speaking in little more than a whisper, she told William about his mother's depression and explained how worried she was.

'She must have had a row with Nicholas,' said Julie 'I knew no good would come of that man.'

'Now Julie don't be so hasty to judge. Mother's behaviour could be down to a number of things, lets not jump to conclusions just yet.'

'Oh I know I shouldn't but you see she hasn't eaten anything since yesterday.'

'Did you ask her if she needed the doctor?'

'Yes and she nearly jumped down my neck. No she doesn't need the doctor, I know that. Oh William if you would only come here and talk to her.'

William smiled to himself at the other end of the line. It was like old times when his mother would take to the bed. As a young boy he remembered the tension as they all tip-toed around the house. Then the massive relief when she would emerge looking well rested after a few days. She did not seem to need a doctor then either.

'As it happens Julie I haven't much on today so I can spare a couple of hours. I'll ask Fr. Breen to cover for me if there's an emergency. Let me see, its 1 o'clock now, I could be with you around half three.'

'Oh that would be great William. I know you could cheer her up. I'll have something nice for the tea. Better go now, she might hear me and want to know who it is I'm talking to on the phone. So goodbye and thanks.'

Then Julie waited a few moments after the phone call before going up to Hattie's bedroom again.

Opening the door gently, she put her head round and told Hattie that Fr. William had rang and he was coming to visit. Then she left in the hope that Hattie might get up and come downstairs.

Hattie Thornton lay exhausted in bed gazing up at the curtains on the large window. Anyone could see from the state of the bedclothes and her untidy appearance that she had had a restless night. Then, in the early hours of the morning a calm had come over her. Getting up slowly, she now walked over to the window and pulled back the curtains.

Since that first time when she had met Nicholas a feeling of detachment to reality had come over her. She had not gone looking for this in fact quite the opposite. She was safe and happy living in a routine of predictability. Having been widowed and passed the age of childbearing, she had packed and locked away a lot of her womanly desires into drawers of mature dignity.

Then out of the blue this man appeared and turned her whole world upside down. With one glance, one touch he could not only open these memories, but could draw out desires that defied time, reason and even family. Passionately, lovingly, magically Hattie's desires had leaped out once again and been thrown wantonly into the dance of life.

Oh how those months with Nicholas had become months of sheer joy. In the beginning his touch, his kisses were just skimming the surface. But as time went on, how familiar he became and how she just melted into his arms.

She would cling to him in the throes of a passionate embrace and then again she would nestle her head lovingly on his chest. He was so masterful and yet so courteous, so strong and yet so tender. Oh everything was going so perfectly until he mentioned that word divorce.

With the pain in her head starting up again, Hattie reached over to the bedside locker and took two Aspro from the packet. Reaching for the jug of water she quickly realised that it was empty. Well she must get up anyway. Didn't Julie just say that William was on his way over?

When William arrived at 'The Rectory' his mother had been up for quite awhile. Washed and dressed, he found her sitting comfortably on the sofa in the drawing room as she waited for him. The ashtray beside her was full with butts of cigarettes. As he bent and kissed her warmly on the cheek, he lifted the ashtray, walked over to the fire and threw the contents in.

'Now Mother, I thought you were making an effort to cut down on these weeds,' he said disappointedly.

'Sometimes I need them more than others and this happens to be one of those times,' she said, raising her voice a little.

Sitting down on the armchair, William sat with a calm intensity of feeling and silently watched his mother. She seemed to have aged a little since he saw her last, and there was a great sadness in her eyes.

'What is the matter?' asked William.

Hattie did not speak, but instead rose from her seat and walked over to the window. Hugging her arms, she stood motionless as she looked blankly into space.

After a few moments of silence William spoke again,

' I don't want to pry but I hate to see you like this. If you could talk about it I might be able to help.'

Tears stung her eyes as the sincerity in his voice reached out to her. Turning from the window she found it hard to speak.

The first word might break her heart. Instead her quivering lips, and her tightly clasped hands struck William to the very core.

'Oh where do I begin,' she said rubbing her arms and letting out a deep troubled sigh.

'Do I tell you that a man came into my life and brought me real happiness after all these years? Do I tell you how much I have enjoyed the weeks and months in his company? Do I tell you he is everything I have ever dreamed of or wished for in a lover and companion? Do I tell you of a man who has the power to wipe out even the memories of your own father?'

William lifted his eyebrows in shock and watched Hattie as she continued.

'Or do I tell you of a man who could make me feel the excitement of youth, and even the foolishness that only a real woman can feel. Feelings that should have been out of reach for somebody of my age.'

Slowly turning from the window, she walked pensively over to the table and picked up her cigarettes and lighter. From listening to what she had just said William suddenly began to see his mother in a different way. For the first time he felt that he was not just her son but her friend.

"Yes I can tell you all this,' she continued, 'but then I have to tell you that he is already married.'

William grew angry at this startling news.

'How did you find out?' he asked suspiciously.

'Nicholas told me.'

'But why did he not tell you sooner?'

'Because the marriage only lasted six months and to quote his own words, 'it meant nothing.'

Taken aback by this remark William asked seriously:

'Oh I see and do you believe him?'

'Yes I do. He's an honourable man who made an unfortunate mistake. However, he is now waiting for his divorce.'

As the word divorce hung in the air a deafening silence filled the room.

Hattie sat down in the armchair opposite him and suddenly the seriousness of the situation became very clear to William.

'But forget about the glamorous side of this for a moment. What I want to know is how… deeply do you feel for this man? I mean do you really love him?'

In a most sincere voice Hattie replied:

'Oh yes son. I know it's hard for you to believe that somebody of my age could actually fall in love, but I have,' she said firmly.

'Do you not think that maybe he has been misleading you?'

A sudden anger came into Hattie's face, she knew William did not quite understand.

'No, I've told you he is a very decent man.'

Feeling a little frustrated with his mother, William replied:

'But why is this only coming out now?'

'Because it was only now he asked me to marry him.'

'But how can he ask you to marry him when he is already married?' asked William trying hard to contain his anger.

'Son neither of us knew this was happening. We did not set out to fall in love. We were just old school mates having found a friendship. We both enjoyed the same things. The night he told me he loved me it came as a great shock. But what was an even bigger shock was, I realised that I had fallen in love with him.'

171

William thought for a moment then looked directly at her and said:

'This is the same man you went to England with?'

'Yes, but he was a perfect gentleman.'

'There's no need to keep defending him,'

'I am not defending him. It's just that you seem to have the idea he's some kind of a villain.'

'No I don't,' he said in a more sympathetic voice, 'I'm just trying to get to the truth of the matter.'

Hattie lit a cigarette and looked deep into her sons innocent eyes.

'What is truth son?' she asked wearily.

William crossed his legs and shuffled uneasily in his chair. Thinking seriously for a few moments he eventually replied:

'Can you turn your back on your religious beliefs and marry this man?'

In the silence that followed William knew deep down how much depended on his question. Hattie sat with head bowed staring at her tense hands. She had thought so much and mulled so many things over in her mind for the last two days that her brain felt raw. Her mind had struggled so hard to unite her head with her heart. But now in her utter weariness, she suddenly felt the presence of someone greater than she. And in that moment she humbly bowed her mind to God's word. For the first time in her life Hattie realised that she had a Master.

After a few moments she raised her tired head. Then, rising from her chair she walked over to the window and looked out into space.

'Oh William why do you think I have been going through such torment for the last two days? There has been a great war raging between the logic of my head and the emotions my heart. For years I have believed in my righteous faith. I have lived by its rules and I thought I understood it. It's bred in my soul as sure as my ancestor's blood is bred in my veins.' Then, placing her hands on the cold window ledge, she continued:

'But up to this it was easy to obey because I was never challenged by anything of such personal magnitude. This came and tore at my very being. It reached into unknowing and it actually exposed the weakness in me. Oh you know it would have been so easy to give in to the allure of the happiness I was being offered.'

Trembling, she turned from the window and in a strong voice she said:

'But in the end my faith would not allow me to be less than I am. Now I know I will have to give up something I can see for something which I believe.'

'Are you sure?' asked William concernedly.

'Yes I am,' she replied positively.

Sitting with his hands clasped tightly together, he bowed his head and cast his eyes down as he felt deeply for his mother's sadness. Tears flowed as she looked over at her son.

Her head fell sideways on her weary shoulders. She stretched her hand out towards him. Then for an instant she allowed herself a last outburst of anger.

'Oh look at you William, sitting there in your priestly clothes. I know the power and the might that stands behind you. In spite of the pride I feel for being part of what you are, the irony is, I passed on to you the very faith that is today crucifying me. I feel so angry and do you know why? Its not that I will lose Nicholas and all the happiness we could have had. But for the first time in my life there's a fire of unyielding faith burning in me, and I cannot put it out.'

Then turning back towards the window she moaned softly in a weary effort to clam down.

William was so moved by the conviction of her words that he got up from his chair and walked over to his distressed m mother. He turned her gently towards him, put his arms caringly around her shoulders, and held her precious little body close. Hattie cried bitterly into his chest. In that moment it seemed as if William became the parent and Hattie the child.

Then he took his handkerchief from his pocket and handed it to her. Drying her red eyes, she blew her nose, took a deep breath and stepped back. After thinking for a moment she said fearfully:

'But do you know what is facing me now William? I can see a great black loneliness opening up before me. I feel the frailty of old age creeping into my bones. I know this is my last chance of such happiness and can you imagine now how that feels?"

'But mother, what are you going to do?' asked William concernedly.

Straightening her back she looked up slowly at him, her brown eyes resuming their usual look of pride.

'What can I do William?' she said determined to retain her dignity, 'all I can do is go back to being Hattie Thornton.'

Chapter 38.

Hattie Thornton walked slowly, thoughtfully, under the tall beech trees. She walked right down to the end of the avenue, to the gates. Then she turned around and walked all the way back. She had made up her mind that it would be too painful for her to see Nicholas again. She also knew because of her genuine deep feelings for him that she would have to tell him just how she felt.

After a lot of soul searching, and a bit of dithering, she decided she would have to write him a letter. Quickening her step, she hurried indoors and went into the sitting room. Sitting down at her roll-top writing desk, she took out her Parker fountain pen and some personalized notepaper and began.

'The Rectory,'
Fairways,
Co. Wexford.
8-3-1978.

Dear Nicholas,
It is with deep regret that I find I am unable to meet with you again, but because of what we have meant to each other, I need to express my feelings in this letter.

The last few months have been the happiest in my life. You have given me so much and you have made me realise the power of real love. I know now that it can pass all barriers of time and age.

Your love gave me back my youth and my feeling of womanhood. The evenings we spent together were all so precious and their memory I will carry with me for the rest of my days.

Nicholas, in those short months, we packed in a lifetime of living.

I believe you are sincere when you say your marriage meant nothing. But marriage to me will always mean something. I know I could have given you the love but unfortunately your divorce does not make this possible.

You see Nicholas, there is something which is more important to me than all these things put together. It is my Catholic Faith.

174

Not just as the mother of a priest, but as somebody who has seriously tried to live it. Therefore I could never marry or continue a relationship with somebody who is already married.

Please do not contact me as I would find it too painful, but whenever you think of me do so with kindness. I am so thankful to you for all the happiness you brought to me.

Your own
Harriet Thornton.

Hattie's eyes filled with tears as she re-read her heartfelt words on the page. Then sadly, as if she was closing a door on one of the most important chapters of her life, she folded it carefully and put it into a scented envelope. Wiping her eyes with her handkerchief, she rose quickly from her chair and left the house.

A few moments later her car pulled up outside the village post office. Miss Hughes, the white-haired spinster post mistress, greeted her in the usual courteous way. Then, after some small talk about the weather, Hattie said her goodbyes. Licking the stamp, she pasted it securely on the right hand side of the envelope. Walking over to the post box she hesitated for a second. Then, lest she change her mind, she pushed it quickly into the small opening. It took all her will power for her now shaking fingers to let it go. With the letter went her childhood dreams, her teenage fantasies, and her deepest felt womanly desires.

Then she listened for the gentle thud as it hit the bottom. It brought the finality of the moment home to her. An unbearable pain of emptiness gripped her lonely heart. Too upset to go straight home, she lit a cigarette and drove around for a little while.

When eventually she got back she was surprised to see Julie standing at the door. Before she had time to get out of the car she rushed over and announced quickly:

'Your accountant Mr. Davis is on his way down. He'll be here around three.'

'Oh the pompous old dear, I wonder what does he want?' she wondered.

As Hattie got changed in her bedroom she began thinking what a great friend Harry Davis had been to her late husband James down through the years. They had gone to school together and to Trinity

College. Although Harry had offered James a chance to join his firm 'Carney and Carlton Accountants Ltd,' James, not being one to take chances, stayed within the security of his position in Guinness.

'I wonder what on earth he could want,' she thought to herself as she arranged a dozen carnations in a crystal vase.

A little while later she smiled broadly as she greeted her old friend at the hall door.

Harry shook her hand and then threw his arms affectionately around her. Then carrying a large leather briefcase, he entered the sitting room in his usual busy way and sat down. He was a stout man with thick wavy grey hair. Although bald at the front, the back of his head was a mass of curls. From the pocket of his navy pinstriped suit he proceeded to take out a packet of hamlet cigars and a silver lighter.

'Well I hope you have good news for me. I could do with some right now,' said Hattie sighing deeply.

' I have news but I'm afraid it's bad,' he said regretfully as he ran his thumb over his nails.

Hattie walked over to the drinks cabinet. This was not her day. After pouring out a whisky and soda for her old friend, she reached for the sherry bottle and poured herself a large one. Walking over to the couch she left the drinks down carefully on the coffee table, lit a cigarette and sat down beside him.

'Right tell me,' she said, preparing herself for the worst.

'Well there is no kind way of saying this my dear, I'm afraid it looks like you are broke.'

Hattie was rooted to the spot. Taking a sip of her drink she said anxiously:

'But how?'

'I'm afraid with the way your shares have fallen it was inevitable.'

'But what about all the money James had invested? '

'Well my dear with your day to day spending, your purchase of this house, plus giving Seamus the one in Dublin and William the new car, I'm afraid there isn't much left.'

Hattie looked a little bewildered.

'Now old girl,' he said, 'patting her hand caringly, 'at the same time there are a lot of people worse off than you are. At least you are not in debt and you own two fine houses."

Hattie was very quiet for a moment.

'What do you suggest I do Harry?' she asked taking a deep pull on her cigarette.

'Well I was thinking about that on the drive down here. Now these are only suggestions mind you, and only made with your deepest interests at heart.'

Hattie squeezed his hand affectionately: 'Go on,' she said nervously,

'Well I suggest you might take in lodgers here, or you could charge Seamus some rent. He is on a good salary now and I'm sure he would be only too willing to help out.'

Just then Julie interrupted when she walked into the sitting room with a tray of tea and sandwiches.

'Julie,' said Hattie, almost in a light-hearted way, 'did you hear that, my good friend Harry here says I should take in lodgers or charge my son rent. What do you think?'

Julie blushed deeply and was unable to reply. She hated when Hattie put her on the spot like that. Such a serious question could not be answered flippantly. She just shook her head and left the room.

'Now you've upset the two of us,' Hattie said ignoring the tea. Standing up she began pacing around the room.

'I can't take in lodgers and I will never charge my son rent,' she said in a loud voice.

'Now don't take your anger out on me,' he said cautiously, 'I'm only here to advise you. Because of my friendship with James and yourself down through the years I have tried to do my very best for you.'

'I'm sorry Harry.' she replied, rubbing her forehead, 'but it has been a very trying day for me. Is there any other way out of this mess?'

'Well.' he said thoughtfully as he reached for a cucumber sandwich, 'come back over here and sit down. We will go over the figures together. Now you could always take a mortgage out on this place and...'

For well over and hour they mulled, argued and threw suggestions back and forth at each other. Then it was time for Mr. Davis to leave for Dublin.

Hattie walked him to his car and the shook hands warmly.

'Thanks for coming Harry, but the next time, don't just come down on business, you know you are very welcome always.'

'Yes I do Hattie but it's not like the old days you know,' he replied, getting into his car, 'we are now getting a lot of corporate business. Sometimes I don't even get time to go home to my own house.'

Then they said their good byes and Hattie watched him leave.

Returning to the sitting room, she was deep in thought. She picked up the tea tray and went out towards the kitchen. Julie was standing with her back to the cooker rubbing her hands nervously together.

'Listen Hattie,' she said earnestly,' I have a good idea. Now, I have a little sum saved and if it would help you are welcome to it.'

Hattie was very moved by her generosity. Putting the tray down on the kitchen table, she went over and gave her housekeeper a reassuring hug.

'Bless your heart dear,' she said smiling, 'But I'll be okay. You know Julie these accountants love to be the prophets of doom. Things are never as bad as they make them out to be.' But somehow Julie did not believe her old friend.

That night the faithful old housekeeper lay awake thinking, and by morning she had reached her own solution. She decided to tell Hattie over breakfast.

'I rang my sister in Bray last night Hattie, and I have decided to go and live with her.'

Seeing a surprised look on Hattie's face, she continued talking quickly.

'Now let me explain. You know yourself that Joyce has been asking me to come live with her for a long time now. She's been very lonely since Robert died.'

Then, reaching across the table, she patted her hand affectionately.

'Hattie I have never really settled in Wexford, you know that. This house is beautiful and I love you and Molly dearly, but I'm really a Dub. at heart. I don't want you to try and change my mind because it's already made up. Now I'm not doing this because of your bad news and of course my offer of that money still stands, but what happened yesterday just helped me make up my mind, that's all.'

Hattie was silent for a moment and then said pleadingly:

'But this is not necessary Julie, I keep telling you everything is fine.'

'Look Hattie, with me out of your hair you will be able to think things out more clearly.'

A sad silence descended on the conversation.

'When were you thinking of going Julie?' Hattie asked quietly.

'I'll leave day after tomorrow, if its alright with you.'

'So soon?'

'Yes, its better to do these things quickly, there is no point in delaying'

For the next two days the two women were inseparable. They reminisced, laughed, joked, and cried, as they reminisced about the 38 years they had shared together.

On Friday morning, as Hattie helped Julie pack the last of her things away, a great sadness descended on the bedroom.

Julie was just about to close her suitcase when Hattie handed her a little present wrapped in very pretty wrapping paper.

'Before you open it Julie,' she said with tears in her eyes,' There is something I want you to know. You were never just a housekeeper to me. If I was to ask God for a sister it would have been you.'

Julie squeezed Hattie's hand tightly. Then they let go and she opened the little box.

Tears welled up in her eyes when she lifted the lid and saw the beautiful cameo brooch she had often admired. This was the lovely gift James Thornton had given to his wife on the birth of their twins. Julie knew only too well how much this brooch meant to Hattie.

'Oh Hattie I couldn't...'she said, her lips trembling.

'Oh but you will,' she said earnestly, 'because they were as much your boys as mine.'

They looked knowingly into each other's eyes and then with tears they embraced tightly. Then the moment was broken when they heard Frank's car speeding up the avenue.

Standing at the front door the two women held hands while they watched Frank load Julie's luggage into the boot.

'Now Miss Clancy, I expect a letter at least once a week from you,' said Hattie with a mock formality in her voice.

'Yes Mrs. Thornton Maam,' she said, replying in a similar way,

'You know you can always depend on me.'

Then smiling, they embraced for the last time.

Julie got into the car and in few seconds she was gone. Hattie waved until they were out of sight. Standing with her arms folded, a sudden lonely shiver went up her back. She turned slowly and went back inside the house.

Later that evening, as she went to prepare supper for one, she discovered there was no milk. Driving towards Kenny's grocery shop, she thought about how she had depended on Julie so much in the past.

Hurrying back out of the shop with two bottles of milk, something caught her eye. It was a red jaguar car parked a little way up the street outside the local Auctioneer's office. Her heart started to beat faster and her face became flushed. She got back into her car quickly, placed the milk bottles on the seat and sat watching.

Within minutes Nicholas Robinson came out of the building with another man and they shook hands at the door.

Oh how she well knew the feel of those hands. She sat watching the familiar way he tilted his head. Memories of his lovely smile came flashing back to her. He looked so handsome and well. She desperately wanted to run to him and have him take her away to where...she did not care.

Thinking he might look up the street and see her car, she put her two hands on the steering wheel and straightened up in her seat. But Nicholas did not turn back or look around. He just opened the door of his car, climbed in and drove away. With great sadness she watched him go. Tears filled her eyes.

It was only now, with Nicholas's love, Julie's company, and most of her finances gone, that Hattie realised the enormity of the sacrifice she had made. Slumping back wearily in her seat she sighed a broken sigh of loss. With her empty cold hands falling listlessly onto her lap, Hattie Thornton now submissively resigned her fate into the loving arms of her Creator.

CHAPTER 39.

Doireann pulled out a chair and sat down to her breakfast. Suddenly the reality of her being pregnant hit home. It was like a nightmare that would not go away, she was actually going to have a baby, a real live person. It would need feeding, clothes, schooling and it would be to her alone to mind it forever.

Suddenly her appetite went and she pushed the bowl of cereal away. Standing up from her chair, she walked thoughtfully out to the stables. She began to wonder who she could talk to about it.

'If only Aggie was alive now,' she whispered, 'she would know what to do, she would have got Daddy to understand.'

Now for the first time she really missed her love and wisdom. Then she thought about telling her Aunt Hattie, but then she thought she would never understand. Doireann could hear her now:

'Well if you'd been let come live with me in the first place none of this would have happened.'

She would probably go on then about the disgrace it would bring to the Furlong family. No she could definitely not talk to Aunt Hattie

Deciding to go for a walk, she went across the yard towards the fields. On reaching 'Paradise' she sat for ages under the trees pondering over everything that had happened.

She had not seen Garrett since that special night in the trailer. He had gone abroad with Propeller. She wanted so much to share her news with him, but the old Furlong pride stopped her. No matter what she felt for him she could not go to him now in her weakness. Then she began thinking about her Mother and how she never knew her. In the photographs at home she was just a very pretty woman standing beside her daddy.

'I was only six months old when she died,' she thought sadly.

Then she remembered how Molly's mother had also died in childbirth. Rubbing her stomach gently a terrible thought crossed her mind:

'I could die having this child too.'

Suddenly realising the seriousness of her dilemma, she decided the only one she could trust to keep her secret was Lady Gowne.

Feeling a little relieved, she got up from the ground and brushed the twigs and moss from her jeans. As she was hurrying back home to change, she met Frank speeding out of the yard on one of the tractors. Just as she was wondering what was up, she almost collided with Biddy at the kitchen door. She seemed to be in rather a distressed state.

'The boss wants to see ya he's in the dining room,' Biddy blurted out.

'What's up Bid?' Doireann said reaching out to her.

Biddy burst out crying and ran past her into the yard.

In the dining room Walter stood with his back to the fireplace.

He tapped his foot impatiently on the brass fender.

'What's wrong?' Doireann asked as she noticed an unusual dark anger on his face.

'Ya never told me about this pregnancy?'

Thinking for a moment he was referring to her, Doireann went weak at the knees. Her face drained of all colour.

'What pregnancy?' she uttered.

'Biddy and Frank's.'

Doireann felt a plank had hit her and for a moment thought she was in a dream.

'How? I mean when?' she asked surprisingly.

'Damn it,' said Walter, shaking his head, 'I knew there was somethin' goin' on. Once I heard them giggling in the dairy ya know. I should have nipped it in the bud then. Did you know they were carryin on?'

Doireann was so relieved that his anger was not directed at her that she pulled out a chair and sat down at the table.

'I didn't,' she said truthfully,' but then I'm not here a lot of the time.'

Fiddling with the teaspoon in the sugar bowl, she listened as the Boss went on.

'We'll be lucky if that one doesn't take the roof from over our heads. The whole parish will be talkin' about us now

Then pacing up and down he suddenly got an idea.

'There's only one thing to do about this, she may get out of here right now.'

Startled by the coldness of his angry words, the reality of her own situation became quite clear. Nervously she knocked over some sugar onto the table

There and then she made up her mind that with this angry reaction to Biddy and Frank, it would be safer if she told nobody about her own condition. She would not show for three months, maybe more, and by then all this fuss would have died down.

'When will Biddy be leavin'?' she asked sadly

'This very day,' said Walter sternly.

'Will we be getting' someone else in? '

The skin tightened on Walter's face as he replied

'And have it happen again with another one, are ya mad? We will not. No you may take over the housework. That's an end to it now.'

Walter took his cap from the back of the chair and walked quickly out the door. Doireann went out quickly to look for Biddy but could not find her anywhere. Feeling a bit tired she returned to the kitchen. With everyone having left earlier in a tense emotional state, it was no wonder that a strange atmosphere had descended on the big house.

That evening, the supper was eaten in almost complete silence. Then Walter went out into the yard as usual to check on a few things. Doireann began clearing away the dishes. In an attempt to break the silence Frank awkwardly tried to whistle.

This only served to infuriate Doireann as she turned from the sink and slammed a large bread knife angrily down on the table.

Looking straight at him with a hard angry stare she said crossly,

'Lord, Frank, what were ya thinkin of?'

'What's up with you?' said Frank, moving back nervously.

'You, you and Biddy what the hell did ya think yez were doin?'

'Ah we were only messin',' he said coldly.

'What were you messin with her for?'

'Why what's wrong with Biddy?' he said with a sly grin.

Trying to get some kind of seriousness from her brother she continued:

' But it's your baby, ya can't wash your hands of it.'

'And what can I do, I can't marry her,' he replied, shrugging his shoulders,' ya heard what the Boss said, she has to go.'

'But you can't just walk away,' said Doireann thinking of the injustice of it all, 'its your baby.'

Frank rose from the table. Walking over to her he shouted angrily;
'No Doireann it's Biddy's. I'm just the father.'

On hearing these words it seemed to her as if Garrett was speaking. Then walking over to an armchair Frank picked up the newspaper and plonked himself down.

'Don't worry about it I'll see that they want for nothin.'

'God Frank your all heart.' said Doireann sarcastically.

Slapping the newspaper down on the arm of the chair, he rose up from his seat. Walking over to his sister, he stood quite close. She could feel his hot breath on her cheek.

'It's alright for you,' he said, 'you and David, yez could always do what yez liked. I can never go anywhere. Meself and Biddy spend so much time here on our own that it just happened.'

With her mind flashing back to the night in the horse box Doireann replied firmly:

'It should never have happened.'

'Well, Miss Perfect, what would you do?' he asked sarcastically as he walked back to his chair.

With the conversation just getting a little bit too close to the bone, Doireann took off her apron and threw it at the sink. Then she said wearily:

'Oh I don't care what ya do.'

Then she left the kitchen quickly, banging the door as she went and hurried upstairs to her room.

The subject of Biddy's pregnancy was never mentioned again. From then on a strange tension could be felt between Frank and the Boss. For the next two weeks Doireann had no time for anything only housework.

She hated being cooped up indoors. No matter how much she cleaned things they seemed to be just as dirty again in a few days. It was all so boring and tedious.

The following Friday, Frank and the Boss set off early for the mart in Carnew. Doireann had been looking forward to this all week. She could take the whole day off. Feeling very well she decided to go over to 'Mount Benedict' to see Lady Gowne and Gadan.

'It's so good to be riding again Maureen,' she said taking the reins from her, ' how I've missed it.'

Then, cantering out to the paddock, and became lost in the thrill as she went over the jumps. Rising up and slapping down on the saddle, she urged the horse on. Then suddenly, as she went to turn him around, she felt a sudden sharp twinge in her stomach.

Pulling Gadan up quickly, she got down and began walking slowly towards the gate. Stopping at the post she doubled up in agony, as the painful twinges grew stronger.

Seeing blood coming through her cream jodhpurs, Lady Gowne hurried over to her and said anxiously:

'Doireann you seem to be bleeding.'

She looked down at herself and cried,

'Damn it, I can't be... oh no.'

'What do you mean can't be? What's wrong? Did you hurt yourself.'

'No it's the baby.'

'Oh my, you're not... are you?'

'Yeah I'm afraid I am,' she said, looking up at Lady Gowne with guilt ridden eyes.

'Oh dear, you should not have been riding my girl. I'm going straight in to ring for the doctor. Now don't worry everything will be alright.'

Lady Gowne ran quickly towards the house.

Feeling scared, Doireann sat down very still on the ground.

'This is all my fault,' she thought regretfully,' I'm being punished now for not wanting the baby in the first place.'

Tears rolled down her cheeks.

'But that was only due to the circumstances. Who wouldn't want a baby?' she thought again.

Over the last couple of weeks she had accepted and even delighted in the thoughts of motherhood. She had grown used to the idea and was quite looking forward to her little son or daughter.

As she sat waiting for Lady Gowne to come back she held her stomach protectively and prayed.

'Please God don't let me lose it,' she prayed.

When Lady Gowne returned a few moments later she pulled up beside her in her Rover car.

Jumping out quickly, she opened the back door and went over to help her up.

'The doctor says I'm to bring you straight into the hospital. Here, I've brought some towels for the back seat.

Now you climb in and lie down there good girl.'

While Doireann was making herself comfortable Lady Gowne took Gadan's reins and hurried him back to the stables. Handing him over to Charlie she ran back and got into the car. Within minutes they were speeding out the gates towards the hospital.

On the way Lady Gowne inquired how she was feeling.

'The pains are easing but I think I'm still bleeding,'

'Do you mind if I ask who the father is,' said Lady Gowne, looking back at her in the mirror.

There was an awkward silence for a moment and then she replied: 'Garrett ... Garrett O'Loughlin.'

Lady Gowne said nothing and Doireann took her silence to mean that she was disappointed with them both.

By the time Walter Furlong arrived at the hospital that evening Doireann had been prepared for a dilatation and curettage and had returned from theatre.

The pregnancy was gone.

As she was coming round from the aesthetic she felt her Daddy's hand on her head. In her half sedated sleep she was sure she heard him say: 'My poor child.' Then she dozed off again.

When she woke the second time Garrett was sitting beside the bed watching her carefully.

'Why didn't you tell me?' he said worriedly, 'I'm so sorry.'

'Who told you I was here?' asked Doireann, struggling to sit up.

'Lady Gowne of course, she really cares you know.'

'Well it doesn't matter now,' she said sadly, holding her stomach, 'It's gone... my baby is gone.'

Taking her hand he said sincerely: 'But it was our baby.'

Remembering Frank's indifferent attitude towards Biddy, Doireann coldly replied:

'Yeah right, look don't worry I'll be okay. I just need some time on my own.'

'No,' said Garrett anxiously, 'Please don't send me away. I want to be with you.'

'But you don't understand, the baby's gone. There's nothing to keep you here.'

Garrett ran his fingers wearily through his thick hair.

Then he moved his chair closer to the bed. With his right hand he reached up and stroked her cheek.

'You're the one who doesn't understand, Doireann I love you and want to marry you.'

Feeling completely vulnerable, her emotions raw from the painful experience of her miscarriage, she could not believe he was serious. Nobody ever wanted to take her out, never mind marry her.

A handsome confident successful man like him could not possibly want to marry plain unattractive Doireann Furlong. No it had to have something to do with the baby, that's it, he too was feeling guilty.

Looking into his pleading blue eyes she withdrew her hand from his, lifted her chin proudly and said coldly

'Well I don't want to marry anyone.'

Then she turned her back to him and stared at the corner. Garrett was hurt deeply by her words and did not know what to say.

He watched her for a few moments, hoping she might turn back to him. But she continued to stare stubbornly at the wall.

Very slowly he stood up and left the ward.

Doireann heard him leave.

If he really meant what he had said he would not have left. He would have stayed and convinced her of his sincerity. Taking the hand he had just held, she pressed it to her lips. Then, the emotional floodgates that held all the tensions, disappointments, loneliness and frustration of the last few months opened, and she cried bitterly.

'Oh Garrett,' she moaned, 'If only...'

That night Walter arrived into the hospital to see his daughter. Stopping for a brief moment he inquired about her health from one of the nurses.

'Well, she has been crying a lot this evening,' she replied, 'but that's to be expected. The loss of a pregnancy can be a sad experience. All she needs now is lots of care.'

'Well I'll see she gets that Nurse, ya can depend on it.'

Then he walked over to the bedside and kissed his daughter on the forehead. Pulling up a chair beside her bed, he patted her hand and began talking.

'Lady Gowne came to see me this mornin' and told me everything. So there's no need for us to go over all that. You just have to put it all behind ya now.'

'Daddy, you're not angry with me, are ya?' she asked worriedly.

Trying hard to hide his disappointment, he patted her hand lovingly.

'No I'm not, you just take it easy.'

Then smiling he added: 'I've been doin' a lot of thinkin' lately and I just may have to get used to all this baby stuff in the future.'

Doireann looked up, surprised at him and then the two of them burst out laughing. Walter stayed on with her for a half an hour and then it was time to go.

'By the way, when are they lettin' ya home?' he asked as he rose from his seat.

'First thing in the mornin',' she said happily.

'Good because ya'll be glad to hear we've a new housekeeper comin'.'

'Oh who is it?' asked Doireann excitedly.

A mischievous look came into his eyes. Then with a certain childishness in his voice he announced:

'It's your Auntie Hattie.'

Chapter 40.

Molly Furlong sat looking out through the window of St. Anne's dormitory. Being up three stories high, she had a bird's eye view of the traffic going past the row of council houses at the end of the town. Further out on the landscape, trees and endless fields stretched to the horizon.

She was feeling particularly lonely because Kate and most of the other girls had gone home for the weekend. She was supposed to go too, but her grandad rang at the last minute to say that Aunt Hattie was not well.

The school building was unusually quiet from the usual hustle and bustle of the pupils.

Molly eventually got up from the window ledge and wandered out into the long dark corridor. The sun shone brightly through the large windows at the other end. Mischievously she decided not to go down the right hand stairs to the ground floor. Instead disobediently, she chose the narrow left hand one strictly reserved for the nuns.

On reaching the stairs, she found it too much of a temptation. With her blue eyes wild with daring she quickened her pace and jumped a couple of steps at a time. Then in a matter of seconds she had landed safely on the ground.

Quickly she straightened her uniform and fixed her long blonde hair. Then, breathlessly, she peeped cautiously around the corner to see if any of the nuns were about. But, thankfully, the coast was clear. Sighing with relief, she then proceeded slowly down the long corridor, walking very ladylike past Sr. Amelia Mary's office.

There was really only one place to go on this lonely Saturday and that was the library. Molly turned the large porcelain knob on the heavy wooden door. The library was a long, wide, bright room with a high ceiling.

In between the four large gothic style windows and on the opposite three walls, were shelves and shelves of books.

Two junior girls, sitting at one of the long tables looked up shyly and stopped giggling when they saw the head girl walk in.

189

Molly could never figure out whether the new position bestowed on her by the nuns was a blessing or a curse. But being a 6th year and head girl definitely had its advantages.

'Poor things,' she thought sympathetically, 'they're like me, stuck in for the weekend.'

Smiling kindly at the girls, she walked over to the shelves. She began looking and moving her fingers idly up and down the spines of the books compacted tightly together.

Some of them seemed to be far above her understanding, others she had read before, and others were just plain boring. So Molly reached for one in particular that caught her eye. It was a large heavy book with black and white photographs of people who lived in a town in France. The title was, 'Bernadette, The Story of Lourdes.'

Pulling out a wooden chair, she sat down at the end table beside the window and began to read.

Opening the first page, she found she was looking into the serious dark eyes of a young girl called Bernadette. The girl's hair was concealed beneath a headscarf tied at the nape of her neck. Her ankle length skirt and shawl seemed too old and dull for a girl around Molly's age.

On page 2, the poverty of Bernadette's home intrigued her even further. She studied ever feature in the photograph.

There was a small room built of stone, formerly a prison. In winter the family had found it freezing and in summer it was the other extreme. Because of these damp living conditions Bernadette had suffered chronic asthma.

Molly felt a strange empathy with her in this regard for on two occasions she herself had almost choked trying to catch her breath. It was a frightening feeling, as if somebody had put a great weight on her chest and no air could get down. It was also the beginning of Molly's lifetime struggle with the condition

On page three, was a striking picture of a statue of Our Lady, carved from a description of what Bernadette had seen. She had gone with her two young friends to gather sticks in the local wood when the heavenly vision appeared to her in a small cave among some rocks.

Molly found herself wondering what it must have been like for Bernadette to stand in the presence of the Mother of God, to have looked on her beautiful face and to hear her speak. To an impressionable young girl this would have been the ultimate in happiness.

'Imagine,' she thought, 'Our Lady could have appeared to the highest person in the palaces of France, but instead she chose to come to the poorest of the poor.'

She wondered also if, through having little, the poor were closer to the spirit of God? She remembered Jesus had often spoken about poverty in the Bible.

Suddenly her reading was interrupted when the two junior girls stood up and, scraping their chairs noisily on the floor, they hurried out of the room. Molly watched them go. Then looking back at the book she turned to the next page and read on.

'The finding of the miraculous waters.'

Our Lady asked Bernadette to go and wash herself in the spring.

Bernadette made towards the river but Our Lady stopped her and told her to go in the opposite direction. The heavenly Mother bid her to dig with her hands in the earth and wash herself with the soil, and to eat of the grass and plants growing beside it.

A quick gasp escaped from Molly's lips and her cheeks suddenly became flushed with excitement. She looked embarrassingly over her shoulder to see if anyone had heard her but to her relief she found she was quite alone. These actions of Saint Bernadette reminded her of Aggie Cullen and caused an immediate yearning emotion to sweep right through her. Suddenly in Molly's mind's she was back once more as a child in the woods in Wexford.

The wisdom of Aggie's words, spoken years ago, were only now giving her the openness to receive the true message of this book. The wise old woman always said people would not understand if they did not search. She remembered Aggie holding the clay in her hands with such passion.

'Feel the life in the clay,' she had said, and she was right. There was life in the soil and Our Lady knew that there was healing in it too.

Now Molly had a great urge to read on. Looking back down at the page she continued:

'The unbelievers, who had mingled with the crowd, only mocked and jeered Bernadette when they saw her covered in mud. With no spring emerging from the ground, they went away saying she was mad.'

Aggie always said that people would have to search with a humble heart.

Molly knew now that it was Bernadette's humility that Our Lady had used to bring forth a spring that was to heal the sick of the world.

At the top of the next page the powerful words: 'I am the Immaculate Conception,' almost jumped off the paper at Molly.

This was what Our Lady told Bernadette when she inquired, on the priest's behalf, as to her identity. But on hearing these inspired words the priests still found it hard to believe.

'Imagine,' thought Molly in amazement, 'even ordained men can have doubts too.'

As she sat reading the book the afternoon sun streamed its brilliant light through the library windows warming her back. Turning more pages, she continued to read on and enter passionately into the story. Her intense teenage emotions making it come alive in her mind. She believed everything that was written, and because of her belief she felt her heart would burst with wonder and joy.

Becoming oblivious of her surroundings, her concentration was broken suddenly by the noise of car tyres on the gravel outside.

Lifting her eyes from the book, she watched as it drove past the library window. Then she began gazing up at the white fluffy clouds in the clear blue sky. She wondered why the story of Lourdes was having such a deep effect on her.

Watching the birds landing on the branches of the trees, she began thinking back. She remembered how as a child she had listened to Aunt Hattie saying her prayers in the Rectory. She would kneel down on the cold hard kitchen floor, and with bowed head, would begin slowly and sincerely,

Oh most gracious Virgin Mary,
I humbly beseech You to grace my home with your presence.
I do not ask for a glance, for Your love would swell my heart.
I do not ask a smile, for its beauty would catch my breath.
Say not a word, for Your sweet voice would bring tears to my eyes.
But as You leave Oh heavenly Mother
I ask only that Your veil brush lightly off the lintel
This alone would be enough to bring pure joy into my soul.

Night after night Aunt Hattie spoke from her heart. The love and reverence in her voice seemed to bring the invisible presence of the Holy Mother into the room. This simple act of faith by Aunt Hattie, Molly now realised, had, over the years, given her the faith to believe in the reality of God and His family. Slowly her gaze wandered back to the book and she turned to the last page.

In the photograph Bernadette, with her white delicate hands joined lay dead in her glass tomb, a beautiful young girl sleeping.

'I bet she's with Our Lady in heaven,' thought Molly happily.

Reluctantly she closed the book and thoughtfully ran her hand over the shiny cover, the heaviness of the library air bringing her back slowly to her own time.

Molly looked over at the clock on the wall. She could not believe she had spent almost two hours in the library. Taking the book up in her arms, she walked over and replaced it on the shelf.

Looking around the empty room, she wondered where she might go next. Then with her soul filled with happiness she thought sadly,

'Where is there to go after getting a glimpse of Heaven? '

CHAPTER 41.

Doireann Furlong stood alone in the lady rider's changing room at the 'Royal Dublin Horse Show.' She looked carefully up and down at her appearance in the long mirror. From her shiny new black riding boots to her immaculate cream jodhpurs, up along her smart-fitting black riding jacket to her groomed hair held tightly in a brown hairnet.

The deep thoughtful eyes looking back at her from the mirror held all the strength and courage of a young woman determined to succeed. Then they took on a glazed expression as her mind drifted into a daydream. In a matter of seconds she recalled the events of the last five days.

Everything had looked so hopeful when she had set out from 'Mount Benedict ' that previous Tuesday morning. Charlie had led a groomed and physically fit Gadan into the horsebox. Then Lady Gowne, Doireann and he had set off on the journey to Dublin.

They were so looking forward to the week's events at Ballsbridge. 'The Royal Society' had provided free accommodation for the riders and Chefs d'Equipe for the week at 'The Burlington Hotel' on Leeson Street.

One of the highlights of the show jumping was 'The Nations Cup' on Friday, the winners to be presented with the 'Aga Khan Cup.' Ireland had a particularly strong team this year with among others, Eddie Whelan on Footnote and Frank Durrow on Heather Bunny.

Then there was the Hunt Ball in 'The Burlington' on Friday night to look forward to as well. Doireann and Lady Gowne had gone shopping only last week and purchased two gorgeous evening dresses.

They had heard through the grapevine that Garrett O Loughlin had also been selected by the committee to compete in 'The Jameson Grand Prix' on Saturday. To Doireann this meant she would have to avoid him at all costs.

The Thornton and Furlong families were travelling to Dublin on Sunday to lend their much needed support and to cheer Doireann on. They were also curious as to how Cuteog's foal, Propeller, would perform.

On arriving at the stable yard at the R.D.S. Doireann had settled Gadan into his stable before they went up the road to check into the hotel. Then she returned to the yard to get ready for the warm up classes.

As the galloped around the course she did not push the horse against the clock, deciding instead to hold him back for the 'Grand Prix.' She was very pleased when she came out in 5th place. When it was Garrett's turn she decided to watch from a distance.

'How well Propeller looks,' she thought fondly.

It surprised and hurt her a little to see that Garrett had achieved the oneness with the horse that she thought was exclusive to her. However, later that afternoon disaster struck. As she was walking Gadan back to his stable, she noticed a swelling on the tendon of his left leg.

'Damn,' she thought disappointedly, 'what rotten luck. He must have knocked it off the horse box on the way up.'

Charlie held the reins while she went quickly to fetch a bucket of cold water and a sponge. As she was bending down to stupe the horse's back leg she failed to hear Garrett coming up behind her.

'What's up?' he asked curiously.

'Oh it's nothin', I think he has a bit of a swellin' that's all.'

'Let me have a look,' said Garrett concernedly as he stepped closer.

His closeness disturbed her and in her anxious state only made her nervous.

'No it's alright thanks... I can manage, I'm fine...Its fine.'

'Do you know you're one stubborn woman,' he said in an exasperated tone.

What with being tired from the activities of the day, and upset about Gadan's injuries, Doireann immediately overreacted to his smart words. Standing up, she angrily slung the wet sponge at him falling short of his feet. As he bent down to pick it up, the horse suddenly lashed out and with his back legs kicked Garrett forcefully in the side. Charlie chugged on the reins and tried to hold the agitated horse.

Doireann rushed over to Garrett lying curled up in a ball. He was clutching his side in sheer agony.

'Are you alright?' she said worriedly, 'I'm so sorry.'

Being totally winded, he was unable to speak and motioned to her with his hand.

By now other riders and grooms had gathered around. Somebody rang for an ambulance and in no time at all, with the blue siren blaring, it arrived. As the ambulance man placed an oxygen mask over Garrett's face, Doireann kept repeating anxious words of comfort and apologies.

Then they went speeding towards 'St.Vincent's Hospital' with a distressed Garrett lying on a stretcher and Doireann holding his hand.

Arriving at the hospital Doireann was asked to wait in the waiting room while Garrettt was rushed into the accident and emergency. Anxiously pacing up and down, she began thinking about everything.

'Oh what if he was to die,' she thought, 'It would be all my stupid fault.'

Suddenly strong feeling's of love for the man raced through her.

'Why am I letting these feeling's of inadequacy come between us all the time, why can't I believe that he loves me? ' she said confusedly.

Wandering into the waiting room, she sat down on a wooden bench. Sitting in the large stuffy room, she began to think back to her childhood.

Having grown up without a mother, she had not had a lot of affection. She knew the Boss had loved her even though he never said it in so many words. Walter was always too busy with the farm. Although Biddy and Aggie Cullen were always there too, it was not the same as having a sister. So over the years she had learned to hide her real emotions and act tough.

But this toughness was always in constant battle with her feminine side. She found it hard to appear frivolous and silly like the village girls, yet she knew this helpless behaviour attracted husbands and lovers. But Doireann wanted more from a man. She wanted to feel equal to him in achievement and passion. She knew she was in love with Garrett, their night in the trailer confirmed that. But with all the disappointments over the last few years she had become dispirited and felt she had failed.

Not only with herself but she knew she had let her family down too. She really had made an awful mess of things.

When a nurse came over to talk to her, Doireann was so deep in thought that she jumped as the young girl laid a hand on her shoulder.

'I'm afraid your friend has three broken ribs. But there is no sign of any other damage or internal bleeding,' the nurse said reassuringly.

' Could I see him?' begged Doireann.

'Yes indeed, they're just moving him up to Allen ward.'

A little while later Doireann walked upstairs and into ward 10. Now she had to face him. This time she could not walk away

Garrett, supported by lots of pillows, was propped up in bed with his chest bandaged tightly. He managed a little smile as she walked towards him.

Trying hard to apologise, she found he was having none of it.

'Look,' he said, in between short painful little coughs, 'we were both to blame. I should not have said what I did, you were obviously under pressure and I should have known better. What was wrong with your horse any way?'

'Swollen tendon, it looks like I may have to scratch him from the competition,' she replied disappointedly.

Garrett looked thoughtful for a moment. Holding his side carefully, he whispered:

'Would you do something for me?'

Immediately Doireann's hopes were up. She thought he was going to ask her to ride Propeller. But then they just as quickly faded again when he said in a sad voice:

'Will you scratch Propeller's name out as well?'

All feelings of trust in her love for him were once more replaced by doubts again. Garrett obviously did not think she was good enough to ride Propeller. Twisting hurtful feelings of inferiority began to gnaw at her insides. She was so disappointed with his suggestion that she immediately agreed.

On Friday morning Lady Gowne and Doireann collected Garrett from the hospital. Then they rushed back to the R.D.S. just in time for the beginning of 'The Aga Khan Cup' sponsored by 'Arthur Guinness and Son.'

The crowd applauded as an Irish solider, mounted on a horse, led a parade of four riders from each country around the arena. Pausing at the President's box, The 'No.1 Army Band,' in turn played each team's national anthem.

As Doireann and Garrett watched with baited breath all their personal problems were lost in the excitement of it all.

After the first round Ireland, France and Britain were level with no faults.

In the 2nd round France faded to 3 faults and Ireland and England were clear again, setting the stage for a dramatic jump off.

Frank Durrow, on Heather Bunny, flew around the course next in 3.4 seconds, the fastest yet. Doireann forgot herself in the excitement and nudged Garrett with her elbow. He immediately winced with pain, but then seeing her excitement, he could not help but smile back at her.

The competition had started in brilliant sunshine. But looking up at the black clouds forming in the sky above, Doireann hoped it would finish before a downpour.

When the final Englishman jumped clear it was all up to Eddie Whelan on Footnote. With great skill and showmanship he cleared all the fences and won the 'Nations Cup' for Ireland.

'I wouldn't have missed this for anything,' said Garrett, his eyes beaming with pride as they watched the Aga Khan present the Irish team with the Cup. Then a loud round of applause followed the Irish team on their victory march around the large arena.

That evening, back at 'The Burlington Hotel, ' Doireann and Lady Gowne were so looking forward to the night ahead. Deciding to treat themselves, they took their time getting ready for the ball. With their evening dresses carefully laid out on their beds, they soaked in hot baths with perfumed oils added.

Having adjoining rooms, they wandered in and out, borrowing and lending, swapping and changing cosmetics and advice. Lady Gowne ordered a bottle of champagne to celebrate the day that was in it.

Then, once they were dressed and ready to go, they opened the champagne, raised their slim glasses of bubbly and laughed, joked and relaxed. Sitting down on the bed, Lady Gowne was suddenly struck by her young friend's appearance. In her deep blue velvet dress, Doireann was unusually attractive.

'Garrett O'Loughlin is a fool if he doesn't sweep that girl off her feet tonight,' she thought excitedly.

An hour later, when Garrett saw Doireann walk through the doors of the ballroom, he had the very same thought. Looking extremely handsome in his tuxedo, he watched her long slim body as she walked elegantly across the floor. Friends and acquaintances came up to greet her. With eyes sparkling, she shook their hands, tossing her thick brown hair back in laughter. Sitting at a table in the corner, Garrett felt his ribs carefully. They were still tender and painful. He knew he would not be able to dance with Doireann and God did he need to hold her tonight.

Remembering that he was also out of the competition, he grew very angry and disappointed. Swallowing down the last mouthful of orange juice, he raised his hand. When the waiter approached with a tray, he handed him the glass and sternly ordered the first of many double whiskys.

It was three o clock the following afternoon when he woke with what seemed like a hammer pounding in his brain.

Struggling to rise, he knew he would have to hurry if he was to make the R.D.S by 4 p.m.

On arriving in the grounds, he met the Furlong and Thornton families returning from the tea garden behind the stands. They had just enjoyed a scrumptious meal prepared by the 'Aer Lingus Catering Services' and were now heading towards their ring -side seats at the arena.

Sitting next to Molly and David, Garrett looked anxiously around the crowd for Doireann but could not see her anywhere. Remembering very little about the previous night, he wondered where she was. He hoped she had not met somebody else.

Inside the lady rider's changing room Doireann came out of her daydream. Looking at her watch, she went to hurry out the door. Suddenly she remembered the baby she had lost. A great sadness came over her but then it was quickly replaced by a sudden anger. Placing her black hat firmly on her head she stormed out of the room.

Moments later, as Doireann sat upright on her horse waiting for the gates to open, she was oblivious to her surroundings. She did not blink an eyelid when over the loudspeaker came the announcement,

'Doireann Furlong on Propeller.'

18,000 onlookers broke out into an encouraging applause. Many more fans looked in on their television sets at home.

Garrett was stunned. He could not believe that she would disobey and deceive him. He stood up quickly, his painful injuries momentarily forgotten. Then he watched in amazement as his woman rode out proudly on his horse.

Both of them had tremendous presence and were immaculately turned out. Propeller's dark coat shone like pure silk. Little stars of light hopped off the silver metal on the stirrups and on the bit as they reflected the afternoon sun. The highly polished saddle squeaked and contracted with Doireann's movements as it held a small tricolour in its place at the back.

Garrett felt such pride and fear for her all at the same time that it was impossible to describe his emotions. Looking across at Walter, Hattie had never seen him so excited and she feared he might take a heart attack.

Then the crowd grew quiet as Doireann led off with a careful clear round. She continued to keep her cool and the 2nd and 3rd rounds were also clear. But the French and German riders had the same impeccable record too.

David tried to calm his excited daughter as she jumped up and down in the stands.

Then followed a nail- biting jump off. The fences, which had already been increased in height to 20cm, were now raised a further 10. When the German rider jumped fence no 5, he rattled it slightly, and to the relief of the Irish fans it came crashing down. Propeller once more proved with his consistency that he was indeed a wonderful athlete and with the French rider doing as well they were both clear again.

Then the final round commenced.

Chris Dion was a couple of years older than Doireann, and had been very successful in international competitions.

Setting a cracking pace from the beginning, she cleared all the jumps up to the second last. The horse's back hooves seemed to barely touch the fence but it was enough pressure to bring the wooden bar down. Everyone gasped with disappointment as it fell crashing to the ground.

Now at last it was Doireann's turn.

Fr. William clasped his hands tightly together in prayer. Frank shuffled from one foot to the other. Molly screwed her eyes up and clutched tightly to the sleeve of David's jacket. Seamus, Eithne, and their children jumped up and down with glee, while Lady Gowne ran her hand anxiously through her hair. Walter, leaned on the railings with his eyes cast down, and, as for Hattie, if ever a cigarette was needed it had to be now.

With the adrenaline racing through her body and Propeller all fired up, Doireann was once more ready to go. Cantering towards the first fence the horse quickened his pace and then, rising up and almost gliding in the air, he cleared it beautifully. Using his turning ability to its full force she urged him passionately on and narrowly cleared the fences. Then there were only one fence left to jump.

Turning sharply, Doirean suddenly felt at one with her horse. Approaching the final combination she lay forward in complete trust on the horse's neck with her rear high in the air. Then effortlessly they flew over the poles. By now Doireann was the darling of the Ballsbridge crowd and managed to sweep them along with her. Around each turn it was as if the crowd too felt her tremendous effort as she cantered around the course, with the courage of the Furlong spirit urging her forward. Then, with the magnificence of his sire and the high spirit of his dam, Propeller lifted his fit heavy body high up in the air. The crowd erupted with an unprecedented applause when, a second later, both horse and rider landed well clear on the far side.

Doireann leaned forward again her right hand caching his big velvety ears, while she patted him affectionately on the neck with the other.

'We've done it,' she shouted excitedly as tears of happiness welled up in her eyes, 'Just you and me boy we've done it.'

Garrett stood in awe of her. From clapping and jumping he did not know which part of him hurt the most. He wanted to run, hug and give out to her all at the same time. Lady Gowne leaned over and ruffled his hair affectionately with her hand.

'Now Garrett you have a team,' she said joyfully

With tears rolling down his face he clasped his hands together and replied sincerely:

'Thanks Maureen.'

Out in the arena Doireann took a few moments to compose herself. With the clapping of the crowd ringing in her ears she was joined by the other contestants.

The President of Ireland shook her hand and smiled broadly as he presented her with the silver cup. Then, with the two runners -up riding behind her, she proudly proceeded around the arena on a lap of honour.

On reaching the stall where Garrett was sitting, Doireann stopped suddenly, handed the Cup to her comrade, and dismounted. Surprised by her actions, he stood up and leaned over very carefully on the fence.

Smiling the brilliant smile of a winner, she walked over confidently towards him.

The crowd broke out into a tremendous roar.

Then, looking straight into his wonderful glassy blue eyes, she said cheekily:

'Now Garrett, I'll marry you.'

The End.